Copyright © 2022 Robert
All rights reserved.

We'll always have Berlin 2025

R Smtt xx

It could have been you!

We'll always
have Paris xxx
love xx

CHAPTERS

Δ.i	5
I	7
II	11
Δ.ii	16
III	18
Δ.iii	24
IV	27
V	30
VI	34
A	37
VII	42
VIII	49
B	53
IX	58
C	62
X	68
D	74
XI	76
E	80
XII	85
F	90
XIII	94
G	98
H.i	100
H.ii	105
XIV	106
H.iii	112
XV	114
XVI	116
1	119
2	126
3	129
4	137

5	139
6	147
7	150
8	154
9	158
10	162
11	169
♭	175
12	179
13	188
14	194
15	200
16	206
(o>~	214
Σ.?	218
?.ㅊ.R	225
?.ㅊ.T	231

Δ.i

"If you had the chance to go back and do this all again, would you change anything?" Tara asked.

The words shook Rhett from the thoughtlessness of his post-coital glow.

He swallowed hard. Maybe this time it would be different...in that maybe this time it would be the same.

"When it comes to us?" His gaze tracked along the hotel bed, tracing the soft contours of Tara's body until his vacant eyes rested at a point behind the opposite wall. "Not a thing."

Tara shifted her focus from the slow-turning ceiling fan. The scraping sound it made on each rotation had long since ceased to register and it was difficult to imagine it was doing anything to alleviate the dense heat of the static night. She had been about to say something but on reaching out to retrieve it, she realised it was too late. It had already sunk like a stone in those deep waters of the mind that absorb lost memories.

Rhett's eyes narrowed and they guided his head back across the landscape of her figure. Her silhouette looked like the horizon at dusk on an alien world, the dim blue light of a stray mobile phone acting as the departing sun. An itch formed on Rhett's forearm. He rubbed at it, unable to locate the shifting irritation embedded on the inverse of his skin.

"How about you?" Rhett broke the silence, the cadence of his voice undulating beyond his control.

"Same." Tara said.

Blood drained from Rhett's scalp. It was thick and heavy, coalescing like sludge around his ribs and pushing down on his stomach. It was clear she did not feel the same.

He watched her fall asleep through blinking eyes. He inhaled her intoxicating scent, holding each breath until purple sparks burst across his vision. He released each breath slowly through a subjugated sigh so as not to disturb Tara's deepening slumber. He reached out and traced the length of her body with his fingertips so gently that any less contact would have been classed as reiki. Even this delicate touch elicited a slight flicker behind Tara's eyelids at the points where she would usually squirm from hyper-ticklishness.

It did not make sense. He had followed Bruno's instructions to the letter. What exactly would he have to do to make her say it again?

"This button here?" Axe asked.

"You look surprised?" Bruno slipped his hand further down Axe's back, expecting at any moment for Axe to rebuke his advances.

"It just looks so...cheap." Axe said, fighting the instinct to recoil from Bruno's touch.

They both laughed. The switch was soldered to two wires, which protruded in a tangled mess from a rough plastic cover. Several thicker wires snaked from its open back into a large bank of metal cabinets. These reminded Axe of high-school lockers and it was hard to imagine they housed the most sophisticated machine ever created.

"I thought it would be better guarded than this. It's just...so...exposed." Axe's arm extended out, his index finger drifting towards the button. Bruno guided him back and wrapped the stray limb around his ample waist.

"There'll be a full initiation procedure when we launch, with passwords and stuff, but up until now, I've been focusing on getting the guts of the system working. At the moment, the real security lies in getting into the lab-" Bruno surprised himself with a resounding burp, causing him to close his eyes and screw up his face. He was not used to drinking so much and now his guts were rumbling their displeasure at the evening's excess. He opened an eye to peek at Axe, who shrugged. "As I was saying before I so rudely interrupted myself. Once you've made it past the university security guard, used a punch card to access this part of the facility, and then unlocked the door to the lab, I didn't think I needed to bother building any other safety measures."

"And it's ready to go?"

"Yeah...pretty much...I think. I mean, you can never be sure until it's fired up but I'm confident it will work. All I need to do now is integrate all the boring stuff like diagnostic tools and data output systems. Once all the legal issues are resolved, we're up and running."

Axe was a little dazed. A part of him had expected the process of turning QuantSim on to be an impossible task for someone acting alone, especially with the wAIt protests taking place outside.

"I'm the only person with the security clearance to be in here unsupervised. I hope you understand how rare it is for me to invite someone to join me?"

Bruno said. "Especially at this time of night."

"I'm honoured." Axe fluttered his long eyelashes.

Axe stroked Bruno's cheek and leaned in to kiss him. Bruno kept his eyes open, shocked at how rapidly things were escalating. He knew how unlikely a coupling they made. Axe had a muscular physique, tanned skin, and blonde highlights in his chestnut hair. The ironic bootleg t-shirt he wore had been selected to portray a sense of fake nerd nostalgia. Combined with his red leather trousers, it would have been a garish outfit on anyone else, but on Axe's frame, it looked like something straight from Braxton Fashion Week. Bruno was obese, had pasty dry skin and a posture that seemed to suggest his spine had dissolved into the excessive layers of fat around his neck and shoulders. On the infrequent occasions he dressed in fashionable clothes, he worried this might be an insult to the people who had spent time and energy creating them. Bruno considered his only positive feature to be his thick black hair, which he often used to hide as much of his face as possible. He breathed in deep and cast his doubts about Axe's intentions aside. He had to heed his father's advice and not end up ruining things for himself by over-thinking or second-guessing the motives of someone who seemed to genuinely value him for his intellectual prowess. Bruno pulled away, realising he had diminished the experience of his first-ever kiss by distracting himself with an internal commentary on the moment.

"Seriously, I don't usually do this." Bruno stared into Axe's eyes. He twitched his nose and eyebrows in an attempt to convey condensed layers of meaning. "In fact, I wouldn't normally go to a club like Furnace but as I said earlier, I'm expecting some rough news from the hospital tomorrow and I was sent a few promo—"

Axe placed an index finger to Bruno's lips. His other hand had clenched into a fist and he was pushing it against his own mouth to catch a burst of nausea. His cheeks puffed out as a soft hiss escaped. It pleased Bruno to see they were both suffering noticeable reactions to the evening's indulgences. Once Axe had composed himself, they exchanged smiles of embarrassment.

"It's OK. I don't care." Axe said. He wiped his mouth. He pondered for a moment how he found himself in the arms of someone so repugnant.

Axe's first song had been a major hit. It had topped the charts for several months and gained him a lucrative contract with Rudd Music. The success had come fast and easy, propelling him into a life that was a world away from the squalor and violence of the tower block estates of outer Braxton. Instead of focusing on developing his career, he had instead lost himself to a binge of promiscuity and excess. He had not realised how much of his fame was attributable to luck and not an ineffable essence of his character that compelled the universe to bestow glory upon him. On returning to the studio, with an extended entourage in tow, his new artistic direction had been met with both critical ridicule and commercial apathy. Release after release had flopped and his label's patience had become threadbare. Sitting in Maxwell Rudd's penthouse office, it had been made explicit that if his next project did not live up to his early promise, management would have no choice but to trigger the exit clause in their agreement. As he spoke, Maxwell had looked over at the two arcade machines he kept in his office. They acted as inspiration whenever he had to decide between profit and loyalty. The first machine, "Other Side", had been a cultural phenomenon with revenues to match. Off the back of it, he had allowed the developer free reign to create the second game, "T.W.O.K". This had been a groundbreaking technological triumph but unfortunately also an unmitigated commercial disaster. Maxwell would never again allow himself to be in a position where one of his employees could have such power over the fortunes of his career. Observing Maxwell Rudd pondering the arcade machines had also given Axe an idea. He had seen their creator a few times around Braxton's alternative clubbing scene. He wondered if he could leverage a growing awareness of his latest project for his own advantage.

Axe now stood on the edge of turning the abstract ideas formed in Maxwell's office into a tangible reality.

Bruno was overcome by a wave of confidence. Maybe brought on by the unusual grey crystals Axe had added to their drinks earlier that night. Maybe because of the look of desire he saw reflected back at him in Axe's eyes. Either way, he could not resist the compulsion to act on the unusual tingling sensations rippling across his scalp.

He leaned in and enjoyed another first, by taking the lead in initiating the second kiss of his life.

Axe hesitated. He had grown to like Bruno in the few short hours they had spent together. He still found him viscerally repulsive but Bruno was no longer the notional entity he had been when their eyes had met across the dancefloor earlier that evening. Bruno had introduced himself after noticing Axe wearing a retro "Other Side" t-shirt and jokingly admonished him for robbing him of royalties. Axe had apologised and bought him a drink as the first step towards reparations. The ease of the conversation had surprised Axe, as had his own excitement as he encouraged Bruno to tell him about QuantSim's potential. If it was able to realise even a small percentage of the positive outcomes Bruno had outlined, it was a formidable device that needed to be managed with consideration and care. Axe weighed all this up against the personal costs of being dropped by Rudd Music. He did not relish the thought of life as of a former popstar, only ever returning to public consciousness as an answer on an obscure daytime quiz show, or as the punchline of a joke told by a second-rate comedian.

Axe shut his eyes and met Bruno's eager advances, committing himself completely to the kiss.

II

Katja was using the news truck wing mirror to apply a fresh layer of lipstick. The glass was layered with grime but she had found a gap. If she positioned her head at the correct angle, she was able to use it to guide her hand across the contours of her mouth.

"And?" She turned to Martha who was fiddling with the camera.

"Yeah." Martha replied with a cursory glance. Her eyes were only partially visible through her spiked purple fringe.

Katja was determined to turn the deputy technology editor's misfortune to her own advantage. She had been his production assistant for three years. In that time he had always arrived in impeccable clothing and a clear focus for the day ahead. That morning, he arrived with a distracted look in his eye and a smudge of strawberry jam on his tie. Katja had wiped away the condiment with an old fashioned combination of tissue and spit. An hour later he was in an ambulance heading for the hospital with severe chest pains.

They were assigned to cover a protest at Braxton University. It was small but had been taking place for a few days. The protestors had made it clear they were not going to budge until the university addressed their concerns about Bruno Mattham's new project. There was not much else going on in the world, with tech conference season over and the autumn product announcements not due for several weeks. As such this protest had reached the level of becoming a newsworthy item.

"You'll have to do it." A displaced voice crackled over the phone as Katja and Martha stood in the back of the van. Katja was unsure which of the executives she was listening to.

"Me? But I've never..."

"Just get it done Katja. It's not like we're reporting on a manned-rocket launch." A distinctly different but similarly inflected voice had taken over to express the collective irritation.

"...and we believe in you, Katja." This voice she knew. It was the once heavy but now tamed colloquial accent of the 9 O'clock news anchor, Amanda Tanner.

Katja took a deep breath and closed her eyes. After five long years of progressing at a glacial pace from unpaid intern all the way up to badly paid production assistant, she was finally going to get the opportunity to appear in front of camera. Her first thought was what it would feel like to tell her parents. Would she still be able to detect the you-could-have-married-a-doctor expression in her mother's eyes?

"Don't screw this up." She mumbled to herself after the call was over.

"What?" Martha said. She squared up to Katja. Itching to take offence at something...anything.

"I was just telling myself not to screw this up."

"Oh....good advice." Martha's rounded shoulders dropped. She realised she would not be able to twist Katja's words to provoke a confrontation...at least not on this occasion.

The members of the recently formed wAIt organisation were already renowned for their dislike of broadcast media. This was even before their inhibited founder, Dr Parveen Panwar, had given her infamous interview on NightStream. An exchange where her wig had slipped without her knowledge. She had tugged at it to relieve an irritation caused by the bright heat of the studio lights. The show was pre-recorded so the producers could easily have let her know there was an issue and allowed her to put across her point in a second take. Instead, they had let her continue with the patchy hair of her scalp visible for all to see. The feedback had been harsh, with all focus on her looks rather than her erudite legal and moral arguments she had posed. It did not seem to matter very much that her hair loss had come as a result of chemotherapy.

Katja had observed a few other local reporters, apparently the only other journalists interested in the story, attempting to secure some sort of exclusive access to Parveen. They all wanted a sound bite from the world's leading ethical scholar to use as flavour in their news items. Parveen had rebuffed them all with little more than monosyllabic answers to their questions. Parveen had been impervious to the usual deference people felt when a camera, a bright light, and an attractive, charismatic reporter invaded their immediacy to bless them with attention.

Katja had been wondering all morning how she could make an impression on Parveen to enable some form of open exchange. She had found herself devoid of inspiration but with time running out, she had to make a move. She decided she would have to fall back on the "nudge-and-snag" strategy. It was risky but she was running out of options. She casually integrated into the group of protestors, hovered close to Parveen and then tripped into her when an opportunity arose. She made sure to angle the sharp edge of her clipboard in a way that had a chance to cause a bit of disruption. A rip in Parveen's clothing or even better, maybe even a slight cut.

"Mrs Panwar. I'm so sorry."

"Ms Panwar." Parveen corrected as she steadied herself from the collision. She had only received her honorary doctorate a few months earlier. She often forgot about the title, as she now. She had not, however, forgotten that she was no longer a "Mrs". Family and friends had all told her to expect her husband to leave once he found out about her diagnosis but Parveen had refused to accept it. She believed in her own worth and had presented him with some persuasive arguments as to why he should stay. After a few days of consideration, the only real surprise had been how long he had taken to come to the conclusion everyone else had anticipated.

"I was wondering if you would take a few moments to talk about your work with wAIt."

"No."

"It would help the VEX News audience gain a deeper understanding of your objectives. Our channel has over sixteen million viewers most days. The Nine O"Clock show is now the largest nightly news show on TV. It might help generate more of an impact than twenty or so individuals standing outside a university campus with a few banners and a megaphone." Katja said.

"Our objections to Professor Matthams's research can be found with detailed reasoning in all our pamphlets. I suggest you look there." Parveen's voice was crisp and formal. She nodded towards one of her fellow protestors who was handing out wAIt literature. Their pile had not reduced much in the few hours since Parveen had arrived.

"We have always found our viewership to be much more receptive to these sorts of issues when presented with a personality who can embody them." Katja leaned back and smiled. As the only female reporter covering the story, she hoped to invoke a spirit of sisterhood between them.

Parveen was aware of the irony of the suggestion she could act as a personality for anything. "The printed information is quite clear." She maintained her curt tone, seeing it as a barrier of professionalism to deflect against Katja's attempt at building rapport. "Neither myself nor any of the others from the movement would be able to articulate it in a more succinct manner."

Katja could sense she was not going to get anywhere.

"There is one thing. I--"

"I have nothing more to say to you."

The interruption was almost enough to make Katja walk away but glimpsing the long scars creeping out across Parveen's sternum had caused Katja's own lungs to tighten. She now felt an urge to protect Parveen from the devious tactics of unscrupulous journalists.

"OK. I was just going to let you know that your bra is showing." Katja said.

Parveen looked down to see two of her blouse buttons had popped off, leaving intermittent views of her chest area for all to see. She had needed to buy a fresh outfit on her way to the protest due to involvement in a minor mishap on the train. The passenger seated opposite her had been enjoying a jam doughnut and coffee when all of a sudden had experienced some sort of 'turn'. He had lurched forward, spilling jam on himself and coffee all over Parveen's blouse. She had been cursing herself all morning for choosing the cheapest replacement she could find. It had been strangely loose in certain areas and uncomfortably tight in others. It appeared this had culminated in a serious wardrobe malfunction, which would no doubt be the only picture from the protests any of the gathered journalists would choose to show.

"I have a sewing kit back at the van. I was going to see if you wanted to borrow it...but as you have nothing more to say to me..."

Katja turned with a flourish.

"Actually. Ms..." Parveen called after her.

Katja looked over her shoulder with faux suspicion in her eyes. "Miss...Miss Leitner."

"Miss Leitner. Perhaps it does make sense for us to talk." Parveen looked down at her watch and snorted. The morning was racing away from her. It would not be long before she would need to get set off for Braxton Central Hospital. "I must warn you, I only have a limited amount of time before I have to leave for an important appointment."

△.ii

Tara and Rhett sat in silence picking at their breakfasts. Rhett's frustration was growing. The conversation was not flowing anywhere near as freely as he had expected.

"What's on your mind?" Tara asked him before cutting off a small piece of sausage and placing it in her mouth. She relished the texture of the blended fat, meat, and coarse rusk as it moved around her mouth.

"Have you ever experienced d j vu?" Rhett asked her.

"Yeah. I hate it. Are you getting it now?"

"No."

Tara thought it odd he would bring it up and then have it lead to a conversational dead end. She watched him sipping his coffee. His eyes focused softly on the window pane.

They had been lovers for a few weeks. A whirlwind romance after getting to know each other at a university networking event. They had exchanged numbers and been on a few dates. They were now on their first trip away. Everything had seemed like it was heading in the right direction until the previous evening when Rhett had become distant and cold. Tara could not quite put her finger on exactly what it was. One moment he had been full of energy and excitement to discover more about her. The next, he seemed to have a preconceived notion of who she was and who she would become.

"Do you ever think about our future?" Rhett looked at her with a curious intensity.

"The future? Yeah, definitely. I am hoping they'll offer me a permanent position at the agency. Once I've completed my multimedia communications training, I should be able to build my own portfolio of clients. I want to represent organisations and individuals who have strong environmental credentials." She said.

"No, I meant our future. Do you think about us...in the future?"

Tara's head flew back and she burst out laughing. She had expected to see Rhett smiling back at her, but instead his eyes had formed into a blank stare. She had not seen this side of him before until this weekend. It was starting to get on her nerves. Where was the outgoing, lighthearted man of a week ago? The one who had soaked himself by jumping in a fountain to retrieve a coin, just because she had changed her mind about a wish.

"You're not serious?"

Rhett looked like he was serious.

"Oh...you are serious?"

A server came over and refilled their mugs with coffee. He paid no attention to what they were saying but they felt compelled to pause their conversation until he had gone.

"Look, Rhett...you're a great guy and everything but it is waaaay too early to be talking about anything like this. We're having fun. Let's see how things go." The urge to "go" was growing inside her. She pushed her cutlery together and forced herself to put on a reassuring smile. They still had a two-hour drive ahead. There was no point in allowing an awkward atmosphere to develop.

Rhett's eyes flitted around the room until they rested on his phone. It was a brand Tara had not seen before with a new type of touchscreen interface. Rhett had explained how it was a prototype from a company that had spun off from some university research. He was confident it would not be long before everyone had something similar. She was quite sure it would not catch on. It seemed like overkill for a device most people used primarily for texting and making calls.

Rhett picked it up. Using it to occupy his trembling hands.

Something was definitely not right.

III

"My name is Katja Leitner and I am lucky enough to have secured an exclusive interview with Dr Parveen Panwar, founder of wAIt, an organisation currently protesting outside Braxton University. I'm here to find out why."

Martha gave Katja a thumbs up to signal she was happy with the sound and visuals. Parveen was now dressed in a chic silk blouse. Katja had asked Martha to purchase it from one of the stylish boutiques in the Sutton Arcade after it became clear Katja's sewing kit would not be enough to salvage Parveen's original shirt.

"Dr Panwar, your group is relatively new. Can you please explain to our viewers what wAIt is?"

"We are concerned about the rapid developments in Artificial Intelligence. We do not think we should allow them to proliferate until we, as a society, resolve the moral and ethical questions surrounding them. The government must then put in place a robust regulatory framework." Parveen said.

"And what does wAIt stand for? Is it an acronym?"

"In a way. There is an acronym in it. The "A" and the "I" in uppercase letters stand for Artificial Intelligence and they are surrounded by the lowercase "w" and the 't" to spell the word "wait". A succinct way of saying we should pause before unleashing the unknown forces of Artificial Intelligence on the world."

"Oooh. Clever, I like it."

"I'll pass your sentiments on to the member of our team who came up with it."

"It might not surprise you to learn that the viewers of VEX News aren't the brightest bulbs you can put in your lamp. Could you give us a brief idea of what Artificial Intelligence is?"

Parveen arched her right eyebrow. She had not expected Katja to display an openly derisory attitude towards her own viewers.

"Oh don't worry, we're not live." Katja laughed as she realised the source of Parveen's confusion. She leaned in towards Parveen in a conspiratorial manner. This reminded Parveen of the way the popular girls at her college had confided in each other. Never including her in the secret. It felt good to be brought into Katja's inner circle. Katja lowered her tone. "We understand the limitations of our viewers. They aren't the type of people to form their own opinions but once influenced by the information services they consume, they hold on to their views with all their might. If you and I could get them onside with your cause, it could be an interesting opportunity for both of us." Katja leaned back and her voice returned to normal. "So if you could explain Artificial Intelligence in your own words, we can edit it down later to something they can easily digest."

Parveen brought to mind an average family of VEX News viewers, spending the majority of their free time absorbing bile and propaganda. Information spewed out at them from one of the few sources they exposed themselves to. Most of them had not read a book since leaving school and were proud of it. They made fun of the very scientific and democratic processes that had provided them their wealth and comfort. It made her uneasy to have to pander to this demographic but despite their deficiencies, they were a powerful block, and their opinion, however obtained, were crucial for developing policy. The protections she sought were also ones that would ultimately keep them safe. Looking at it in this way, manipulating them into serving their own best interests did not seem such a devious tactic.

Other members of the wAIt organisation had advised her many times that they would not achieve their objectives by winning the intellectual debate. They needed to move the discourse into an exciting and visceral realm, highlighting the stakes through a strong narrative. This was not something their group had the inherent skills to achieve. If they could win friends in the media, maybe they could create the momentum needed to force the government into action before it was too late.

"Over the years the definition of Artificial Intelligence has been ambiguous." Parveen said. "And to a certain degree, it still is. It can encompass any task or activity performed by a machine or program that if carried out by a person, we would say intelligence was needed to accomplish it.

"We are not primarily concerned with this type of AI. This already fuels some of our commercial activities, such as the algorithms scouring databases to recommend what commercial offers you receive, or those that determine how much interest to charge you on a loan.

"We worry about a more potent AI developing. One where a machine is given a general and flexible intelligence, which surpasses the understanding of the people who created it. If this type of AI is unleashed, we simply have no way of knowing what the consequences of it would be."

"I see. If it becomes cleverer than we are, we would be unable to predict how it would behave and what it would do?"

"Exactly."

"You currently have some limited support, albeit from a dedicated number of individuals. Why do you think your movement hasn't gained much traction?"

"I wouldn't say our support is limited. There may only be a handful of us out here protesting today but we have many people in the background quietly underpinning our movement." Parveen said. She looked over towards the small group holding placards and leaflets outside the entrance to the University. Looking at them through the cold midday drizzle in their mismatched charity-shop clothes, they did not appear to be a formidable bunch. If you could not see their slogans, you could imagine them supporting anything from climate change to economic equality. A lot of them would probably turn up for whatever "awoken" cause was currently gaining traction, especially if their latest crush had expressed an interest.

"Don't worry about that. We'll get a good angle and edit it in a way to make it look bigger." Katja smiled, noticing Parveen's glance.

Parveen was not sure whether she approved of this type of manipulation but with such high stakes, she had to defer to someone with more messaging experience.

"Why now? Why did you feel the need to create wAIt in the last few months, and why have you been actively protesting outside Braxton University these last few days?"

"All these issues were purely theoretical until recently. We were working under the assumption that we were decades away from developing anything even close to being considered a threat. Then around four months ago Braxton University issued a press release. Professor Matthams had developed an AI powerful enough to simulate an entire universe."

Katja responded instinctively with widening eyes and a sharp intake of breath. After a moment she exhaled and a frown spread across her forehead. "I don't know what that means."

"We are not entirely sure if it is true, because the underlying concepts are so abstract. It appears only Professor Matthams has a full grasp of the theoretical frameworks required to achieve this. But if his claims are true, with a flick of a switch he could create a world equally as sophisticated as our own using a quantum cloud framework array."

"That sounds pretty cool." Katja said. She could not imagine what benefits this would bring or why it might be a problem but she did sense a specific opportunity for herself. She could become the media face of the controversy surrounding this new technology.

"Maybe but there are also lots of things to consider. This digital universe would be as rich and varied as our own and within it life could develop once, or several times. Ultimately it could evolve to sentience. We need to make sure..."

"Wait." Katja caught her inadvertent reference to Parveen's organisation and laughed. Parveen bounced her index finger in front of her face and smiled at the acknowledgement. "You're saying a computer could have the capacity to think and feel?"

"The latest theories of cognitive science often compare the brain to hardware and the mind to software. But a software program is just information. In principle, there's no reason why you should have to encode the information of consciousness in neurons. The qubits underpinning Professor Matthams's machine could perform the task just as well."

Katja nodded as her own neurons processed this new information and manifested it as a conscious thought within her mind.

"We need to make sure," Parveen continued, 'that we understand the moral and ethical implications of this before we play god. wAIt is not trying to rule out this type of technological progress. All we are saying is we should pause for a few beats before powering it up."

"I can see how that makes sense. There's a chance there might be some unintended consequences so we should think things through before ploughing ahead. The benefits will still be there after we have taken some time to reflect on potential negatives."

Parveen was impressed at how quickly Katja seemed to pick these concepts up. She also liked the way Katja made her feel. It was very different from her preconceived notions of how a journalist would act. She softened to the idea of having Katja operate as a trusted contact within the media industry. Her train of thought was broken by a commotion outside the entrance to the University. A tall but obese man was making his way through the protestors. They were hindering his progress and chanting wAIt slogans at him. He was in his late twenties but had the aura of a much older man. Large sunken circles framed his jaundiced eyes. They made him look like an unattractive old piano player trying his best, but failing, to evoke the spirit of a rockstar.

"That's Bruno Matthams there.".

Katja followed Parveen's finger and located Professor Matthams. She had seen images of him before but he looked nothing like the promotional pictures taken at the height of the hype around his arcade machines. He had gained significant amounts of weight and seemed to have aged decades rather than years since his time in the spotlight.

"Oooh. Would you mind if I shot off and tried to get a comment?"

"No...not at all...go."

Katja and Martha gathered their equipment.

"Did you get anything you can use?" Parveen's voice undulated with an unexpected bout of shyness. She recognised the feeling but struggled to place where she had experienced it before.

"Nah - all too verbose." Parveen's shoulders slumped at Katja's response. Noticing this, Katja continued. "...but I think it is something that could rouse our viewer's interest if we pitch it at the right level. wAIt is the type of thing they would normally be against, but it might be fun to see if we could get them to come round to your way of thinking."

Parveen fought off the uncharacteristic bashfulness that was overwhelming her. She grabbed Katja's elbow. If she could just recollect when she had experienced this emotion before, she might be able to control it better.

"Keep in touch. We might be able to add some value to each other." Parveen palmed her business card into Katja's hand.

"Thanks Dr Panwar, I certainly will."

"Call me Parveen."

Katja winked and then hurried away. The wink finally triggered Parveen's memory. She had not felt these feelings of excited self-consciousness since her earliest interactions with her ex-husband. She remembered their initial meeting as they sat opposite each other, flanked by their respective parents. Zahid had offered her a surreptitious wink when it was clear she was the only one looking at him. She had fought her shyness back then as well and had returned his gesture with a delicate flutter of her eyelashes.

Parveen sighed. She watched Katja gaining ground on Bruno. She feared she may never get a chance to speak to her again. Parveen glanced at her watch. It was time to set off for her latest hospital appointment.

Martha wheezed along behind Katja. It was a struggle to keep up in their pursuit of Bruno. She cursed between gasps for breath. Running was definitely not something covered in her contract.

△.iii

Rhett had heard very little from Tara since they returned from their trip to the environmental protest in London. They had exchanged a few brief texts. Every time he had attempted to call her, she had let it ring through to her answer machine. She would later message him an excuse about why it was inconvenient to talk. It was getting to the stage where he felt he should take the hint. Under normal circumstances, he would have...

...but these were not normal circumstances.

It was inconceivable to him that Tara could treat him this way. He knew they were destined to be together. The life they would share be one of love, exhilaration, and laughter. How was she unable to see this? How was he unable to convince her of this fundamental fact?

It had all been so easy until the trip had changed everything.

A vibration on his outer thigh shook him from his thoughts. As he glanced at the caller, a jolt of hopeful glee surged through his body. It was Tara.

"Hey, how you doing?" Tara's voice seemed devoid of its usual tonal range.

"Yeah, great. How about you?"

"I'm good. Been busy...but good."

The conversation was strained. After a few half-hearted bursts of small-talk, interspersed with awkward silences, they both knew where it was heading.

"I was hoping we could get together this weekend?" The usual confidence in Rhett's voice had drained away.

"Yeah...well..." Tara cleared her throat and coughed into her hand. "I don't really think it is a good idea. I mean, I really like you. I think you're a great guy and I had a lot of fun with you but I'm not really in a place right now where I'm looking for anything serious."

"I see."

"I'd like it if we could stay on friendly terms. I know we'll see each other around. Obviously we'll both be at Flick's birthday party next month so I hope things don't get weird between us."

"No. Of course. I'd like that too."

Rhett completed the final few seconds of the conversation on autopilot as he struggled to comprehend what was happening. It was impossible for Tara to be acting this way. She had not even given him a chance.

He sat in silence for a while, his eyes tracking a band of sun creeping across the wooden floor.

He picked up his phone and dialled Tara's number. It rang for a long time until she answered.

"I'm sorry about this but...it....it just does not make sense." He said.

"What doesn't?"

"I know you are in a place right now where you're looking for something serious."

"Don't make this hard, Rhett. I'm just not feeling it." Tara said.

Rhett imagined Tara's eyes rolling upwards in exasperation. It was an expression of hers he knew well and always accompanied her current tone of voice.

"You have to give me a chance. I know how good we will be together." Rhett said.

"It's not going to happen."

"It's not going to happen?" Rhett was unable to stop himself from raising his voice. "It has to happen. We're destined to be together."

Tara remained silent.

"I'm sorry." Rhett regained control of his emotions. "Can we just forget this conversation ever happened? Maybe meet for a coffee tomorrow after work?"

"No." Tara felt like she was treading water in a stagnant pond and was sinking under the weight of ever more reeds tangling around her ankles. "It's really creepy to hear you say things like you think we're destined to be together."

"I don't ever want to do anything to make you uncomfortable."

"Good...well...then I think it's best if we keep our distance...at least for a while" Tara was already calculating the social impact of having to avoid Rhett. She could probably skip Flick's birthday as long as a suitable present accompanied her apology.

"OK"

"OK. Goodbye."

Tara put the phone down. She had been pleased with the way the initial phone call had gone but she now felt uneasy and insecure. She opened a bottle of wine and pushed away the thoughts. She had to hope this episode with Rhett was now part of her past. The tension in her shoulders dissipated as time and alcohol moved her further away from the moment.

"Goodbye." Rhett had said without realising Tara was no longer on the call.

Rhett sat for a long time in silence with the phone still positioned at his ear. The band of light was now streaming across his right knee and onto his left thigh.

Something was seriously wrong.

He let his arm drop so he could see the screen of his phone. He thumbed through his apps until he found the one which Bruno had added to his device. He typed a message and then waited.

Bruno had not responded to any of his previous attempts at contact. He hoped he would not have to grab Bruno's attention in the same way he had done before. He was not worried about any of the risks this course of action would create for himself. The one thing he was not sure of was if he would ever be able to bring himself to end Tara's life to send Bruno a message.

IV

Bruno quickened his pace across the Braxton University hexagon in response to the eager voice following him. He was in no mood to speak to the media. His head hurt and his mouth was dry. He still had some artificial sensations of euphoria rippling intermittently through his scalp. His body refused to oblige in his attempt to evade his pursuer, forcing him to an abrupt halt. His breathing faltered to a wheeze and his heart thumped at his throat. Beads of thick sweat had formed across his lustrous hairline. He could feel them working their way down his face through the contours of his flaky skin. This was not the type of moisture his dehydrated cuticles craved.

"Mr Matthams. I'm Katja Leitner from VEX News. Do you have a moment?" Katja was also out of breath.

"Actually, it's Professor Matthams." Bruno said. He was only ever concerned about his academic title when something else was aggravating him. "And it's not a good time. I've been working all night so if you don't mind, I'm just going to head home to freshen up. Then I have an important personal commitment to take care of."

"Working all night? Really?"

"Yes. You might have heard that QuantSim is on the verge of a significant breakthrough. It's not the type of work you can dip in and out of. You have to stay until the project itself presents a natural opportunity for a break."

"It must be lonely work?"

"Not really. I mean, I do work alone most of the time. I have to...there isn't anyone else who is capable of understanding the theoretical, conceptual, and practical aspects of my work...but I wouldn't say this makes me feel lonely. I am normally so engrossed in what I'm doing that I don't have time for things like loneliness."

"Is your assistant not able to provide you with some sort of companionship and understanding?"

"My assistant?"

"Yes. You were seen entering the facility with a coworker in the early hours of this morning." Katja said. Her conversations with some of the protestors were paying off. Bruno squirmed in response to her words. "They must be of critical importance to the work for them to have to work so late at a time where QuantSim is on the verge of a significant breakthrough? Tell me. Do they understand the theoretical, practical, and conceptual aspects of your work?"

Bruno opened his mouth to answer. Nothing came out.

"The thing is." Katja continued. "A source has informed me that there isn't anyone matching the description of your colleague with the security clearances required to access the facility. I am certain my source is mistaken but I am sure it will not take long to clear things up when I speak to Vice-Chancellor Mashwani later today."

Bruno was not too concerned about the Vice-Chancellor finding out about this type of security breach. He was far too important an asset to the university to receive any form of serious reprimand for this kind of incident. Even so, it was always preferable to keep these things under wraps. There was no point wasting goodwill on matters like this.

"What do you want?" Bruno asked.

Martha had now caught up with them and was going through her own recovery process. Bruno gave her a look of disdain, unsympathetic to the fact he had been in much the same state mere moments ago.

"I want to find out a bit more about QuantSim. I think our viewers will find it quite interesting." Katja said.

"Really? VEX News viewers?" Bruno gave her a quizzical look.

Katja leaned in towards Bruno and softened her voice. It reminded Bruno how his father and uncle talked to each other on occasions they did not want him to overhear. It felt good to be included for once.

"Yeah." Katja said. "We just need to present it in a way they can understand. If they can find out what drove the man behind it to create such a complicated technological advancement, it might make it easier for them to see why it matters."

Bruno had always wanted his work to be recognised beyond a small clique of academics. Experience had taught him that it was impossible for anyone but those with the keenest of intellects to grasp the fundamentals. However, if he could get a wider audience to understand the practical benefits and the broad concepts involved, he might be able to push things forward. His life would be so much easier without Dr Panwar and wAIt on his back. He needed a media partner and Katja Leitner seemed like she could be a formidable ally. She was ambitious, smart, and he liked how she was willing to use any leverage she had to get what she wanted. Besides, there were not too many journalists currently interested in presenting his side of the story.

"OK - I'll give you an hour but only on three conditions." Bruno said.

"Go on."

"It's off the record, it's over breakfast and you pick up the tab."

"I can certainly agree to that Professor Matthams." Katja smiled and winked. If she was able to forge some form of exclusive access to both sides of the QuantSim debate, it could be a foundation on which she could build a career. She noticed Bruno looking her up and down and gave him a flash of her trademark smile and a wink of collusion.

"Call me Bruno." He said.

V

The smudge on the window turned out to be on the outside. Vice-Chancellor Zahid Mishwani had attempted to wipe it away with his index finger. Instead of making the window cleaner, he had inadvertently added an additional smear to the glass. He pulled out his red silk handkerchief, which matched his tie, and rubbed it clean. He wrote a reminder to get the window cleaning contractors to come before the beginning of next term. His list of to-dos was an ever-expanding register. It only ever reduced when the yellow pad of paper it was written on invariably went missing. Sometimes on a train, sometimes in a taxi but it never stuck around much longer than a week. In this way, he was able to convince himself of his own productivity without ever accounting for it.

He looked back out the window and scanned the protestors. He was looking for the woman who had commanded the greatest amount of his attention throughout his adult life. He had thought that once they had divorced, her influence on his time would diminish significantly. He had not reckoned on her becoming the greatest critic of his university's flagship project. She had made a case against him leaving her after they found out about her cancer diagnosis. He thought this had been unfair. It had only been a few months since he was appointed the Vice-Chancellor of one of the most prestigious universities in the world. He simply did not have the capacity to manage this important part of his career and care for someone with a terminal condition. He hoped her interest in his professional affairs was not in retaliation for their personal matter. She had not readily accepted his logic, believing she still had a lot to give and that she would overcome the odds and make a full recovery. Now it was clear she had been proved right, he wondered if there could be some kind of compromise. If they could put in place a reconciliation of sorts, it might come with the added bonus of the wAIt problem evaporating into the ether.

He was distracted for a moment as the lights in his office flickered. It found it wasteful to have them on throughout the day but he had no control over the settings of the automated system controlling them. His office had always been quite dark and it seemed it never attained a level of brightness so that the lights would deactivate. The flickering had occurred several times that morning. On each occasion, he had thought about contacting someone about it but as soon as it ceased, it dissolved back into the still waters of his mind.

The ancient trees lining the hexagon were turning their famous hues of red, gold, and orange. It was this image that was shown in most pictures of the university. The age and continued health of the trees highlighted the stability of the learning establishment he now oversaw. It was the oldest university in the country. It competed with two or three others to be regarded as the best academic institution in the world. He now had a chance to build on its remarkable reputation so it could stand alone at the pinnacle of academic excellence. So many important figures had sat at what was now his desk, including some of history's most revered academic minds and political leaders. He had ambitions in the latter sphere. This was an important step in achieving those aspirations.

He located Parveen amongst the crowd and all thoughts of compromise departed from his mind. Her image triggered memories of how formidable and accomplished she was in her dual disciplines of law and ethics. Dr Panwar would never align herself to a cause based on a personal grudge, nor would she abandon it for anything other than a valid moral reason. He pushed the fantasy of her acquiescing to the depths of his mind.

He could see her standing next to the VEX News mobile media van chatting to a young reporter. He considered it odd that this was the media outlet she had chosen to speak to after a lifetime of criticism against the industry as a whole. She had hardly selected one of the most stringent examples of journalistic integrity but he knew she was sharp enough to understand this. He had to conclude there must be an ulterior strategy behind her decision. The reporter Parveen was talking to had requested an interview with him earlier that day. He had not seen any advantage to granting one, so had asked the press department to issue a standard response. It might have been different had Maxwell Rudd himself been the one to make the offer.

He noticed the other main cause of irritation in his life emerge from the university entrance. Professor Bruno Matthams had a prodigious intellect. Unfortunately, it was so advanced, it was difficult for anyone to understand exactly how his technology worked. What was clear, was that if it did function in line with Professor Matthams predictions, QuantSim could bring untold benefits to the world. More importantly, if it were to do so it would propel Braxton University to preeminence in terms of academic prestige. It could also open up significant opportunities for Zahid's own career development. However, as was always the case with things he could not himself understand, he was suspicious of Matthams claims. He suspected he might be overpromising to gain funding for a technology that might end up being nothing more than a solution in need of a problem.

"Vice-Chancellor Mashwani." He said as he answered his phone. He never tired of referring to himself by his full title.

"Vice-Chancellor, it's Geoff Watts from building services here. I've just received a strange call from Foss Energy."

"You don't need to bother me about cold callers trying to sell utility packages." Annoyance seeped into Zahid's tone. He had more important things to deal with than the minutiae of the building's maintenance and service contracts.

"No, it's not that." Geoff said. He was not pleased with Vice-Chancellor Mashwani's manner. He was on the verge of hanging up but realised this was a situation requiring the input of a senior decision-maker. He took a breath. "They have informed us that the university began drawing significant amounts of energy in the early hours of this morning. The amount is enough to destabilise the whole grid. They would like to know if we intend to continue to draw the same amount of power or if it is a temporary situation."

"Have you identified the source?"

"No. That's why I am calling. We were hoping you might know something about it. In the event that you didn't, we thought it best to inform you sooner rather than later."

Zahid's eyes scanned the hexagon for the whereabouts of Professor Matthams. "I am not aware of anything. Can you keep trying to find out what department is pulling all that load?"

"Of course. We'll keep you updated."

Zahid rapidly located Bruno's position. He was now talking to the same reporter his ex-wife had been with a few moments ago. He squinted his eyes, furrowed his brow and pursed his lips as he continued to contemplate his most controversial employee. He wondered if it made sense to try and get down there to catch him. This was resolved when he saw Bruno disappear behind the golden foliage of the hexagon's famous line of trees.

VI

Bruno placed a piece of sausage in his mouth. He relished the texture of the blended meats, fats and cereal on his tongue. Eating had made him feel much better. He was also enjoying speaking to someone about his work without having to deal with all the esoteric aspects of technical theory.

The lights in the cafe flickered for a moment. Martha was struggling to keep up with the speed at which Bruno and Katja were exchanging ideas. Martha had thought of Katja as another in a never-ending line of spoilt brats. They would take on production-assistant roles, supported by the wealth and network of their family. It was something to do until they found someone suitable to marry, at which point they were gone. Seeing Katja in action had changed Martha's opinion. She now had a new sense of respect for her potential as a journalist. Katja would sometimes wink at Martha in a lull in the conversation and when Bruno was not looking. This created a warm sensation in Martha's stomach and made her feel like they were guardians of a shared secret.

"Fascinating." Katja leaned back as she absorbed the latest burst of information. "I have heard some people have concerns. They worry we will not be able to predict the consequences of these systems once they reach a certain threshold."

"Are you talking about the singularity?" Bruno asked.

"The what now?"

"The singularity." Bruno repeated. He said it with greater articulation as Katja wrote it in her notepad. "It is a hypothetical point in our technological advancement where computers are capable of building better versions of themselves at an ever-increasing rate. This should lead to their performance becoming vastly superior to anything we could ever conceive of. This exponential technological growth will be out of our control, irreversible and will change us in ways we cannot foresee."

"It sounds scary." Martha said, wanting to add something to the conversation.

"Yes, it could be but that's why my project offers us the best of all conceivable scenarios. We can create a simulated universe within the confines of a quantum framework and then let it run unhindered. If we set the parameters right, a similar kind of life to our own should evolve within it. If a singularity is an emergent property of our underlying physics, then we should see it evolve within QuantSim.

"If it doesn't emerge then we can tweak the settings and run the simulation hundreds... thousands...even millions of times. We're only confined by how much energy it consumes. If it doesn't manifest in any of the simulations then we can postulate that there are hard limits preventing a singularity. At least within the constraints of the fundamental laws of our universe...or our intelligence...or some other multiversal constant."

"I'm with you...barely." Katja confessed. "I have to admit, I'm hanging on by a thread. It is a lot of material to take on board in such a short space of time."

"You're doing well. I can tell when someone is not getting it. Unlike most of the post-grads I've had the misfortune of mentoring, I can see the pennies dropping behind...both sets of eyes." Bruno said. He had the awareness to include Martha in the compliment.

A server came over and refilled their mugs with coffee. He paid no attention to what they were saying but they felt compelled to pause their conversation until he had gone.

"If however..." Bruno continued. "...QuantSim shows a singularity is an emergent property that follows on naturally from the formation of intelligent life, then we will be able to monitor the positives and negatives of it within the simulation. If those consequences are catastrophic then it is something we can avoid here in reality. If they are positive then we can work towards them and even expedite them based on what we learn from the more advanced civilisations that have developed within the framework."

"Will that not take a lot of time?"

Bruno smiled. "See, this is another way that I can tell how smart you are. You are asking all the right questions."

"Thanks". Katja was unable to stop herself from feeling a sense of pride. She was being praised on her intelligence by a person perceived by many to possess one of the greatest minds in history.

"The beauty of QuantSim is how we will be able to tweak the 'time" parameter within the simulations. We can set a universe in motion and billions of years will pass within it, in what to us would only take days or weeks. There are some hard limits on energy consumption and quantum stabilities but once the technology has matured, we should be able to run hundreds of them simultaneously."

"I see...and even if a singularity doesn't emerge, we might be able to learn something if a more advanced civilizations evolves within the simulations? We could get cures for diseases or other insights the likes of which are currently beyond our imaginations to conceive?" Katja said.

"Exactly." Bruno slapped his palm on the table. He had finally got through to someone who worked in media. He became aware of his watch as it rattled around his wrist. The hour hand jumped out at him. He realised he was running late for his consultation at Braxton Central Hospital.

"It doesn't sound like there is much of a downside. Why are people like Parv...I mean Dr Panwar against it?"

He knew.

"I don't know." He coughed into his fist and cleared his throat. "Listen, I have to get off to an appointment but please take my card and maybe we can talk later."

Katja sipped at her coffee as she watched him struggle his way through the tight arrangement of tables. Martha took the opportunity to visit the toilet and then go outside for a cigarette. Katja reached into her purse and pulled out Dr Panwar's card and placed it next to the one Professor Matthams had just given her.

She could feel things were changing in her professional life. She also knew that to maximise her chances of success, she would need to concentrate completely on her career. She picked up one of the stray coins Bruno had left as a tip for the waiting staff. She walked over to the phone booth in the corner of the restaurant, and dialed her boyfriend's number.

"Listen...we need to talk."

A

Bishop Anthony Gaumond lay in his hospital bed surrounded by a small entourage. It consisted of his chaplain, several ambitious priests, and some medical staff. Archbishop Hayhurst's private secretary had promised he was on route to deliver sacrament. It was now unlikely he would make it in time. The medical team had exhausted all their options. There was now nothing to do other than for Gaumond to await his inevitable demise. He had advised his consorts to turn their prayers to the welfare of his spirit. The thought of death elicited no dread. He knew his Lord and saviour was waiting with open arms to welcome him into the light. He was ready to let go.

He ached to let go.

...but he had to fight to hold on long enough so he could see the boy. His grandson was a prodigious mathematical talent with a sharp mind for logic and science but he lacked an appreciation of the more fundamental matters of faith. There was no point in a child excelling in academic disciplines if their soul was subsequently neglected. A brief but successful scientific career seemed meaningless if it came at the expense of eternal salvation. Gaumand wanted one last chance to instill a sense of belief in the final living member of the family line. It was a challenge he had spent a significant amount of his recent glut of spare time ruminating on. After much study and cross-referencing amongst various disciplines, he felt he had come up with a solution. He might not be able to convince his grandson via traditional theological methods. He was hoping a strategy of melding these to a strong logical framework might open his heart to the awesome power of faith.

Gaumond's tiredness seemed to take on the tangible consistency of a viscous liquid, oozing up from his feet, through his legs and along his spine. It had no colour but it radiated its own comforting heat. It made its way into his cranium and began to pool in his eyelids. These sank across his pupils until the thick fluid consumed his vision. The room around him faded to black.

"He has arrived." A familiar voice cut through the sludge like vinegar droplets slicing through oil.

"No matter. It is too late. Let him sleep." Another voice commanded.

It took a monumental effort for Gaumand to raise himself back above the surface. He emerged with a sharp intake of breath, absorbing the revitalising oxygen pumped into his nostrils via a plastic tube.

"Let me speak to him."

"Bring the boy forward." Chaplain Clove said. He beckoned towards the back of the room, attempting to convey his position as the Bishop's legitimate successor.

"Alone." A strength was growing in Gaumand's voice.

"Everybody out." Chaplain Clove bellowed.

The medical team exchanged furtive glances. They did not like to let someone so young watch death unfold alone but they had to respect the Bishop's wishes. The assembled group shuffled into the corridor leaving only Gaumand, Chaplain Clove and Rhett.

"Alone." Bishop Gaumand repeated.

Chaplain Clove opened his mouth to protest but before saying anything reconsidered. He closed the door as he left.

Rhett had never been prone to crying but seeing his once physically commanding grandfather lying in a hospital bed, shrivelled and frail, unleashed a wave of emotion. He sobbed, unable to return his grandfather's intense stare. His own eyes focused through his tears on the chequered black-and-white tiles of the floor. He felt as if his mind was floating outside his body, above and behind the back of his head. It was not a sensation he had ever experienced before.

"How old are you now Rhett?"

"Thirteen granpapa." Rhett sniffed.

"Well it is time to grow up. Don't let the emotions overcome you. Be aware you are feeling them but understand they are transient. There is a more fundamental part of you that can acknowledge their existence and their power, but is not controlled by their ebbs and flows."

Rhett's internal sensory and perceptual systems reconfigured in an instant. His conscious mind snapped back into the region of space taken up by his brain. The words had delivered to a greater extent than Bishop Gaumond could possibly have hoped. A sense of self-awareness reverberated violently through Rhett's core. He inhaled with a sharp intake of breath in response to the new sensations and then exhaled through parted lips. He wiped away the residual moisture on his face with his sleeve. He directed the bright focus of his gaze into the eyes of his grandfather.

It was Gaumond's turn to inhale sharply. He was shocked by the intensity exuding from his grandson. He felt confident his final words would not be wasted. "There's something I have to tell you."

Rhett nodded.

"There is no God."

Rhett's first reaction was to feel a deep frustration at all the hours he had wasted servicing the ritualistic obligations required by his family's religion. He was now being informed by the patriarch how meaningless it had all been. His second reaction was to be aware of the first reaction happening to him and then to let it pass.

"You seem shocked." Gaumond had misread Rhett's response.

"I'm surprised to hear such a sentiment coming from you."

Gaumond chuckled. His laughter turned into an extended bout of coughing. Rhett handed him some water as a concerned Chaplain Clove poked his head around the door. Through his wheezing, Gaumond signalled for him to leave.

The water helped and Gaumond's breathing returned to a rasp.

"At least it is very unlikely there is a god... extremely unlikely...so infinitesimally unlikely it is indistinguishable from there being zero possibility of God's existence. Hence, it is fair to say that there is no God.

"However, a wise philosopher named Pascal once pointed out that irrespective of how low the odds, a rational person should believe. If there is a God who in his infinite wisdom and mercy, grants eternal bliss to the souls of believers then there is unlimited potential gain for the finite loss of the activities required to earn his grace." Bishop Gaumand said. He could see his grandson processing the information by the way his eyes were darting around the room without taking in any visual information. " Don't you think this reconciles the logical frameworks of science and the theological systems of faith into a glorious and beautiful union?"

Rhett shrugged, still waiting for his mind to run through all the logical paths created by his grandfather's assertion. Bishop Gaumond exerted tremendous effort to place his palm upon his grandson's cheek.

"Believe in science, my boy. Believe in God, my child. Believe in both with all your heart, my love. But know deep inside yourself that every conceivable scenario leads to the same conclusion. Do everything you can to ensure your soul shines bright so God can single you out from the dimness of the crowd."

He smiled sweetly at the only child of his only child. He felt a sense of deep satisfaction that he had covered all the bases of eternal life. His corporeal existence would continue through the strands of his DNA embedded in the boy. His spirit would live on through the threads of faith that reached out into the holy domain from a lifetime of prayer. The swell of thick liquid was beginning to resume its irresistible surge through his body. He had no more reason to fight the oncoming subsumption of his increasingly redundant physical frame.

"What about if there is a God who punishes people who have faith? What if he gets angry when time is wasted time on such trivial matters?"

"What?"

"Don't the sum total of all probabilities and consequences regarding the existence and motivations of any given deity or deities cancel each other out thus rendering the wager moot? " Rhett was articulating his conclusions out loud, unable to filter the flow of his thoughts. "A rational man would acknowledge the riddle for the bit of fun it is and then live his life without specific reference to it."

Dread rushed through Bishop Gaumond's mind. He had forgotten he could feel that way. It only remained for the briefest of moments before a large wave of black treacle engulfed it.

...and then...

...nothing.

Bishop Gaumond's hand dropped from Rhett's face and swung limp by the side of the bed.

Rhett's posture sagged. In that moment, he wanted to feel love and joy for the life his grandfather had lived. He could only feel pity. He was a man who had lived his life based on sound logic but unfortunately that logic had been built around false axioms. A sense of guilt was the next emotion to creep up on him. It would return to him from time-to-time throughout his life. He should have humoured his grandfather in those final moments. It was already too late for the truth to matter, so it made no sense to have sent him into the abyss with a mind full of doubt.

The encounter left a lasting mark on Rhett but it was not the one Bishop Gaumond had sought. Rhett became obsessed by the question of supernatural motivations. If there was a higher power, whether omniscient or limited in the scope of its knowledge, whether omnipotent or bounded in its powers, whether interested in human development or uncaring, whatever its makeup or motivation, how could he maximise the chances of at least getting its attention?

He knew the conundrum held no practical relevance but he would return to it periodically throughout his life. It was an intriguing thought experiment. He would use it to occupy his mind when he needed a break from the other abstract matters he would make a career out of considering. If he could solve it, it might be enough to assuage his guilt and make up for the suffering he had caused his grandfather in those final moments.

VII

"Hmmnay hmmnay blah blah yerp..."

Bruno was staring at the moving lips of his oncologist, Dr Vargas, aware of the sounds coming out of her mouth but their meaning was not registering in his brain. She was listing the series of tests he had undergone over the two visits he had made to Braxton Central Hospital in the preceding week. He knew she had to go through the full procedure and although all he wanted was for her to spit out the results, he was aware any interruptions or protestations would simply delay the speed they were delivered to him. He had tried to hurry her along at previous appointments and this had just led to calm explanations of how her methods were the consequence of years of research and how he should trust in their efficacy. He nodded along with slight upward curls in place at the edges of his mouth, conveying to her he was fully following and comprehending each of the statements she was reading robotically from a list in his file. She made sure to get a positive verbal response before moving on to the next item.

"Is everything clear?" Her head remained angled towards the file, meaning her eyes made contact with his over the rims of her dark spectacles.

"Yes." Bruno had previously attempted to mix his affirmative responses up by replying to her with words like 'sure", 'totally" and "of course" but these had elicited concerned facial expressions. He had learned to respond in the clearest and simplest way possible to any of her questions.

"OK." She ticked the final box and then took a moment to inspect the back of the paper, which she knew would be blank. It was something she always did as a delaying tactic while she gathered herself to deliver terrible news after the formalities were over. "I am afraid the diagnosis is the worst of the possible outcomes we discussed. You have a T4 N3 M1 cancer which means it..."

"...it is a stage four cancer which has spread to several lymph nodes and other parts of the body." Bruno interrupted, speaking as if in a trance.

Bruno had been expecting this news and was prepared for it. He had just sensed that the cancerous cells had infiltrated his blood and his bones, which ached its message to him in the earliest hours, in those moments where he was not still sleeping but also not yet fully awake. At least, he had convinced himself he was expecting the news. There was still a small part of him that was unsure as to whether he had really been prepared for it but now the information was truly out there, he was slightly surprised that he had not in fact been fooling himself.

"How could it have happened so quickly? I had a medical a few years ago and OK, I was not given a sparkling bill of health and I was told I had to start looking after myself better...which..., I didn't really do...but there was no hint of this."

"I'm sorry Professor Matthams but we still do not have a full understanding of how this disease develops, and unfortunately the tests performed in a routine medical would not have tested for this type of illness anyway." Dr Vargas scanned her notes to see if there were any factors that might have given any clues to this diagnosis on his last medical but having gone through it thoroughly with him several times already, knew nothing would stand out.

Bruno sat in silence, gazing at his hands, which were joined together by his interconnected fingers and resting on his lap. Dr Vargas had been trained to remain silent during these moments and although she still found it hard because it went against all her social instincts, she waited patiently for Bruno to show signs of being ready to continue their discussion.

Bruno knew what had caused the malevolent mutations in his body...well, he didn't KNOW...but he KNEW. He could imagine the streams of excited subatomic particles flowing through him as he calibrated the quantum hardware required for QuantSim to function. He could see them passing through his organic matter with hardly any form of interaction but due to the volume, every so often one would strike at the DNA of one of his cells. The chances of any of these interactions resulting in the cell metamorphosing into a hostile entity were infinitesimal but the cumulative effect of the countless hours he had spent in this state meant that some sort of adverse action was almost certain to take place. He looked up to see Dr Vargas waiting patiently for him to compose himself but he had no desire to discuss any of this with Dr Vargas.

"I'm guessing not...but are there any options in terms of treatment?" Bruno uncoupled his fingers and ran them through his hair.

"There are things we could try but to be brutally honest with you, at this point the treatments will be worse than the symptoms of the disease and although they might prolong your life by a short period, that extension would be extremely uncomfortable. So in terms of offering you the best chance of maintaining a decent quality of life for your remaining months, my advice would be not to undertake any treatment."

Bruno cursed the irony of having ignored the potential dangers inherent in the new technology he was building in order to speed up the process of completing it. That haste had directly led to an overall decrease in the time available for him to complete his work. It would now be highly unlikely that he would ever see QuantSim in action. His upper lip began to tremble and the corners of his eyes developed a salty sting. He fought the tears and forced himself to take comfort in the fact that although he would perish, his work would endure...at least, it would if Dr Panwar and wAIt ever allowed it to. This was now his biggest fear. Who would act as an advocate for the technology once he was gone? Was there anyone who even had the capacity to understand it enough to make it work when he was no longer around?

"Right. I'll do what I can." Bruno said aloud to himself, exhaling explosively.

"What do you mean?" Dr Vargas asked him.

"Sorry...I was just talking to myself. I'll just have to stay positive and do what I can to make the rest of time I have left mean something."

"That's a very admirable attitude." Dr Vargas said, hoping to maintain the positivity.

Dr Vargas spent some time explaining to Bruno how things would progress. After he had confirmed he understood everything and that he knew she was always available to address any concerns he might have, at least during office hours, she directed him back to the waiting room with a small bundle of leaflets and documents. She had arranged for him to meet with a counsellor directly after the appointment was over and so he picked up a magazine and flicked through it, while waiting for his name to be called once more.

He marvelled at the irony of how QuantSim had directly led to the onset of his cancer and how his research into the condition had directly led to his final breakthrough in making QuantSim function autonomously. He had been stuck on trying to ensure each of the qubits was able to carry out a predetermined function within the quantum mainframe but after learning how cancer cells rely on mutational outliers called subclones to accelerate progress. These side branches are the things that make cancer so hard to treat because they allow it to adapt to different scenarios and respond dynamically to attacks. Cancer's diversity of structure is what gives it options - and this was what was needed to give QuantSim the ability to truly operate as a sophisticated, self-perpetuating virtual universe. He stopped trying to imbue them with limited operability and allowed the software inputs to cascade back through them, altering their state and adapting their function. If he had not started building QuantSim, he might never have developed cancer but if he had never developed cancer, he might not have been able to solve the final problem in making QuantSim fully realise its potential.

His train of thought was broken when he sensed out of the corner of his eye that someone was staring at him. Bruno was used to a small level of fame due to his work on the games Other Side and T.W.O.K, and the recent controversy around QuantSim had raised his profile somewhat, so he had some experience in fending off unwanted attention. He shifted his body away from the offending person and tried to cocoon himself in the pages of the magazine. It was only at this point he realised it was upside down. He rotated it slowly as if looking in more detail at a photo and then repositioned it so it was the right way up. In the midst of the convoluted maneuver, he snuck a look in the direction of his observer and a flicker of recognition flashed through his mind but after a second surreptitious glance, he could not place the face. He did notice however that they had moved to a seat much closer to him.

Bruno continued to leaf through the magazine until he stumbled across an article on QuantSim. He was loath to read anything about it in the press as invariably they would misunderstand some aspect of it or misconstrue his objectives but as there was little else to do, he began to scan the copy. It was at this point he saw a picture of the face opposite him and her name was written underneath. His brain suddenly remembered he had seen her hanging around outside Braxton University amongst the protestors. Dr Parveen Panwar of wAIt was in the same waiting room as him and seemed intent on some form of engagement. He realised her looming presence was irresistible and so with a resigned sigh, he slowly lowered the glossy papers he was hiding behind and nodded solemnly at her.

"Breast cancer. Remission." She with a comforting smile, pointing at herself with her thumb.

Introducing yourself with your specific condition was not something Bruno had experienced before, but somehow in this setting it instinctively made sense and all the wariness he previously felt towards her vanished. It was as if there was a secret language and set of practices that all cancer patients innately understood as soon as they received their diagnosis.

"I've pretty much got it everywhere. Category T4 N3 M1, untreatable...terminal." Bruno said.

Parveen pursed her lips and sucked in sharply, inadvertently producing a dull whistling sound. She checked herself and the absence of it created a thick cloud of silence between them. It seemed primed to release a lightning bolt asking "how long", but also ready to dissipate should Bruno choose not to answer the question which could never be verbalised. This seemed to be another of those unwritten modes of communication intuitively understood by fellow sufferers and Bruno felt safe answering what had not explicitly been asked.

"6 months...maybe...of any quality."

Parveen's head bobbed up and down and her eyes blinked slowly. She knew her cause combined with his situation would likely lead to Professor Matthams never seeing the fruits of his genius working in practice.

"You see now why some of us can't..." Bruno paused for comedic effect as he bent and twisted his fingers in a vain attempt to represent mixed capitalisation within his next word. "...wait."

He was hoping for at least a chuckle of recognition but when it didn't come he raised his eyebrow as a prompt.

"Yeah, I get it Professor Matthams." Parveen said flatly.

"Do you?...Do you though? I have stretched the possibilities of our scientific understanding to levels not expected for generations...if at all ever. This new technology exists only because of me. It has not simply come five years early or ten years early, and all I have done is act as a catalyst to bring it forward. QuantSim could not and would not have existed without me and now you are obstructing me from seeing it in action...from seeing what wonders it could reap...from seeing if it could give me...give us all more time."

"I understand that Professor Matthams..and I also understand these personal considerations do not come into questions of legality and ethics. If the claims you make about there being the possibility of sentient life evolving within QuantSim, no matter how slim, then we have a duty to create protections for those lives."

"...but they would not have existed otherwise. Is it not our duty to allow them the greatest opportunity possible...to exist?"

"I don't know Professor Matthams. I don't have the answers to those questions but I do know we need to have those answers before we embark on this path. What if we are condemning a host of sentient beings who can feel, and think, and experience torment just like us, to lives of anguish, pain or slavery...or things we are unable to conceive of with our limited imagination? If our own history is anything to go by, would you want to be responsible for having initiated our existence?"

Bruno shuddered as he contemplated some of the atrocities of recent history, let alone the full abominations dating back to the emergence of the species.

"I think it would be worth it." He said.

"Yes, I see that. You think...you feel...you reason...but you don't know. You are undoubtedly a genius, Professor Matthams, but you are not infallible. Your ability to create the system does not automatically give you the right to turn on the system, or make ethical judgements about it. In that sense it belongs to society as a whole. As one of our great thinkers once said, you can only see as far as the hills because of your ancestors who built a platform over the trees."

Bruno let out an involuntary snort at Parveen's inaccurate recollection of the phrase, but he understood her point, so tried to make it look as if he had been clearing his throat.

"I know." Bruno placed the magazine on the chair next to him and leaned towards Parveen. "I know all these arguments but it still doesn't stop me from feeling this overwhelming sense of despair and frustration."

A tense moment of silence landed as Bruno and Parveen stared intently at each other. Parveen had never understood the depths of feeling the QuantSim creator had for his project and she sympathised with how his condition altered his ability to be patient. However, this was no reason to abandon her morality. It was her sacred duty to rise above the needs of the individual and protect the greater good of the collective, irrespective of whether the collective was extended to include beings residing in a virtual reality, unaware of their creators.

"Dr Panwar." The tannoy broke the silence and alerted Parveen that Dr Vargas was now ready to see her.

"I understand your impatience Dr Matthams, I really do...but these matters have to be resolved using the correct legal tools." She gathered her things and stood up. "I do wish you the best of luck with your condition and I just hope you can work with us for the benefit of society. You still have a lot to offer and there is still time for your legacy to expand. If you were to really commit to the legal process, you could help expedite it."

Bruno watched her walk towards the exit and after she had gone, he lifted the magazine back to being level with his eyes even though in reality, he stared straight through it. He understood her reasoning on an intellectual level and as tempted as he was to go ignore due process, he vowed to take her advice and make sure everything was clearly defined and documented so those who came after him could utilise his work once he was gone.

VIII

Bruno rushed down to see who was banging on his door. He had been in a deep slumber aided by a sedative given to him by the counsellor he had seen earlier. It had taken him a while to understand the banging was not another aspect of the harrowing dreams he had been experiencing all night. These were fairly common on nights after partying at a place like Furnace and in combination with the personal news he had received, they had taken on a strange gothic quality. They were full of vast moorlands, ancient buildings, long corridors and blocked archways, ghouls and demons shocking him repeatedly from the depths of the shadows. He used his finger and thumb to wipe the crust of sleep from the corners of his eyes, remembering the tears welling there as he lost consciousness the night before. He opened the door a crack to see Katja Lietner standing on his doorstep.

"What is it?" He closed his nightgown and tied it while stifling a yawn.

"I'm sorry to bother you but the news desk told me we have some exclusive breaking news about you."

"Is it about my diagnosis?" Bruno was not sure why this would be considered newsworthy.

"I don't know. Senior management are keeping this completely within their inner circle until they release it on the 9 O"Clock news. I was hoping you might be able to shed some light on it."

Katja was aiming to secure her own exclusive in terms of getting Bruno's reaction to whatever the breaking news happened to be. It would only be a matter of time before other journalists found out his address but for now, she was the only one who had any clue to his whereabouts. VEX News had been scrambling to find it but she had kept quiet, his personal details scorching the lining of her purse on the card he had given her earlier. She had a limited period to get the inside scoop from his perspective and she was not going to waste the opportunity.

Bruno looked at his watch and quickly turned on the TV just in time to hear the final chimes of Braxton's imperial clock tower, indicating the news bulletin was about to begin.

"Hello. My name is Amanda Tanner, you're watching the VEX Network and this is the 9 OClock News. Our first story tonight is a breaking story about Professor Bruno Matthams of Braxton University. He is currently working on a controversial project called QuantSim. This controversy is set to grow rapidly after VEX News received the following video."

The screen switched to footage taken on a covert recording device. It was a limited quality and had been stretched to fit the screen but its contents were easily recognisable.

"Here I am inside the famous Haston Facility at Braxton University." Axe was speaking into the camera as he walked through Bruno's workshop.

Bruno was unable to stop himself from feeling a twinge of sexual desire while looking at Axe even while the painful evidence of how he had violated his trust was playing out in front of him. It was a strange cocktail of feelings, which itself was soon washed away by an even more curious combination of excitement and dread.

"This amorphous lump of human flesh over here is by most accounts the most intelligent man ever to grace our planet...Professor Bruno Matthams." The camera rotated to point at Bruno who was asleep in his office, loosely covered in a make-shift blanket of industrial tarpaulin, which was normally used for rapid prototyping. He was wearing nothing but a pair of white briefs and as hurtful as it was, Bruno could not dispute Axe's description of his body.

"Last night the two of us met at Furnace and after consuming a few drinks and a few...well...I don't want to say it here, but you all know what I mean..." Axe winked at the camera with his left eye. "...the two of us came back to his supposedly highly secure offices and then we...well...I don't want to say it here, but you all know what I mean." Axe winked at the camera with his right eye.

"Can you believe this ugly bastard thought he had enough value to land this?" Axe placed the camera on a desk and spun around, showing off a figure honed by thousands of hours of hard work in the gym and difficult dietary sacrifices.

"I mean, he might be a genius but for something like that to land something like this, he'd need to have achieved be some sort of god." Axe cackled at his own joke. "I think we need to make him pay for his arrogance. Don't you?"

Axe walked over to Bruno and pursed his lips and kissed Bruno on the forehead. He quickly wiped his lips as he scrunched up his face in disgust. He mimed the action of vomiting all over Bruno.

"Most of you will have heard at least something about Matthams as the creator of the smash hit game Other Side or his flop T.W.O.K, but what you might not have heard about his latest cutting edge but controversial work with quantum computing and simulated realities. Should he run it? Should he not?" Axe made an over-the-top yawning gesture. "Boring."

Axe moved towards the button Bruno had shown him the previous evening.

"World....The time has come to push the button." Axe lifted his hand high in the air then stopped. "...but before I turn this on, make sure you go out to the shops tomorrow and buy Barnstorm's latest single, Turn It On, featuring me, Axe Vyne, on vocals. I promise you, you will not be disappointed."

He dropped his arm with a dramatic flourish and placed his index finger onto the unassuming red switch and slowly applied pressure until it clicked. He turned back to the camera, widened his eyes and elongated his face as he mouthed the word, "whoops". The deep bass beats of the song he had mentioned began to play in the background.

"Bye shagger." He said as he spun the camera back towards Bruno.

The camera was then turned back on himself as he made his way to exit the lab. A sense of panic seemed to flash across his eyes as he pulled on the door but on finding that it opened easily, he visibly relaxed.

"Bye shaggers." He said into the camera and then the video cut to a black screen with Axe's animated logo spinning over the top of it.

Katja looked over at Bruno who was slumped forwards with his head in his hands. The news report continued in the background but Bruno was no longer paying attention to it. Katja sat next to him and patted his back in an attempt to comfort him. His phone was ringing and it took an age before he realised ignoring it was not going to make it stop.

"Yes...yes....no....yes." He coughed into his fist and cleared his throat. "OK, I'll come straight over."

B

Tara had always had a keen sense of her own normality. The third of four sisters, she would see her siblings and her friends generate countless frustrations and miseries for themselves through the continual erosion of their ego as it scraped across the harsh frictions of rough reality. It was not to say Tara felt in any way inferior to the people around her, if anything she felt superior at having been blessed with the wisdom to accept and appreciate her consummate conventionality.

"You're a very beautiful little girl." Her elderly relatives would tell her.

"I'm not, I'm just normal." She would reply, knowing inside that this was true and being completely at peace with it.

"You're so clever." Her parents would say when she achieved some entirely trivial milestone in life such as tying her shoelaces or riding her bike without stabilisers.

"Nope. Everyone manages to do that at around my age...unless they have specific difficulties." She would say, not accepting the commendation because the underlying achievement warranted none.

"If you study hard, you can do anything you want in life." Her teachers would offer encouragement to try and motivate her to study more.

She had learned quickly enough that her protestations evoked discomfort in those attempting to compliment her so she would smile sweetly in response but internally she rebuffed the notion of infinite possibilities laying ahead of her. She knew her position in every measurable respect lay within a standard deviation of the bell curve she had studied in statistics, as a capable but average student, and she was happy with that. Her academic achievements came about purely because she conscientiously worked through the curriculum, not from any flashes of deep insight or passion for the subject.

She would work hard. She would get a good normal job, the specifics of which were essentially irrelevant, as long as it offered sufficient challenges and paid commensurately. She would find a nice husband of similar normality and have nice normal kids. She would live a very average and very happy life, unencumbered by dreamy notions of a different life that could, would or should have been. She saw her sisters agonise over whether or not the choices they made were in fact the correct ones, and it seemed strange to her why they would waste so much effort on matters of such minor consequence.

There was not enough difference between James and Phil to worry too much about who they had as their boyfriend. The contrast between choosing to learn French or German was tiny. The repercussions on your life were the same whether you did the qualification in hospitality or the course in office management. She would always invest time listening to their woes, all the while wondering why they worried so much about such trivia, none of them ever realising they never had to return the favour of providing support for Tara's choices.

Her school days were carefree and full as she slotted seamlessly into the middle tiers of her social circles. She had solid friendships and interesting relationships, had fun on all the trips, was invited to all the parties and was asked by nice boys to all the dances. The schoolwork was challenging but with effort, not too much, she was able to achieve good grades, in the same way most others would have if they had applied themselves adequately.

She was firmly entrenched in popular culture, falling in line with the particular fashions and trends as they came and went. She would get the same haircut as the pretty side-kick in her favourite show, fancy the third most popular member of every charting boyband, and have seen, read or been to every film, book, show or concert that warranted attention from her peers. The only slight variation from the norm was how here interests were skewed somewhat towards science fiction. She was not absorbed into the growing popularity of "nerd culture" but she did enjoy reading literature and watching things where scientific and technological boundaries were stretched to the max.

She liked the practical aspects of the arts and gravitated towards digital design and her work was always completed on time and fully compliant with the brief, even if it lacked the elusive "edge" some of her peers and tutors seemed to revere. Her abilities earned her a place to study multimedia at Nottingham University, far enough away from family to offer her freedoms but close enough to allow her to fall back on their support when the unknown unknowns of life invariably came her way.

While studying for her degree, she became much more interested in environmental matters and was an active member of EcoSoc, taking on the role of secretary in her final year. She found it frustrating that it was clear what had to be done to take the planet to a sustainable position where the economy could function to provide everyone with a comfortable existence without destroying the delicate natural ecosystem, and yet nobody seemed to have the will to make the necessary changes for it to happen. She was not willing to join them herself but understood the way organisations like Greenpeace, Extinction Rebellion and Occupy felt it necessary to protest in an active manner. She drew the line at offering support to the fringe groups such as the recently formed ViroMental, which sought to effect change through any means necessary.

She had a few brief affairs, several one-night stands and one long relationship, which ended shortly after graduation by mutual consent when they found that professional opportunities had landed them in separate geographies. They professed to love each other but it turned out not to be strong enough to overcome a ninety minute commute between their respective new homes.

She applied for several internships and although she did not receive an offer from her preferred agency, she did have a number of others to choose from. She eventually decided on a small PR company in Birmingham, which had a strong client portfolio of ethical and environmental charities. She was far enough away from family to enable her to assert her independence but close enough to pop back and get her washing done every now and then.

After a couple of months in dingy bedsits to acclimatise to the area, her living arrangements became much more pleasant when she moved into a small house in Edgbaston with two other young female professionals who offered each other fun, friendship and support. Samantha was training to be an accountant and Nina had a project management role in a property company. The roots of their social network spread through the city and everything in Tara's life was progressing in an agreeable and standard manner.

"Our company received a few tickets for the Birmingham University gala…" Samantha said through a mouthful of spaghetti, a bad habit of hers mimicked by Nina and Tara when she was not there. "…and nobody was really fussed about going so I bagged three for us. It might be quite boring but I thought we might as well check it out and maybe head out to a club after…oh, and it's free booze."

"You had me at free booze?" Nina raised her eyebrow, clicked her tongue and pointed at Sam.

"Really? At free booze? So I had you at the very last part of what I said?"

They all burst out laughing and then a second wave spread through them as they all reached for their wine glasses at the exact same time.

It did not take the three of them long to realise the university had stretched the definition of their event to its limit. It was more of an opportunity for networking between local business and academics, with the gala element being provided by a short and largely ignored set by a local comedian, and some music from a local school orchestra. The young women felt a little self-conscious in their formal gowns but soon made the decision to make the most of the evening after consuming copious amounts of the boxed white wine on offer.

"Tara?" There was a light tap on her shoulder. The owner of the finger seemed familiar but she could not remember why.

"Brett?" She ventured.

"Rhett." He smiled and nodded, accepting the first impression he had made on her had not been as potent as the one she made on him. "We met at the opening night of Winston's exhibition."

"Yes of course." The tone of her voice betrayed her sincerity. "Great to see you again."

Samantha and Nina hovered behind him, waiting to see if Tara would indicate a desire to be extricated from this enforced interaction. She had gifted Rhett the purest form of generosity by granting him her full attention, which meant that at least for now she was happy to spend some time with him, and so her two friends stood down from their state of alert. They were confident she would make it known to them if at any point circumstances changed.

"What brings you to an event like this?" Rhett swept his arm across the room with exaggerated dramatic flourish. The lights in the room flickered momentarily, which added to the spectacle.

"Why does anyone come to the Birmingham University Outreach Gala? I was looking to be challenged on an existential level, hoping for a transformative and exhilarating experience to redefine the relationship between my mind and my soul. I was expecting to be exposed to an array of stimuli so vigorous and powerful that I would be overcome by wave after wave of awe and wonder."

Rhett laughed. The most amusing aspect of her joke being that unbeknownst to her, she had accurately described his feelings when he looked into her eyes.

"...either that or because I heard there was a free bar." The self-deprecating delivery of her punchline and the lilting cascade of her infectious laughter convinced Rhett that beyond the instantaneousness of the physical attraction, he could easily fall in love with her...and although he would have denied it, it was obvious to anyone who observed him basking in her presence, that he already had.

Tara wasn't sure where this had come from. She would often think about making jokes like this, especially when mulling over her social performances in retrospect but she never went as far as actually saying them. There was just something about being with Rhett that was making her feel different about herself. The way he was looking at her made her feel something new.

He made her feel special.

For the first time in her life, Tara felt like she was more than normal, and much to her surprise, she liked it.

IX

The leather creaked as Bruno sunk as deep as he could into the vintage chair, experiencing sensations he had not endured since his earliest days in academic life. He sat opposite the Vice-Chancellor, ostensibly his boss but due to Bruno's tenured position was little more than one more administrative annoyance. Another in a long line of bureaucrats who flapped around while people like himself did real work and made actual academic progress. They came and went in five-year cycles that began with bursts of energetic motivation and ended in resignation of both descriptions. Bruno would suffer through their political ambitions and desire for legacy, knowing they fulfilled a necessary function, but he never lost sight of how all their sound and fury would ultimately signify nothing. It was important not to get sucked into their pet projects or political machinations otherwise vast quantities of time could be lost to irrelevant concerns. After each of these temporary figureheads departed, they would leave nothing behind but another plaque to polish. Bruno had always known he too would one day also have to depart, his recent diagnosis bringing this truth into sharper focus. The difference was that after he had gone, his work would remain and endure, acting as a foundation for future discoveries and developments. This fact was the thing that gave his life purpose and meaning above all else and meant Bruno had little need to worry about the whims of the institution's executive.

Today was different. Bruno's tenure was on the line and the Vice-Chancellor had undeniably been given adequate cause to explore each and every avenue at his disposal. It was clear today how much his position as Bruno's boss was much more than ceremonial. In homage to his former experiences in such disciplinary matters, Vice-Chancellor Zahid Mashwani was projecting the commanding presence of a headmaster chastising an unruly pupil.

"Well..." Zahid slammed his palm on the table.

Bruno shook his head weakly.

"How could someone, who is by all accounts and measures the very definition of a genius, go and do something so stupid?"

"I'm sorry." Bruno mumbled.

"What?" Zahid was struggling to believe the immaturity Bruno was displaying, unaware his own demeanour had contributed to Bruno's regression.

"I'm sorry." Bruno raised his voice and looked the Vice-Chancellor directly in the eyes, displaying his own, which were welling up with tears.

"Sorry?...I'm not sure sorry is going to cut it this time, Professor Matthams."

"What else can I say? I may have a high aptitude in certain areas but that doesn't translate across all aspects of my life. I find it easy to understand complex fundamental concepts...allowing me to manipulate the mathematical constructs governing them... but there are basic social facets I just can't comprehend." Bruno's voice broke down as he finished the sentence.

"It must have been clear to you that the..." Zahid snapped his fingers as he searched for the right word. "...balance...between you and Axe Vyne was not there. There's no way he could have assessed your true worth...and that's always going to be a problem for you. People will never be able to see beyond the superficial and take time to understand the value beneath." Zahid looked up and down Bruno's obese figure, already contemplating how to clean the sweat from the antique leather of the chair. "...and you have the added problem of only a very few people on the planet having the capacity to even comprehend your abilities, even if they were to invest the time.."

"I know...I do know...but he seemed interested...genuinely interested in my work and all the other stuff like Other Side. I dared to believe...allowed myself to believe that I might finally have found someone who valued me for what I am behind all this." Bruno puffed out his cheeks and tracked his hands up and down his frame. He then lowered his head with his eyes fixed on a spot just below the floorboards. "Why shouldn't he be able to see that my intelligence was equal to...if not more valuable than his physical attributes? Why couldn't it be a fair exchange?"

"We're not teenagers Professor Matthams. You know how this world works?"

Bruno's chin slumped fully into the padding of fat created by lowering it into his chest.

"OK...OK...We're not going to get too much further discussing the whys. I suppose we'd better turn our attention to the practical ways we can respond to this."

"RIght." Bruno inhaled deeply and lifted his head to reveal a fresh brightness to his eyes.

"So what exactly is going on within QuantSim?"

"Well...that's the problem. We can't really be sure. I've established the node network so the application now manifests within the uncertainties inherent across the entanglements of the superpositioned quantum foam. However, the current architecture only allows for downstream cascading so there is no system log or tracking API."

"I see." Zahid tapped his chin and looked thoughtfully at the smudge on the window.

"Really?"

"No."

"Basically, I set it all up so it can run a full scale artificial universe but I have not created anything that allows us to monitor what is going on inside the simulation."

"What do you presume is going on inside?"

"Probably nothing. The most likely scenario is that it has spawned a cold and empty universe that will run its course over the next few weeks or so and then die."

"Is there any chance it could contain simulated life?"

"It is likely that it will simulate some basic lifeforms...so something equivalent to bacteria...but I can't imagine anything more complex being simulated. We are not yet certain of the probabilities when it comes to the development of life, even in our own universe, and that is one of the questions this was designed to answer. However, you would have to expect it to be extremely...infinitesimally...low. "

"So...we could just turn it off?"

"Yeah. I don't see why not."

"It's just that some people, such as my ex-wi---" Zahid cleared his throat. "...some people, Dr Panwar of wAIt is one notable example...are saying there could be some ethical implications to turning it off."

Bruno's head snapped back sharply at the news Dr Panwar and Vice-Chancellor Mashwani had formerly been married.

"She's entitled to her opinion but in all honesty, I think it just shows her fundamental inability to understand the statistics."

"Great...because the power consumption of having this thing on is costing almost as much per day as we were previously spending in a year."

Vice-Chancellor Mashwani looked down at his intercom in annoyance as it began to buzz. He leaned across his desk to access the awkwardly placed activation button. "You know I am not to be disturbed during meetings."

"I understand." His secretary's voice crackled through the speaker. "It is just that there is a lawyer here with some police officers. They are insisting that they see you immediat---"

The doors to Zahid's office flung open and a familiar face burst through. Dr Panwar marched towards him flanked by three uniformed police officers. She was holding an official looking document in her hand, which she slapped on his desk with dramatic flair.

"I have here an emergency injunction that expressly forbids you from turning off QuantSim."

Bruno was startled to see Katja and her camera operator Martha following close behind. Katja gave him a wink before turning to camera and commenting on the scene to her viewers.

C

The Gaumond family history was one of tragedy and heartbreak. Bishop Gaumond's wife had died giving birth to Hue, their only son and Rhett's father. Hue had been a solemn child who in his early years had followed in his father's footsteps in respect of matters of ideology and dogma. He seemed destined to enter the clergy and rise through the ranks to equal or eclipse his father's achievements in the same way Anthony Gaumond had exceeded the eclesiastical accomplishments of his own father before him. Puberty hit Hue relatively late and when it did his attitude altered dramatically. It was almost impossible to imagine this formerly puritanical child could have grown into a tenaciously faithless and feral adolescent. He was impossible to reason with or control and he soon fell into a life of petty theft, mindless violence and drug abuse. He would often disappear for long periods of time and Bishop's Gaumand's only means of keeping him safe was through prayer and intercessions. It was during one of Hue's lost months when he was fifteen-years of age that he met and fell in love with sixteen year-old Amelia, Rhett's mother.

Amelia had come from a home of similarly ostensible privilege with an entrepreneurial father and a socially aspirational mother. She had struggled to fit in with the role they had outlined for her and as her interests diverged from ones useful to the advancement of the family, she was increasingly left to her own devices. Her siblings willingly embraced the banal politics of infiltrating high society and so her involvement was not deemed a priority. Hue and Ameila had connected instantly, facilitated by the respective weights of their perceived familial burdens. They were each other's first kiss and only hours after experiencing this tender rite of teenage passage while overlooking a lake, as a diminishing sun sparkled at them from its rippling waters, they lost their virginity to each other on a urine-soaked mattress during the fading flushes of a chemical high.

The reality shock of Ameila's pregnancy prompted them both to make every effort to clean themselves up and push all of their energies into supporting the life they had created together.
Ameila approached her parents alone but wary of how this scandalous narrative could negatively affect their flourishing brand, they suggested an abortion. Amelia's reticence prompted an ultimatum and her refusal quickly led to ostracism. It was a monumental effort in her fragile state but she was eventually able to kill them off in her mind. By the time Hue and Amelia presented their situation to Bishop Gaumand, he was informed that Ameila had been abandoned at an early age and had never known her parents. Much to Hue and Bishop Gaumand's own surprise, he embraced this development in

his son's life and vowed to tap into God's infinite well of grace to welcome them back into the flock. He thanked God for allowing him to prove himself through the test of a prodigal son.

The two lovers played their part as they transitioned back into the civilised domain...or at least they did in public but the opiates held their grip, and they could not resist having a surreptitious taste from time to time, even with the knowledge of the potential harm it could do to the baby growing inside Ameila's womb.

Rhett was born in a private eclesiastical hospital within Bishop Gaumond's diocese with the eager grandparent in attendance. Against all odds, Rhett appeared to be an extremely healthy child. The radiating glow of happiness that engulfed this extended family of four was pitifully brief as the following morning it had reduced to two when Amelia and Hue were found dead having overdosed on some unexpectedly pure celebratory hits of heroin.

Rhett was a robust and precocious child but Bishop Anthony Gaumond found it difficult to bond with him as he reminded him too much of his son. He tried his best to maintain contact and hide his underlying sorrow but it invariably led to ever-diminishing exposure to the boy. As such Rhett was brought up by a series of au pairs, tutors and Gaumand's eclesiastical subordinates. Bishop Gaumand was confident in his abilities in extending the reach of his Lord's mercy throughout his ordained jurisdiction but due to his failure's with his own son, he was filled with doubt in regards to his ability to positively influence his grandson. He came to the conclusion it would be in Rhett's interest for him to be sent away to a suitable boarding school at the earliest opportunity and so it was, at seven years old, he was escorted on the train by Chaplain Clove to the place that would be his main residence for the following eleven years.

Rhett and his grandfather would correspond frequently through handwritten letters and it was through this medium that Bishop Gaumand felt most comfortable trying to instil a sense of faith in his grandson. However, he struggled to answer the increasingly philosophical questions posed to him by Rhett, which were becoming as difficult to counter or predict as the moves he made in the correspondence chess they played. It became clear to both of them that Rhett had surpassed his grandfather's intellectual abilities before he was in his teens..Rhett felt the need to downplay his own abilities in their theological debates and had to formulate a new chess game for himself that involved losing believably from time-to-time so as not to upset his grandfather. Still, Bishop Gaumand never gave up belief that his grandson would also find his own way along the path of faith, continually attempting to guide him with different arguments, and approaching the topic from new angles derived from study and debate amongst his peers.

Rhett excelled at school. He was exceptionally clever and it soon became clear that not only did he have a prodigious intelligence, he was also gifted in sport, arts and music. He was able to play several instruments, the piano being his preferred option when he was forced to specialise. He captained the football team in winter terms and the cricket team during the summer. He had an easy charm and he was consistently regarded as one of the most popular people in his year group, if not the whole school. He enjoyed all his academic and extra-curricular activities but his real passion lay in physics and mathematics. He had a keen desire to drill down as far as possible to determine what it was that made things tick and why there was something and not nothing. He had always known he was destined for greatness and the only open question was where he would gift his attention. He came to believe theoretical physics was the ultimate challenge and it was this that ultimately won out as the field he chose to pursue.

His trips home became ever more infrequent and he stayed in boarding school during most holidays and when this was not a possibility, he would go and stay at the estates and manors of his friends. As such, when his grandfather died, little in his life changed and the generosity of the church ensured he was able to complete his studies without interruption and his grandfather's prudence had secured a financial buffer to support him. Despite their lack of emotional closeness, Rhett maintained a fondness for his grandfather and thought about him often. He also never forgot the conundrum that sprung into his mind in the moments after Bishop Gaumand's death.

He had his pick of universities to choose from and after doing his undergraduate degree in Cambridge and his masters and doctorate at Durham, he was lured to Birmingham University by a charismatic Dean who offered him access to all the funds he could possibly require to continue his study of the mysterious properties of dark looped gravity.

He had a few relationships but these always tended to be almost forced upon him by enigmatic admirers after they had spent significant resources pursuing him. He often felt like he was viewed as a prize or trophy rather than being appreciated for the person he was within. It was as if his potential mates viewed him as a commodity, whereas he wanted something more organic and authentic, probably a symptom of his secret passion for romance literature and poetry. He fully expected one day to be swept off his feet and experience a unique and passionate love along the lines of Romeo & Juliet, Wuthering Heights or Love In The Time Of Cholera. He thought his destiny was to feel things that could only be expressed by the likes of Shelley, Byron and Colleridge. He vowed not to settle for anything less.

He fell into a comfortable life and built up a strong network of friends within the city. He was active playing football at a semi-professional level and played in the first XI for West Bromwich Dartmouth Cricket Club.

"You can't keep skipping these events." Dean Okoro popped her head around Rhett's office door. "You're box office, so we need you to come and sprinkle some of your stardust at the Outreach Gala otherwise attendance is going to drop. We can't keep funding all that fancy equipment you are so fond of without the donations we receive from industry sponsors."

Rhett promised he would go. He actually enjoyed the opportunity to meet new people and learn about their lives. He was simply so busy with everything going on in his life that other commitments would prevent him from fulfilling that particular obligation as often as he was supposed to.

He took along his friend and colleague Tate, who was doing a thesis on artificial intelligence and with whom he had become close by playing for the same cricket team. They were happily working the room at the gala, playing a game where they tried to guess who was a serious potential donor and who was only really there for the free booze on offer.

"Look at those three." Tate pointed in the direction of some young women who had just arrived. "Seems like they thought this was going to be a real gala."

Rhett smiled as he watched them make their way to the bar. He was pleasantly surprised when he realised he recognised one of them. He had been hoping their paths would cross again ever since he had seen her at an event organised by a mutual acquaintance. He made his way over and tapped her lightly on the shoulder.

"Tara?"

"Brett?"

"Rhett." He corrected her. He was a little perturbed that she did not remember the brief conversation they had shared. "We met at the opening night of Winston's exhibition."

"Yes of course." Tara felt a twinge of embarrassment from not remembering him clearly. She would have expected to have taken more notice of someone so handsome, but she had to admit, she had consumed more than her fair share of opening night freebies on that specific occasion. "Great to see you again."

Brett sensed Tara's friends were hovering behind him, giving her the opportunity of an early escape but he was pleased when they seemed to retreat and leave the two of them alone.

"What brings you to an event like this?" Rhett swept his arm across the room with exaggerated dramatic flourish. The lights in the room flickered momentarily, which added to the spectacle.

"Why does anyone come to the Birmingham University Outreach Gala? I was looking to be challenged on an existential level, hoping for a transformative and exhilarating experience to redefine the relationship between my mind and my soul. I was expecting to be exposed to an array of stimuli so vigorous and powerful that I would be overcome by wave after wave of awe and wonder."

Rhett laughed. He was impressed by her sassy confidence. He had expected a much more conventional and staid response.

"...either that or because I heard there was a free bar." Tara winked as she delivered her punchline.

There was something undeniably special about the woman sipping wine and smiling at him. It was as if she was more present than everyone else in the room, distorting the fabric of the reality around her and demanding his attention with magnetic allure.

For the first time in his life, Rhett felt normal in comparison to another human being and much to his astonishment, he realised he liked it.

X

Katja and Parveen were sitting in the luxurious office of Maxwell Rudd, the Chief Executive of VEX News and one of three heirs to the family-controlled media conglomerate. Maxwell was the middle child but the current frontrunner to get the nod from his mother to take over as President of Rudd Corporation once his mother finally decided to retire...or more likely, died on the job.

"So what's the big deal? They're just characters in a computer game, aren't they? I don't see you campaigning outside the arcades, protesting every time one of the chicks get killed on "Other Side" or..." Maxwell scowled at the cumbersome machine in the corner of his office. "... when one of the characters dies in T.W.O.K."

T.W.O.K. was an arcade game and the acronym stood for "Taken Without Owner's Konsent". It had been developed by Bruno five years earlier and was still lightyears ahead of its rivals in terms of its gameplay, interface and open world format. Players took control of a character called Ra l De la Rosa, a lowlife thug involved in the lower rungs of the Ergodi City underworld. The objective was to undertake various criminal missions that saw him rise through the ranks and ultimately become the city's crime lord. The other games on the market had not developed much more than PacMan or SpaceInvaders so T.W.O.K. was a revelation. The only problem however, was that it was not a profitable concept.

Maxwell and Bruno had a mixed history with Bruno being responsible for both Maxwell's biggest success and his greatest failure. They had met ten years earlier when Maxwell had taken over the newly formed RuddCade Gaming, an amalgamation of the leisure arcade and gaming wing of the company. It was Maxwell's first opportunity to lead a department in the family business and it had been chosen for him due its relative unimportance to the overall performance of the company. He could be left alone to cut his teeth in the corporate world, learning the ins and outs of business administration in an environment where his mistakes would have a limited impact. It was a standard right of passage in the Rudd family for all the offspring to have a similar assignment and Maxwell was determined to make the most of his opportunity and exceed all expectations.

Bruno had been working part-time at RuddCade Gaming while studying for his undergrad degree but it had quickly become apparent that his coding skills far surpassed any of the professionals who worked there full time. Maxwell took a chance and asked him to create a new arcade game. Bruno went away for a weekend and came back with a fully functioning game called Other Side. The concept was simple in that players controlled a chicken that had to navigate its way across a road with various moving obstacles in its way. It was unlike anything that had existed before and the best thing about it, from Maxwell's perspective, was that it had an addictive quality and people were content to spend hour after hour dropping coins into it for another go while they drank beers or coffees. One of its most interesting features was a haptic interface where people could put on a small cap and control the game by head movements, thus freeing up their hands to drink and eat snacks while playing. The venues were happy to have them and on average they recouped the outlay required to buy them in under a month. After that it was pure profit all the way, to be shared between RuddCade Gaming and the establishments. It was so successful that merchandise was developed from the main character and for a while, wherever you went you would see someone in an Other Side t-shirt or baseball cap. An animated series was developed and a novelty song was released, which beat Axe Vyne's second single to the number one spot. In his first year as an executive, Maxwell saw his department increase its revenues by several thousand percent, earning him much praise from his mother and establishing RuddCade Gaming as a serious enterprise.

Bruno was elevated to a superstar in Maxwell's eyes but despite serious offers of cash, he refused to join the company full-time, preferring to continue with his studies and progress his academic career. Maxwell was able to convince him to take a sabbatical for six months in exchange for giving him complete creative control over the creation of a new game.

Bruno had conceived a new style of game whereby the standard rules of play were discarded. Instead of limited controls and objectives, it would take place in an open-world format where players were free to do anything they wanted. They would be offered the opportunity to interact with other characters by undertaking missions but they would also be free to just wander around, exploring the world and creating their own stories. The ultimate aim was to link them together using the telephone network so players could interact with each other in this vast world in real time. An interface was even developed whereby players wear a small cap, similar to the one used to control Other Side, and interact with the game via a rudimentary neural interface. It was quite basic but could pick up distinct thought commands such as 'run", "jump" and 'shoot"; and translate them as actions in the game. After a summer of obsessing over the hardware, which itself pushed the envelope in terms of what was technologically possible, and after having to develop an entirely new programming concept in order to code the game's host of new features, Bruno emerged shortly before deadline with a working game. It was launched with great fanfare in a limited number of locations and although it surpassed every game before it and was exciting and enjoyable to play, commercially it was a disaster. Setting up the manufacturing process had required the investment of almost all the profits from Other Side and although the unit cost would have reduced if the consoles had been produced at scale, the fact that games would last hours on only one coin meant that the costs could not be recouped. The emersion of the interface also prevented players from consuming the drinks and snacks that could have offset some of the costs. No venues were interested in a machine where people stood zombified for hours on end without even emptying their pockets of loose change. As such, only a hundred or so arcade machines were ever created and Maxwell's stock crashed within his family as precipitously as the traded shares of RuddCade Gaming. He was only saved by the fact that Other Side continued to make money, albeit with diminishing returns each year. It was enough for his family not to give up hope and after parting ways with Bruno and working more prudently from then on, he was finally promoted to the broadcast arm of the business after a brief hiatus in charge of the company's music label.

Maxwell had initially ostracised Bruno and vowed never to have anything to do with him again but over the years his opinion had mellowed, and he now maintained a soft spot for him. Encountering Bruno so early in his career had caused Maxwell to take his abilities for granted but with the benefit of several years more experience, he had come to realise how exceptional and rare people like Bruno really were. People who could make things happen and get things done.

"It's not the same." Parveen placed her palms together and lifted them to her lips as she thought about how best to explain it. "The code controlling the henchmen in T.W.O.K. are very simplistic algorithmic rules. They do not have any internal awareness and in fact do not exist in any meaningful manner other than as pixels on a screen. Any anthropomorphism takes place purely inside the minds of the player.

"On the other hand, the simulated life forms within QuantSim have the potential to evolve as fully realised sentient entities with self-awareness and agency comparable to, if not surpassing that of our own."

Maxwell was nodding along as she spoke but there was a vacancy behind his eyes that betrayed his attempt to convey understanding. Parveen looked at Katja for support.

Katja leaned forward. "Have you heard of the concept of sonder?"

"I'm afraid my vocabulary is somewhat limited in comparison to that of the journalists I employ. Please enlighten me." The tactic of highlighting his economic superiority was one Maxwell often employed to mask his feelings of intellectual inferiority..

"It's that feeling you get, normally when you are in your early teens when you realise everybody around you, even strangers, are living a life just as complex as yours."

"Sure." Maxwell's eyes glazed over for an instant as he nodded. He was only just experiencing the sensation she had described in that very moment.

"Now project that into QuantSim. The simulated life within there also has the capacity to experience life and their environment in exactly the same way as you are perceiving yours now."

"I see."

"Dr Panwar and the wAIt organisation feel that we don't yet have the legal frameworks in place to account for how we deal with this ability to create entire universes of civilisations and species. She just wants to make sure that we have explored the moral and ethical questions in full before we embark on a journey that essentially turns us into gods."

Maxwell betrayed an involuntary smile as he contemplated the notion of becoming a god. It was something he would probably enjoy, but he was not sure how he felt about other people, especially Bruno Matthams, having unrestricted access to that power. "So you're telling me that right now, there is a whole universe of sentient, conscious beings living their lives within a box in a lab in Braxton University?"

"The problem we have at the moment is we can't be entirely sure. Professor Matthams built the underlying architecture to ensure that was a distinct possibility. However, the system was initiated before he had a chance to integrate an interface to allow us to know what was going on inside." Parveen replied.

"How do we want to play this?" Maxwell looked at Katja.

Katja had rapidly risen through the journalistic ranks at VEX News after gaining exclusive access to both Professor Matthams and Dr Panwar, both of whom refused to work with any other reporter. There were rumours floating around that she was now in line to host her own current affairs show to replace NightStream, directly after the 9 O"Clock news. Maxwell was even beginning to consider whether or not the two of them could soon be in a position to offer each other some different forms of commensurate value.

"How do you think your viewers will respond?" Parveen interjected.

"Don't worry about that." Maxwell raised his eyebrows and smiled. "They tend to just fall in line with however we choose to spin the story."

"Given Matthams history and the controversy surrounding T.W.O.K., I think we should remain neutral for the moment. I say we push for him to have to build the interfaces required... "

...heavily supervised…" Parveen interrupted.

"Yes, heavily supervised...to see exactly what is going on inside. Once we know, we take it from there."

"Sound good to you?" Maxwell asked Parveen.

"Yes, I will also start building a case to introduce some emergency laws surrounding the operation of such systems pending a full legislature being put in place during the next session."

Maxwell switched off as the conversation turned to the minutiae of the legal aspects of the process.

"Great." He cut Parveen short. "Let's crack on."

The two women understood they had been dismissed and gathered their things. Maxwell picked up a sheet of paper from his intray and pretended to scrutinise its contents. As they were about to depart, Maxell called after Katja.

"Miss Leitner..." He waited for Parveen to continue out of earshot before continuing. "...Katja, I was wondering if you might be free this evening for dinner so we could discuss the 9:30pm slot."

"Sure." Katja smiled and winked at him. He was significantly older than her but his wealth and power were enough to counterbalance the intimacy weighting of the equation firmly in his favour. She could definitely see them developing a mutually advantageous connection.

D

"If you had the chance to go back do this all over again, would you change anything?" Tara asked.

Rhett was abruptly shaken from the peaceful thoughtlessness of a post-coital glow.

"When it comes to us?" He allowed his gaze to follow the contours of Tara's body, his eyes eventually resting vacantly on the opposite wall of the hotel room.

"Not a thing." Rhett said.

Tara shifted her focus from the slow-turning ceiling fan, which scraped softly on each rotation. A futile tool against the dense humidity and static heat of the endless night.

"I love you." Tara surprised herself at the words escaping from her thoughts and forming on her lips.

She was not the sort of person to say something like this so early in a relationship, even if she would sometimes suspect she had begun to experience it, but for some reason it felt right. She was glad to have released it into the world, and while it was still connected to her somehow, it also now existed with an independence of its own.

"I love you too."

Rhett pulled Tara towards him and kissed her. A deep sense of peace and satisfaction overwhelmed him. His mind raced with thoughts of how the universe itself must have been constructed just so the two of them could share this perfect moment. Their love, an emergent fundamental property of a reality desperate to find potent new ways to experience itself.

Tara nestled her head into the soft ridge between Rhett's chest and shoulder, unaware of the excited turmoil her words had initiated beneath the swirls of her auburn hair. She assumed the elevated rate of his beating heart was a residual response to their recent physical exertions. The decelerating intensity of its comforting rhythm lulled her mind gently towards slumber.

Rhett breathed in the subtle hints of sandalwood and ylang ylang from her shampoo, still lingering faintly after the chaos of the day had masked it with a combination of her sweat and the grime of the dense city air. He watched her fall asleep, rapaciously consuming her intoxicating scent, committing every detail of the moment to memory, knowing he would return to it in search of those precious three words time and time again.

XI

It had been over a month since Bruno had been allowed back into his lab. The initial decision by the University had been to keep him away but an overwhelming public desire to see what was going on inside QuantSim's artificial universe was gaining momentum. The media was awash with stories of the myriad ways the system could have developed and how within an unassuming unit in an obscure corner of Braxton University, there might lie untold technological advancements and philosophical insights. There was also a converse narrative playing out about how it could turn out to be a Pandora's Box and therefore should be left alone, which added to the excitement and increased overall public awareness. The agenda was very much being led by VEX News with the "Leitner Late Show" a proponent of at least attempting to gain an understanding of the broad outlines of the mysteries within. Anyone with any level of knowledge about the probabilities involved in respect of a universe developing complex life was certain they would simply be presented by an intellectually interesting, but ultimately lifeless cousin universe to their own.

Vice-Chancellor Zahid Mashwani had drafted in experts from around the world, and at great cost, to try and construct a way of determining the inner workings of the system. Much time and energy was wasted until it eventually became clear how far beyond the scope of understanding the technology was for anyone other than Professor Matthams. There had therefore been no option but to invite him back to continue his work and interface with the project that had consumed the last five years of his life.

"I'll only come back if I can get a substantial raise." Bruno had demanded.

"Nope." Zahid had replied.

"I want total oversight of the project without external interference." Bruno had stipulated.

"Impossible." Parveen had responded and followed up with a full breakdown of the new legal framework under which he was now expected to operate.

"I must be allowed to have complete intellectual ownership of all existing and future developments pertaining to QuantSim." Bruno made it clear this was a deal breaker.

"Not gonna happen." Zahid had informed him. "You will do this because you cannot walk away from the work and you understand how important it is for its potential to be realised."

Bruno slumped his shoulders in the defeated realisation that Zahid knew him well enough to call his bluff. He could tell from his demeanour that the chancellor was unaware of his illness. He had expected Dr Panwar would have let the information slip, even though it would have been a gross invasion of his privacy but she had not betrayed his trust. His respect for her had grown considerably as a result.

"Can I please at least have a T.W.O.K. machine installed in the lab. I'm going to be pretty much holed up in there every hour of the day so it would be nice to at least have something to distract me in my downtime?"

Katja told Maxwell about this request and he had gifted one to Braxton University. Bruno was not too pleased about the VEX News logo having been installed on the start-up screen, a passive aggressive joke by Maxwell, but he knew he would be able to modify it without much difficulty. He was even glad of the opportunity of escape this initial burst of tinkering would offer him.

His work took him more than treble the time it otherwise would have had he not been forced to try and explain everything he did to the committee of academics who were tasked with controlling his work. They were led by Mick Deacon who had been drafted in at considerable expense, chosen because of his glowing reputation as an accomplished academic in the field of computer hardware and programming. Despite being the correct choice as the most likely person to be able to comprehend Bruno's work, it was clear his team were unable to fulfil their function. They were able to understand some of the key concepts underpinning the system architecture and they could work out how to operate the system if given clear instructions, but to reverse engineer it or replicate it was way beyond their capabilities. Bruno amused himself sometimes by requesting approval for nonsensical updates, the hours spent by the committee in attempting to come up with an answer freed up his time to get on with the real work at hand.

If he could have, Bruno would have spent every waking moment working on the QuantSim interface, knowing that he was racing against an internal clock of mutating cells. He was starting to develop strange new aches throughout his body and the type of pain was like nothing he had experienced before. It was not yet excruciating, although it was on its way towards those levels of discomfort, but it was different. It had a radial, pulsating quality and it was easy to get used to it until it sporadically flared up to ever greater levels of intensity. He soon discovered that despite his desires and motivations, it was impossible for him to spend all his mental capacity working on a single problem and so in order to take some breaks from QuantSim, he let his brain reset by spending time playing T.W.O.K.

His knowledge and experience had developed exponentially in the five years since he had built T.W.O.K. and after playing the game, he enjoyed spending time tinkering and upgrading the systems in the arcade machine Maxwell Rudd had sent him. He often wondered if he could integrate the game into the QuantSim framework, which would lead to some significant enhancements in the scope and realism of the open world format. He also started thinking about developing the neural interface to offer two-way feedback, which would allow players to submerge themselves more completely in the game. The more he thought about it, the more certain he was that there were no significant blockers to developing the technology. He was excited by the potential, not just for T.W.O.K. but for immersive monitoring of other complex systems.

One day he asked the committee of academics to gather around his monitor so he could demonstrate the new interface system. He was confined to working on a small sandbox copy of a portion of the universe until Vice-Chancellor Mashwani and Dr Panwar had signed off expanding the monitoring and diagnostics throughout the entire live QuantSim network. The committee looked on in awe as he zoomed in and out of a small portion of a galaxy where they were able to view the stars and their orbiting planets in as much detail as they wished. It was like watching television but with the ability to zoom in and out at will and to place the camera in any position they wished. They were even able to drill down into the simulated matter to the subatomic level, going as far as being able to see the underlying fabric of its dark loop gravity. Statistics and real-time analysis of the underlying QuantSim physics could be accessed via a simple menu system. There were a few questions about the strength of the basic forces and whether the simulation reflected mathematical frameworks accurately. Everyone seemed satisfied with the capabilities of the system and excited about the opportunities it presented in terms of hypothesis modelling and testing. They did not really understand it, but they felt privileged to be so close to something so significant.

"Any life?" Bruno was asked by Mick Deacon.

"Not in this section but there are some interesting pockets of primordial solutions that if given time might combine to form some sort of proto-life."

"So it is an empty universe?" Mick Deacon sighed and the rest of the team began chatting amongst themselves.

"It doesn't look likely that we will find life in this iteration but we will not know until we are given full access to the entirety of the simulated universe." Bruno clarified.

Mick Deacon squeezed his deputy on his shoulder to attract his attention. "Can you please go and inform Vice-Chancellor Mashwani that we have finally made progress and are ready to show him the QuantSim interface we have been working on?"

"We?" Bruno asked Micke Deacon out of earshot of the rest of the committee, arching an eyebrow as he did so.

Mick Deacon shrugged and they exchanged a smile. Their initial combative relationship had soon receded into something akin to an uneasy friendship and mutual respect brought about by necessity. Mick Deacon realised Bruno was a force of nature in terms of his abilities and intellect and was honoured to work with him so closely. Bruno's motive for maintaining developing a strong rapport was much simpler. He realised Mick Deacon was a necessary inconvenience he would have to work with to get anything done.

E

The romance between Tara and Rhett developed slowly but with a seeming sense of inevitability. They started seeing each other a couple of nights a week and gradually integrated into each other's lives as they met each other's friends. Rhett was welcomed slowly and cautiously into Tara's family and Tara learned all about Rhett's difficult ancestry as he opened up to her more and more over time. Tara's housemates enjoyed having him around and he was mindful that despite his frequent visits, he was still a guest. Rhett had thought Tara's housemate Samantha and his colleague Tate might hit it off so he had brought him round to one of their infamous Tuesday night barbecues. He was trying his best to facilitate a conversation between the two of them all night but finally gave up when he walked in on Tate and Tara's other housemate Nina kissing in the bathroom.

Tara's career was going well and she was offered the position of public relations account manager for a global renewable energy consortium. She relished the opportunity it gave her for travel and the sense of pride she experienced from feeling like she was playing her part in accelerating, even if ever so slightly, the inexorable shift away from fossil fuels towards a sustainable future. She saw her work as an important antidote to the increasingly militant posturing of environmental groups like ViroMental. It was her firm belief that change could only come about through winning hearts and minds with sustained and reasoned campaigning rather than through ultimatums and fear. She was able to travel frequently, never fully in denial about her own above-average carbon footprint but never entirely owning it. Rhett missed her while she was away and often worried her job might ultimately lead her away from him, but not openly complaining as he understood it was an intrinsic part of making her the woman he loved. She did have a few casual romantic encounters on some of the early trips but none were anything other than superficial expressions of a youthful desire for the exhilarating thrill of novel experiences. She reasoned these liaisons away by building a retrospective narrative around the fact that her and Rhett had never explicitly defined themselves as exclusive.

Rhett's own career was progressing according to plan and his own experiments in dark loop gravity were leading the scientific world towards novel and exotic understandings of the very fabric of their reality. He had begun working more closely with Tate in order to employ the benefits of artificial intelligence to modelling and assessing the extreme corners of the physical world. The speed at which computational power and artificial intelligence were progressing had even led Rhett and Tate to work on a paper together exploring how it might one day be possible to model the entire universe within a simulated environment.

"We could move in together." Tara suggested one morning.

Samantha had been offered a new job at her company's head office and was relocating to reduce the amount of time she needed for her commute. Nina and Tate had recently got engaged and were in the process of buying a home together so it felt like it was the end of an era and time to move forward constructively with the practical aspects of life. Rhett had suggested this to Tara several times but she had not been keen. It was only now external events seemed to be pushing her down a predetermined path that she decided it was time to grow up and do what was expected of someone her age. There was really no real excuse for not taking the plunge with Rhett. There would likely be little difference between spending her life with him and any of the other potential suitors she might meet along the way.

Rhett was absolutely delighted with the development. The sense of Tara being 'the one" had continued to grow within him and its roots infiltrated every aspect of his being, informing every decision he made. He lived in a paradigm where he was certain Tara felt the same and placed their relationship as the core foundation on which every other aspect of their lives should be built.

Life together was comfortable and they soon settled into a contented routine. Both were reaping the financial benefits of advancing professional careers, meaning they were able to afford a slightly more expensive house than Tate and Nina in the same upmarket suburb of Birmingham. Neither of them would openly admit it to each other or themselves, but this friendly competitiveness with their friends was something they both relished, especially as they were always able to stay a few steps ahead.

"Will you marry me?" Rhett asked.

Tara slapped her hand to her forehead and it slipped down her face, revealing eyes full of scorn and embarrassment. They were standing on the dance floor at Tate and Nina's wedding.

"Yeah I will." She said through gritted teeth. "...but get up and don't make a scene. This is someone else's day."

Tara was happy to be marrying Rhett. She loved him.

She really did.

...but it always seemed to her like love played too central a role in the way society organised itself. She always felt like there should be something more to existence than what actually only amounted to a fairly basic biological function.

Still...she did not envy the single life and merely the thought of having to endure all the societal pressures of having to find a partner if she was on her own exhausted her. Life was so much easier being in a relationship with a kind, highly-intelligent and extremely sexy man...whom she loved. What were the alternatives anyway? If she was with someone else, the various dials might be set slightly differently but overall the sum total of the settings would likely be much the same.

The wedding day was the happiest of Rhett's life. Everything was moving not only along the correct trajectory but also at the right speed. He was marrying the woman he loved. He could not imagine there being another person on the planet who he could potentially love to anywhere near the degree he loved this woman. He had found his one and only soulmate.

Rhett's work and research were also progressing well. He had just completed a career-defining trip to conduct an experiment at the MRTD (Massively Regressive Tachyon Distributor) at CERN in Geneva where he had succeeded in using an anti-tachyon pulse to hook a loop of dark gravity. He had secured his position in scientific history by tweaking one of the threads which make up the interwoven fabric of reality. The resulting gravitational vibrations had been of a magnitude at the upper end of his calculated possible outcomes, which had caused a minor international incident. The shockwave had led to a minor earthquake, which in turn triggered an avalanche that caused significant damage to the upmarket ski resort of Praz de Lys.

He had also postulated a new hypothesis while working with Tate, which suggested that if artificial intelligence were capable of simulating realities, then those realities themselves should also develop the same capacity and spawn simulated realities of their own. This meant the vast majority of realities were likely simulations and probabilistically so too was the one in which they resided. He was at the forefront of two scientific disciplines and fully realising his potential both professionally and personally. He breathed in deeply as the bridal chorus began to play and felt a sense of existential awareness enveloped his soul as Tara walked down the aisle towards him. There was only one thing missing.

"I'm pregnant." Tara squealed as she looked down at the lines on the test.

"We're pregnant." Rhett corrected her as he kissed her tenderly on the forehead.

Tara loved her daughter...and she loved her second daughter equally as much when she came along.

She really did.

However, although she would never openly admit it to anyone, she envied the sense of completion that other parents seemed to attain from having children. It was as if their whole sense of purpose had focused on their progeny and their sense of self had been eradicated as a result. She could not shake the nagging feeling that she should find value in herself as something more than a foundation from which her children extended themselves...but if this was the pinnacle of existence for all her mother friends, why did it not offer her the same sense of completion?

Rhett was as perfect a father as he was in all other aspects of his life. He took on more than his fair share of parenting duties and he would love to sit out in the garden at night, with a sleeping infant balanced on his chest, gazing at the twinkling bursts of starlight as they undulated through the atmosphere. He would subconsciously hum soothing lullabies as his conscious mind worked through the ways in which he could test his latest theories. In these hours he also often returned to the question he had asked himself on his grandfather's deathbed but now it had a slightly different slant. If he did live in a simulated reality, how could he prove it? If he was just one of a plethora of simulated realities being run by bored, uncaring or less capable beings, was there a way to communicate with them or at the very least grab their attention? In these moments, with his child on his chest and his grandfather on in his thoughts, it was impossible for Rhett to conceive of anything that could upset the idyllic life he was leading.

"Is there anyone with you?"

Rhett had been staring blankly at the news when the constable had pressed the doorbell. The city had been alight with the sounds of the emergency services responding to a significant event and the constant sound of their sirens had saturated the air for hours. Thick piles of smoke had billowed up into the sky and spread out along the undersides of the cloud, dirtying and sullying their pristine whiteness until the heaviness encouraged them to expel a gritty rain. All the media channels had been awash with coverage of the story of how several bombs had exploded simultaneously on an unverified number of trains as they entered New Street Station. It was confirmed to be a coordinated attack by an extreme environmental group called ViroMental. Several of their own members have given their own lives to the cause. They had already issued a statement justifying these acts of self-destructive violence as being the only way to get their message across to an incompetent government and an apathetic wider population.

Rhett had been frantically trying to contact Tara since the first explosion rocked him awake from a nap he had been taking on this rare occasion where he had the house all to himself for an extended period of time. He had missed the presence of his wife and kids but also enjoyed the peace and quiet their absence afforded him. Tara had been away visiting her parents with the kids for a few days and had been booked on one of the trains due into the station at the time the attack took place. Rhett did not need the police officer to say it out loud to confirm his worst fears. He already knew.

"Just tell me." He said, his voice high-pitched and strained.

The young officer looked on in sympathy as Rhett sunk to the floor and sobbed.

XII

Katja had gained exclusive access to document the moment when it was discovered what existed within the vast expanse of the first simulated universe. Public excitement and media buzz was reaching a crescendo as the entire world had taken an interest in the events unfolding at Braxton University. Every individual felt they had a stake in the outcome as they stood on the cusp of discovering new and exciting technologies that could enhance and transform their lives. Terminally sick patients dreamed of medicines to cure their illnesses, the elderly secretly wished for the keys to eternal life and to join the youth in their eagerness to experience new forms of entertainment and leisure. Anarchists expected to see working examples of utopian civilisations to act as frameworks for their own upcoming revolutions. There was not a single person on the planet who had a problem large or small who had not given in to the hope that QuantSim would be about to offer them a solution to their strife.

The QuantSim lab had been taken over by the Leitner Late Show team, which was run with ruthless zeal by Katja's former camera operator Martha, who had been promoted to producer. She liked to tell herself she was still a punk at heart but the trappings of that lifestyle were becoming less and less apparent in what she chose to wear. She gave Katja a thumbs-up to let her know the commercial break was about to end.

"Professor Matthams, what realistically can we expect when the button is pressed and the monitoring systems are extended beyond the sandbox environment to cover the entire QuantSim network?" Katja winked at Bruno as she thrust the microphone towards him.

"We have to be realistic. The likelihood is we will just see a universe with similar celestial bodies to our own. Hopefully this will give us the ability to understand some of the more obscure cosmic phenomena such as black holes and neutron stars. This will give us the exciting opportunity to help us start to calculate how our own universe might one day end up."

"Yes, yes. That's all interesting stuff but could life have evolved in QuantSim?"

"It is quite likely that there will be some form of bacterial life somewhere in there." Bruno was more excited than he was letting on. Dr Panwar had advised him to play things down so as not to generate any additional potential for disappointment.

"What about more complex forms of life?"

"Unlikely." Bruno shook his head.

"But possible?"

"Yes."

"Intelligent life?"

"It is not entirely out of the question but the chances are extremely low."

"You heard it here first viewers." Katja looked directly into the camera. "We might just be about to witness the first example of intelligent life beyond our own." She looked back at Bruno. "Could this intelligent life have developed into a civilisation, maybe one more advanced than our own?"

Bruno quickly forgot Dr Panwar's advice, getting caught up with Katja's enthusiasm and showmanship. "Look, there is a chance that somewhere inside the quantum mainframe within this casing..." He pointed at the grey cabinet housing the QuantSim quantware with a pen he was holding. "...that life might have become so technologically advanced so as to have arrived at a singularity."

There was an audible gasp from the large group of lawyers, academics, politicians and media executives who had squeezed into the lab, including Maxwell Rudd. It was the first time he and Bruno had met since the T.W.O.K. fiasco but they had got on well enough, aided by Kata's presence and determination to see them put the past behind them. The term singularity had become common parlance due to the recent media coverage of QuantSim and Vice-Chancellor Mashwani winced at its use. He had echoed Dr Panwar's concerns and expressly instructed Bruno to manage expectations. He had been feeling uneasy about the special guest VEX News had booked to press the button but Bruno's inability to follow his instructions had done a lot to assuage his guilt.

"Well, I don't think we need to waste anymore time. I'd like to hand you over to Vice-Chancellor Mashwani who will now introduce our special guest, who will press the button that extends the monitoring facilities throughout the entire QuantSim network. Hopefully answering once and for all the burning question as to whether or not sentient life and civilisation exists within it."

"Ladies and Gentlemen..." Zahid's throat suddenly became uncomfortably dry and he had to pause to cough and take a sip of water. "Ladies and Gentlemen and VEX News viewers. I would like to welcome the man who will press the button of the hour....the singer of this summer's smash hit "Turn It On"...Mr Axe Vyne."

Axe rushed in through the door as the catchy beat of "Turn It On" burst out from some speakers installed by VEX News. Bruno rolled his eyes and then looked over at Katja, opened his arms and mouthed, "what the...?" at her. Katja just gave him a smile and a shrug before winking and bobbing her head along to the song. Bruno then looked over at Maxwell Rudd who flashed him a view of his radiant teeth and gave him a thumbs up. He should have known that Maxwell would take any opportunity to promote one of Rudd Entertainment's artists.

Axe made his way through the crowd offering out hugs and high fives and finally planting a kiss on Bruno's lips. He was wearing lipstick and some remained on Bruno's lips. He rubbed it off angrily, more frustrated at being unable to control his attraction to someone who had betrayed his trust so completely than the invasion of his personal space.

"This is what we've been waiting for." Axe looked into the camera and offered up his index finger to the lens. "Before I press it, let me just remind you that my latest album "Collaborations" comes out tomorrow and my single "Turn It On" is still available in all good stores. OK shaggers, here we go. Three...two...one..." He pressed the button.

The assembled guests looked on in anticipation as Bruno watched Vice-Chancellor Zahid Mashwani click through a few menus on QuantSim's control panel. It looked like he had got in a muddle so Bruno moved over to offer him some help.

"Can you talk me through what you are seeing?" Katja had arrived with her microphone and a camera light was now shining on the two men.

"It doesn't appear to be working." Zahid looked quizzically towards Bruno.

Bruno took control of the system and clicked around on screen, he leaned in more closely and his arm moved around rapidly but without any sense of real purpose. He typed in some instructions and started checking that all the wires were attached properly to the monitor.

"Keep talking." Katja said through a forced smile.

"There's nothing here." Bruno said quietly.

Zahid roughly grabbed Bruno's arm. "This had better not be some sort of trick."

"No.This is strange. QuantSim seems to have just...I can't explain this...stopped itself."

Parveen leaned over to speak to Bruno and Zahid. "I don't need to remind you that it is illegal to turn QuantSim off until we have established whether or not sentient life is active within it."

Bruno looked over to the energy consumption meter and saw that it was drawing no power from the grid. The menus were blank and all the physics within the universe seemed to have simply unravelled into nothingness. He could see Maxwell in the background shaking his head in disappointment.

"This is not something that anyone here has instigated." Bruno said. "I cannot be exactly sure right now...I'll need some more time to look into it...but the fact of the matter is that the universe within QuantSim has simply vanished."

"Could it be that it has come to its natural conclusion, either through a heat death or big crunch?" Mick Deacon suggested.

"No." Bruno snapped back at him. He felt Mick was offering unrealistic solutions so he could draw attention to himself rather than because he had anything insightful to add. "It is beyond that. I will need some time to study what has happened." Bruno had drained of all colour and small beads of stagnant sweat had appeared on his forehead.

"Well viewers, this is a shocking new development in the ever-evolving story of QuantSim. We will be the first to update you with any breaking news but for now, here are some messages from some of our commercial partners." Katja's smile and the camera light faded in perfect synchronicity. This was not going to be good for her reputation. She scanned the room, needing to know Maxwell's reaction but all she caught was a glimpse of the back of his head as he walked out the room.

F

Rhett tried to be mindful of his feelings, realising they were just transient experiences happening to him, not intrinsic aspects of who he was. His rational brain knew they did not represent a permanent state. He knew they would pass. He acknowledged them. He felt them. He respected them. He tried to let them pass.

They would not pass.

He would need more time. The tidal nature of his sorrow meant he would experience it in waves. There were periods of calm and in them a magnificent chestnut stallion of hope could be seen cantering along the shore towards him, only to be swept away with the next swell of grief. He had expected to sense a diminishing impact as each surge of emotion subsided but if anything, the trend seemed to be moving exponentially in the opposite direction.

He was aware of this. It was a transitory situation. He knew it would pass.

It did not pass.

He had barely seen anyone for a while other than Nina and Tate who had done their best to maintain regular contact, but were at a loss as to what else they could actually do to offer constructive help. The only other interactions he had were checkout cashiers, his world condensed to two locations less than twenty metres apart. Tate had encouraged him to go and see a professional grief counselor and although he had agreed, he never managed to get round to it. Not because he was actively against it but because he simply was no longer capable of keeping appointments. He had stopped all forms of exercise and his sedate lifestyle, combined with his unhealthy eating habits and poor personal hygiene left him looking and feeling like a mess. After a few month's leave, he felt a weight of expectation to return to work and this led him back to the office.

"I didn't expect to see you here...so...soon." Tate had fiddled with his tie as he spoke to Rhett in the corridor outside their offices.

"If you want to come back, you are welcome to, but we want to make it clear you can take as much time as you need away from work. You are under no obligation to return." Dean Okoro had gently said to him as they sat in her office together with a representative from HR.

Rhett had brushed off all their concerns in a light and breezy manner, which had not fooled anyone, nor were they fooling him by playing along. Everyone seemed to just tacitly agree it was a productive method for him to move forward with his life. They had no personal experiences to draw on to allow them any insight or authenticity when communicating with Rhett over such tragic personal events. The only course of action was to continually offer their support and trust that one day he would heal. From Rhett's perspective, being at work was much better than trying to distract himself by watching daytime TV and scrolling endlessly through social media. Emerging hours later feeling exhausted and hollow after falling down whatever rabbit holes the Internet presented him.

Rhett had decided to pursue the strategy of faking it until making it in respect of his mental health. He would act as if he was fine in the hope his inner world would one day catch up with the outward image he projected. As he sunk deeper into his depression, he pushed himself further into his work and this became his sole solace in life. It would offer fleeting moments of distraction but it was unable to instill in him the sense of meaning it had done before. The days drifted by with no sense of change or progression and he struggled to feel as if he was really residing fully within space and time.

"I'm really sorry about this..." It had been two years since Rhett had last sat in Dean Okoro's office with someone from the HR department. "...but the changing nature of our political landscape has led to the need to make drastic cuts across the board. Unfortunately your work in dark loop gravity is deemed not to have enough of a quantifiable short-to-medium-term return on investment, despite the significant strides you have made in our understanding of reality."

"I understand." Rhett smiled but his eyes would haunt Dean Okoro and the Deputy Head of HR for the rest of the day, each of them shuddering when it intermittently flashed across their memories.

"We still see you as an important and integral part of the team and there is still a role for you in teaching and post-graduate support." Dean Okoro had the habit of bouncing her pen to the rhythm of her speech pattern when trying to convey a sense of upbeat positivity.

"We have to clarify however that there will be a commensurate drop in salary." The Deputy Head of HR's addition to the conversation caused Dean Okoro to roll her eyes. She had hoped they could have spoken about pay at another time.

Tate and Nina were a great help in finding a new place for Rhett to live. He was unable to maintain his mortgage on the house and Nina suggested it might make sense, even if he could have afforded to stay, to move away from a place so soaked in memories. Tate did not think it was a good idea for him to move into university accommodation, which had been one of the options discussed, but they did think being close to campus would help him have access to its support network. He finally selected a newly built two-bedroom apartment in Brindley Place. It had a small balcony overlooking the canal and was close to where he had lived in his bachelor days. It was ten minutes walk from his faculty building and although peaceful, he was within throwing distance of the bustle and activity of Birmingham city centre.

"Maybe it's time you got back out there." Tate glanced up from stirring his coffee as Nina delivered the suggestion. "It has been four years now."

"No." Rhett replied.

"It's just there's this great new app where..."

"No."

Nina and Tate shared a look and in it they both agreed not to pursue the matter further.

Rhett would sit on his balcony at night and look up at the stars as he contemplated how the burning pain of his emotions would remain with him forever. He remembered his grandfather's faith and in his weakest moments allowed himself to direct a few words into the cosmos...but how could he know he was being heard?

One night as his thoughts returned once more to the mindless actions of the terrorists who had not only sacrificed their own lives for their cause They had robbed him not only of his happiness but increasingly his sense of self and without that, what point was there to anything. He wondered how it must have felt in their final moments, never knowing if their destructive actions would ultimately deliver their message effectively... and then a bolt of inspiration shot through him.

One night his thoughts returned again to the mindless actions of the terrorists who had not only sacrificed lives for their cause, including their own as well as those of innocents, but had also left a trail of emotional destruction in their wake. He was not sure if the fate of those who had fallen could be worse than that of the ones left behind. He wondered what could have driven them to undertake the ultimate offering? What could have crossed their minds in those final moments? Did they experience an existential dread as they feared their act might not be enough to drive their message through? They were certainly brave, but were they also foolish?

In his continuing emotional pain, and as he contemplated their actions, he realised it might not such a stupid idea to cross into the numbness of oblivion. It might actually be the only solution.

Rhett was suddenly hit by a jolt of inspiration.

He knew what he had to do. There was no other option. He would have to end it.

He would have to end it all.

With the decision made, he was filled with a sensation he had come to believe was nothing more than an imagined former state. He felt a sense of peace.

The only question left now...was how?

XIII

Bruno smashed his fist down on the desk, causing Mick Deacon to jump and spill his coffee all over his workbench, shorting the wires of the circuit board he had been soldering. Bruno had just run another diagnostic of the QuantSim mainframe and everything was in perfect working order. There was no physical reason why it should have been functioning one minute and then in the next instant when they extended the monitoring systems through the network, it should have stopped. He apologised to Mick Deacon and offered to buy him a fresh drink from the cafeteria. On the walk over he realised his next step would have to be an analysis of the way in which the quantware interacted with the underlying bosonic architecture. His train of thought was broken by a sudden bout of breathlessness. He was forced to the floor of the corridor as he tried to regulate his breathing but after an hour, he had to conclude this was not just a 'turn" but the latest symptom in an ever growing list attached to his condition. Having a sense of not being able to suck in enough oxygen to fuel his actions would now become a permanent feature of his life.

The buzz around QuantSim disappeared almost instantly after the live broadcast. The general feeling was that everyone had been subjected to some form of elaborate hoax or scam. It appeared to be just another way for the media to generate content without real substance, in the same way they had with all their scare stories about computers being unable to handle a change from one decade to the next, or how a black hole might form when a new particle accelerator was switched on and smashed a beam of protons into a thin metal foil. The instant feelings of disappointment in falling for the hype had given way to impotent rage and then a desire to push it out of mind and move on with day to day life. Security around the lab was loosened and Vice-Chancellor Zahid Mashwani allowed Professor Bruno Matthams access to his equipment with minimal supervision. Zahid had suspected for a long time that Bruno had been overzealous with his predictions. It was a familiar pattern amongst many of the academics he had worked with whose superior intellects made it difficult for their bombastic claims to be verified until the results of their experimentations ultimately fell short of their expectations.

Bruno's work was significantly hampered not only by his declining health, but also by his inability to power up QuantSim. Dr Panwar had made sure this was only an option if he was able to present his reasoning to, and obtain agreement from, an ethics committee chaired by her. This left him in the envious position of having to pour over historic logs and perform isolated diagnostics on a section by section basis. It was laborious and painstaking work and often involved hours of waiting around while the numbers crunched in the background. It would all have been so much quicker had he been allowed to utilise the computational potency of his quantum network. He was also becoming increasingly conscious that time was running out for him to make an impact, something Dr Panwar was sympathetic about in the regular conversations they had, but never enough to cause her to stray from her robust ethical framework.

Bruno had taken to spending most of his downtime playing T.W.O.K. He still sometimes marvelled at how he had been able to build something so sophisticated at such a young age. The tricks he had used to allow a standard microchip to create the illusion of an open world were remarkable. Some of the techniques he had used were so advanced he could not even remember how he had done them or if he would be able to recreate them in the same way if given the task again. He had modified the machine in his lab so he could interface with it using an experimental two-way neural link he had been working on. He had taken apart several of the original controllers and modified them with some lab components to create an array of electrodes that he could stick on various parts of his skull. They would read his thought patterns, allowing a much more nuanced way of manipulating the main character, and more importantly they sent electrical impulses back into his brain so he could experience the game in his mind, rather than just controlling it on a screen. It was groundbreaking work and something that he might have considered exploring once leaving Braxton University, if the circumstances of that departure had been somewhat different...but despite the rapid gains and exhilarating possibilities of his new control system, the thing that really excited him the most was the potential of running T.W.O.K. on a quantum mainframe. There were so many things he could achieve if only he had more time...and oh how he rued how much of it he had wasted in the past.

"How are you getting along?" Zahid shocked Bruno from a deep immersion in a T.W.O.K. mission.

Bruno pulled the electrodes from his head and blinked a few times to reorientate himself into the room. He had successfully been controlling the rudimentary movements of Ra I De la Rosa through Ergodi City by thinking about the direction he wanted him to walk and a return of focus to the lab was confusing to his optic senses and left him a little nauseous. His cheeks flushing from having Vice-Chancellor Mashwani find him involved in a leisure activity..

"I'm just waiting for some numbers to crunch. If I could just turn the damn thing on, things would move a lot faster." Bruno said.

"That's not going to happen, Professor Matthams." Zahid's jaw was tense. He wondered how many times he would have to clarify this point.

"I've just fed some of the raw data from the operating system logs into the machine. I'm waiting for it to spew out the results." Bruno thumbed at the machine in question without looking at it.

"Looks like it's ready." Zahid pointed at the flickering array of green characters displayed on a large monitor behind Bruno's head.

Bruno turned and looked at the screen. He was astounded by how much time had passed while he was playing T.W.O.K. It only seemed like it had been an hour or so but for the results to be ready, it must have been much longer. Bruno blinked as he assessed the information on the screen. To anyone else it appeared to be a meaningless array of random numbers and letters but Bruno was able to discern a pattern within it. It was so clear and yet so utterly improbable he did not want to let on to Vice-Chancellor Mashwani that he may have spotted something. He leaned backwards and sighed.

"Anything?" Zahid asked.

"Nothing." Bruno did his best to form a frustrated grimace on his face and nodded his head in a way he hoped would convey frustration and disappointment.

"Shame....well, keep at it." Zahid left the lab with the sense of lightness he always felt from knowing he had done his duty for the week by checking in on Bruno. He would not have to think about him again until the following Tuesday. Zahid had noticed that Bruno was looking increasingly ill and he wondered if he should encourage him to see a doctor but brushed off the thought as something beyond the scope of their professional relationship. There was no point in creating further reasons for them to interact.

After he had gone, Bruno turned all his attention back to the screen. He had to work on the assumption that what he was seeing, no matter how improbable to have occurred by chance, must be a random pattern in the data. Otherwise the implications were simply mind-blowing. It simply could not be what it appeared to be.

Could it?

G

"You seem to have turned a corner in the past couple of months?"

Nina smiled broadly as she and Rhett sat with inconveniently-large and garishly-mismatched mugs in their favourite artisanal cafe overlooking the canal. A group of young men who were obviously drunk and part of a bachelor party were struggling with the nearby lock but the allure of observing their shenanigans had waned and Nina turned her attention back to Rhett. She had ordered a mint tea, which Rhett always considered a waste when in the presence of a skilled barista. Nina had cited issues with digestion, which she explained was not being helped today by the nausea-inducing colour contrasts of the individual pieces of crockery they were being forced to drink from. A subtle depth to her frown during her explanation had caused Rhett not to persist with his trademark faux-rant on the subject of suitable beverage choices for any given establishment.

Rhett was generally feeling much lighter than he had when they had last met up. The heavy weight of ennui had been lifted off his shoulders now he had a plan and a purpose. He had focused his attention on making a good impression in his new position at the university and had hit the gym to get back in shape, even going as far as to join a martial arts class. The t-shirt he was wearing was now tight around the chest and biceps rather than the waist, and the incessant desire to sleep during the afternoons had been replaced by an urge to run, jump and move around.

"Did I tell you I've been invited to take part in a round table discussion at SubAtomCon in a couple of months?" Rhett said as Tate returned from his trip to the bathroom.

This was not entirely true. He had called in a few favours from his network to get put on the panel. He had observed some interesting data from his allotted time on the university's access to the national telescopic satellite array. In order to end things in the way he wanted, he really needed to get his hands on a specific piece of technology. The first step in doing that was to have a legitimate reason to be in the city it had been built in.

"Where is submarine come?" Nina asked, fully aware she was pronouncing it incorrectly.

"Switzerland." Tate took over to obtain the gentle ego boost of explaining something to his wife. "It is a conference they put on every year at CERN...near Geneva...to discuss the latest findings of the LHC and the MRTD...that's the

Massively Regressive Tachyon Distributor and the Large Hadron Collider."

"I am not a complete idiot. I know what the Large Hadron Collider is...or at the very least I know it excites Rhett enough for him to want to collide into it with his own large hard-on."

A burst of laughter escaped from Rhett's lungs. Nina could not remember the last time she had felt comfortable enough to tease him and was pleased he had responded well. Thinking about it later, she realised this was the first time she had seen him genuinely laughing since ViroMental's attack on New Street Station.

Tate begrudgingly acknowledged Nina's joke as she swung her fist across her chest and scalded herself under her breath. "Damn, I should have said small hard-on."

"Are you coming this year?" Rhett asked.

"No." Tate instinctively looked towards Nina's stomach.

Rhett's eyes darted between his two friends and then widened. His palms floated to his temples and his fingers glided across the prickly sides of his freshly cut hair. "No?" The shape of the word remained on his lips long after the sound had departed.

"Yep." Nina smiled and a tear welled up in her eye. "Finally...and we were kind of hoping you would do us the honour of being her godfather?"

Rhett saw the future unfolding in front of him, the smell of the baby as he held it in his arms, changing her nappy to give his friends a break from that monotonous chore, letting her secretly play on his phone after her parents had severely limited her screen time...becoming her favourite uncle.

"I'd love to." He said, his eyes radiating joy.

Inside however, he felt a wave of sadness, knowing that if everything went according to plan, none of these things would ever take place.

H.i

It was great to be back in Geneva and entrenched in the scientific community. Rhett had often considered spending a semester or two working there but life and love had always got in the way. He had been able to spend a lot of time there however, with frequent trips to share insight on various research projects and to attend some of the many conferences held there. He decided to treat himself to a whirlwind tour of Switzerland's culinary delights after completing his obligations at SutAtomCon. He ate fondue on Rue de la Coulouvreni re and had a double chocolate dessert on Rue du Rh ne. He savoured their tastes and smells as if experiencing them for the final time. As he contemplated the froth on a milchkaffee from Chou on Rue des Eaux-Vives, he marvelled at how engaged his audience had been when discussing the esoteric and abstract topic of how loops of dark gravity might in fact be an emergent manifestation of a more fundamental quantum foam.

He was seated in the hotel bar, already enjoying his second glass of Qu llfrisch Hell by the time Dr Faletogia rushed in to join him. He was full of fluster and apology for his tardiness even though he was only several minutes late. Rhett nodded at the bar to indicate they should bring another drink for his companion.

"Not for me." Dr Faletogia waved his hand to cancel the order. "A glass of Apfelschorle, please." He patted Rhett on the shoulder and gifted him a broad view of his receding gums, his lips allowing only a hint of the teeth beneath them. "I have to be back at the MRTD in a few hours. There have been some indications that a Cloit Contortion is underway so I want to make sure I am on hand."

"Really? A Cloit Contortion?" Rhett had already noticed the signs from his own observations but he did not want Dr Faletogia to suspect his invitation for them to meet up was anything other than a coincidence.

"Yes." Dr Faletogia looked away for a moment. "You know what...you could come along and observe, if you like?

"I'd love to."

"I thought as much." Dr Faletogia handed him a laminated pass with Rhett's name and photo on it. "It wouldn't do for the person who theorised the phenomenon not to be there at the moment the data was gathered. Data that could then go on to be used to provide empirical proof of its existence."

It seemed Dr Faletogia had already suspected Rhett might want to visit the site where he had made his academic name.

"...but promise not to cause any destruction this time." Dr Faletogia joked, referencing the earthquake Rhett's previous experiment had triggered.

"I'm not promising anything."

Rhett was comforted to see the control centre for the Massively Regressive Tachyon Distributor was much the same as it had been when he was last there three years before. He sat in the project director's office, which looked down through reinforced glass onto a large room with around thirty workstations. These faced a wall of cinema-sized screens, each displaying the various pertinent information critical to the operation of the apparatus. The team referred to a successful attempt as a "grab". This area was dubbed 'mission control" due to its resemblance to the familiar set-ups they had seen on TV when watching a rocket launched by NASA.

The scale of the Massively Regressive Tachyon Distributor was difficult to conceptualise for anyone not intimately involved in the project as there were no comparable references in everyday life. At its center was a tube of only 30 centimeters in diameter but within it, a vacuum as intense as one found in deep space needed to be maintained for its entire length. This meant the tube was surrounded by several metres of graviton-sensitive ferrous alloy suspended in concrete. The tube tunnelled towards the centre of the earth in an elliptical spiral to give it a length of over 100 times the circumferences of the globe. Strong magnetic fields tricked the quantum world into acting as if the tunnel was a straight line and as such the entire force of the earth's gravity could be utilised to create the correct environment for the emergence of a tachyon or anti-tachyon stream. This stream could then be used to probe the most fundamental parts of reality and as Rhett had demonstrated, could even manipulate them.

"Before we initiate the grab, I would just like to let you all know we are joined by a special guest tonight...Dr Rhett Gaumond." Dr Faletogia spoke into the microphone, which allowed him to communicate with the project floor. The whole team stood and turned to face the project director's office. Rhett stood and gave a quick wave to acknowledge them as he received a short round of applause.

The whole atmosphere quickly changed as everyone focused on their specific roles. Establishing the environment in which a stream could be initiated was an intricate endeavour requiring hundreds of synchronised actions and a minor lapse of focus could lead to the whole attempt needing to be aborted. External conditions had to be just right with the ambient gravitational sea experiencing within their cosmic locale being completely calm. The latest observational tools at their disposal were significantly more advanced than when Rhett had last been there but they still only allowed a short glimpse into the future in terms of when a suitable window of opportunity would arise for a grab. It was therefore imperative they minimised failed attempts as each one could be costed in the region of millions of euros. Dr Faletogia had instilled a sense of structured process and disciplined concentration to the project, which had led to a series of eight successful grabs in a row. If they were to achieve a ninth, it would be a project record, leading to a small bonus for the entire team and unbeknownst to anyone else in the room, a six-figure bonus for Dr Faletogia.

The whole process took a little over an hour and as they neared the final minutes the lights dimmed.

"Watch that magnetic resonance Denise." Dr Faletogia barked into the microphone as the main screen saw a green circle drift outside of its designated spherical border. "I said watch that fucking magnetic resonance." His voice was teetering on the edge of rage.

Dr Faletogia had not been the sort of person to lose his temper and in fact had never done so in public since his earliest days at school. This had changed once he had assumed full control of the MRTD. He had been trained to think the best way to achieve compliance was through rationale debate and structuring shared objectives but the thrill of having people respond to his emotional state was alluringly addictive. The circle used to monitor the system returned to within the acceptable parameters and Dr Faletogia's temper cooled. The adrenaline of the outburst remained.

"Great work, Denise."

The delicate balance they needed for everything to work had finally been achieved, so after a final visual check of all the screens to ensure no splashes of red were on display, Dr Faletogia leaned over and pulled the lever to activate the final influx of power. The whole room blinked into darkness for a second as the MRTD took every last watt of energy from the grid. The lights faded slowly back in and then the main screen blinked back on, displaying the current state of the tachyon stream.

It was active.

The room erupted into a cheer and Dr Faletogia wondered if he would ever lose the sense of excitement he felt every time he pulled the activation lever.

Everyone could relax now as once the MRTD was initiated, its regressive redundancies allowed it to self-regulate while it probed the tiniest interwoven fragments of reality's fabric. The way in which it grazed the quantum froth was algorithmically defined and so it was now just a matter of monitoring for unforeseen issues and other than that, waiting patiently for the results to come in.

Dr Faletogia looked over at Rhett who had moved over to one of the control stations and was tapping some instructions into it. He thought for a moment whether he should go and check on what he was doing but then brushed off his concerns and turned his thoughts to the plot of land he was going to buy with his bonus so he and his wife could build their own house. He was sure Rhett was simply checking the station's diagnostic displays to best identify the signs of a Cloit Contortion.

Rhett was surprised that Dr Faletogia was doing nothing to intervene as he reprogrammed the MRTD's algorithm. He even found himself feeling a little aggrieved of having wasted all that time training to be able to physically overpower anyone who tried to stop him completing his task. He had a little look around the room to take it all in before initialising the new instructions to invert the stream from tachyon to anti-tachyon and guide it so it combined with the wake of the Cloit Contortion. If he was going to end it all, he needed to do so in an epic manner and if all that awaited him was oblivion's sweet embrace, then so be it.

He tapped the screen one more time, and then…

…nothing.

It would take a few moments for the new alignments to kick in and as he leaned his waist into the workstation and gripped the sides, bracing himself for the unknowable onset of nothingness, he discovered how Nina's joke about how his excitement might manifest itself had been astonishingly prescient. He had developed an erection, which now pressed against the console.

The team began to stir as it became apparent that something was amiss and Dr Faletogia glanced anxiously in Rhett's direction, and then…

…nothing.

H.ii

Rhett tapped the screen and then…

…nothing.

It would take a few moments for the new alignments to kick in and as he leaned his waist into the workstation and gripped the sides, bracing himself for the unknowable onset of nothingness, he suddenly felt a sense of existential dread. He frantically began dabbing at the screen to try and undo his actions.

The team began to stir as it became apparent that something was amiss. Dr Faletogia stood up and moved in Rhett's direction, and then…

…nothing.

XIV

A faint burning sensation irritated Katja's nose as she sat in the corridor outside Bruno's office. It was being caused by the vapours released by the chemical disinfectant that had just been used to clean the floor and the feeling was now experiencing was not dissimilar to the times she had attempted to add mustard to her food. Her father had always insisted she would enjoy it once her palate matured and she would periodically test his theory but as yet, his prediction had not come true. She had to assume every academic institution had exclusive access to the same brand of cleaning products, for it was only in those establishments, whether it be a nursery school or a leading university, where the same pungent aroma seemed to hang ubiquitously and constantly in the air. After finishing her compulsory school exams, Katja's teachers had encouraged her to continue on to higher education but she saw it as a waste of time for someone entering into journalism. She would sometimes regret the decision, like when a new graduate arrived in the workplace, overflowing with the latest theories and best practice methodologies, making Katja feel like an imposter in her own job. It did not take long however, once these novices floundered and stalled, for her to realise neither academic learning or on-the-job experience actually counted for much. It all centred around temperament, personality and above all else, ambition. She knew deep down she would have succeeded either way and at the very least, the route she had taken had minimised her exposure to that damn acrid smell.

"Katja, thanks for coming." Bruno wheezed as he lumbered down the corridor. He had to sit beside her for a moment to catch his breath. She noted the extra rolls of fat under his chin and the additional layers of flab forcing open the buttons of his shirt.

"I've been working so much here trying to figure out what went wrong, I haven't had much time to hit the gym." Bruno was hoping Katja would respond to his self-deprecating humour but she knew better than to take any such comments in any other way than face value. Her eyes remained full of concern.

"So what was it you wanted to talk to me about. I was intrigued when you said we could only discuss it in person." Katja said.

Ratings for the Leitner Late Show had reduced dramatically since the failure of QuantSim and in the absence of any new leads on breaking stories, Katja was really hoping Bruno could deliver something to help boost this blip in her career.

"I need to let you know that everything we talk about today is off the record." Bruno noticed how his words caused Katja's shoulders to slump and her chest to deflate. "Don't worry, I'm sure it will lead to something usable soon enough but for the moment, we just have to keep this between the two of us."

The laboratory was eerily quiet and the harsh light from a single fluorescent tube cast eerie shadows across the room. It seemed cavernous compared to the last time Katja had been there. Her nostrils now filled with the aromas of tinny sweat, stale gaseous expulsions and boxes of left-over take-away in various states of decomposition. She acknowledged the irony of her previous complaints now she had more personable odours to contend with. Bruno offered her his office chair but the visible patch of moisture led her to politely decline. She pulled over a small stool from nearby. As she settled into the discomfort, which she welcomed because of her revulsion to the alternative, she noticed they were seated in front of an array of three monitors attached to a greasy keyboard. There were several wires leading from the bank of displays into the heart of the QuantSim cabinet. A few other makeshift modules were also connected to the system. These seemed to have been built from bespoke components Bruno had crafted himself rather than the type of part you would find in an electrical store. She noticed that the only other powered-up device was a T.W.O.K. arcade unit at the other side of the room, which itself seemed to have been opened up and subjected to some extensive modifications. The machine reminded her of Maxwell who had one in the gaming room of his apartment, a place she had not visited for quite some time.

Bruno pointed at one of the screens.

"I was doing some diagnostics on the operating system when I came across some peculiar readings. If you look here you will see that QuantSim did not just stop, the architecture of the program seemed to fold in on itself and was reabsorbed into the underlying quantum framework." Bruno could see Katja's forehead now had several deep lines running across it. "Are you with me?"

"Not...really...sure...but keep going and hopefully the jist of it all will sink in. I can then ask you some questions to clarify if I am on the right track or not."

"Great." This was one of the reason's Bruno had chosen Katja as his confidant. She had the capacity to understand things quickly and when she did not, she was not the sort of person who would waste time pretending she had. "It is as if the code had collapsed in on itself and then disappeared into the hardware. In effect, the programme itself punctured through its own software architecture and accessed the quantware. The whole system then regressed back to its most fundamental state...the underlying quantum foam."

Bruno could see Katja was not too far away from understanding what he was describing, at least conceptually. He imagined the inside of her head as a series of motors and cogs that were spinning wildly but without the required purchase to move her comprehension forward. He needed to shift the clutch to get her in the right gear.

"An analogy would be that some word processing software had spontaneously decided of its own accord to put in place a regressive algorithm that not only deleted itself, but all other applications including the operating system, leaving the hardware in the same state it had been when it came off the production line, with all the original factory settings in place...and then powered down the whole computer."

Katja was silent for a while as she tried to make sense of Bruno's explanation.

"I worked on a story last year about some college kids who created a free game." Katja tapped at her upper lip and leaned forward. " It was quite a simple, but pretty addictive concept and everyone was told it was free of copyright so could be shared at will. Then one day, I think it was the founder of Denbridge University's birthday, every computer with it installed suddenly stopped working. All you could see on your screen was a single input field. It would remain like that until you typed in "Denbridge University Rocks"...and then everything went back to normal. Do you mean something like that happened?"

Bruno was pleased by Katja's question. It meant she had grasped the basics. "It is a bit like that but instead of the game being designed to do it by a group of mischievous students, imagine if it had spontaneously decided to create the problem of its own accord."

"Could it just be a bug in the way it was built or could someone else have maliciously added something without your knowledge?"

"It is theoretically possible it could be either of those things, but I basically hard-coded QuantSIm so there is nobody else with the access or the ability to do something like this without leaving behind an obvious trail. In respect of a bug, it would be a stretch to suggest I would create flawed code..." Bruno looked over at Katja and raised both his eyebrows to indicate he was fully aware how fallible he was. "...but there's also something else making me think it isn't one of those two options."

"Go on."

"In the analysis from the data of the final moments before QuantSim shut down, we can see a strange series of stable points within the quantum swirls. This would be extremely unlikely to appear by chance if the problem had been caused by a malicious attack or a bug.

Prior to the actual rift being established between the software and the underlying quantware, it is as if there were a series of little tugs on the subatomic layer. That might not be so strange in and of itself but there are seven of these tug clusters. The number of tugs in each cluster seems to count down according to the series: thirteen, eleven, seven, five, three, two, one."

"Is that significant?"

"Yes, these are all prime numbers. OK, maybe we could just about believe this was a random occurrence but the time between each group of tugs doubles compared to the previous ones."

"Right?"

"...and if that was not enough, the time between each tug within the bursts follows a pattern that evokes e."

"E?"

The number e is one of the most important numbers in mathematics and is approximately equal to 2.71828."

"Approximately?" Katja teased.

"It's an infinitely recurring decimal so yeah, I gave you quite an approximation actually." Bruno replied without picking up on Katja's tone.

"What does all this mean?"

"I'm not exactly sure yet but it seems to be shouting out to us that whatever it was that caused QuantSim to implode came from inside QuantSim and had a conceptual understanding of important aspects of mathematics. It seems as if there was a mischievous intelligence active within QuantSim and it was trying to let us know it was there."

"Do you think it could be an indication of sentient life?"

"It seems so but then the question is, why would sentient life decide to destroy itself in that fashion?"

"Yeah. That would seem to go against all our understanding of life's urge to preserve itself. Maybe it didn't realise what the consequences would be....like sending the message got out of control?"

Bruno nodded at Katja for a moment as he considered whether to end the conversation there or tell her more about what he had discovered. He decided he might as well keep going now he had been able to look into her eyes. He would need Katja for his ultimate plan to work and he simply had to trust her. If she betrayed his confidence then all would be lost anyway. There were no other feasible options. He had to take a leap of faith.

"As you know, we need to get clearance from Dr Panwar and Vice-Chancellor Zahid Mashwani before running QuantSim again...but in order to gain a deeper understanding of what happened, I did something a little naughty and without authorisation. I rolled the system back to just before it collapsed in on itself and let it run for a few seconds. The exact same error occurred and QuantSim shut down in exactly the same way but this time I was able to pinpoint the coordinates in the simulated universe where the activity took place."

"So now you have something to go to them with, they should allow you to officially turn it back on?"

"That's the problem. Now that there is a strong indication of sentient life having emerged in there, Dr Panwar is less likely to approve of it being turned back on until all the ethical questions are clarified in law."

"So what now?"

"Well...now we know the coordinates, we could roll it back one more time and observe in detail the final few moments before everything came to an end. We could find out exactly what happened. Are you up for that?"

Katja nodded without hesitation. She leaned forward and patted Bruno on the back. A layer of tension left Bruno's shoulders and a warmth radiated across his chest. It felt good to finally have a partner in crime.

H.iii

Dr Faletogia looked over at Rhett who had moved over to one of the control stations and was tapping some instructions into it. He thought for a moment whether he should go and check on what he was doing. Even though he trusted his old friend completely, he decided he would be remiss in his responsibilities if he did not make sure he was not inadvertently doing something that might cause a few issues.

Rhett saw Dr Faletogia walking over to him and continued with the task he was performing. He had expected he might be confronted and was ready to deal with such a scenario.

"What are you doing, Rhett?" Dr Faletogia asked as he looked down at the screen Rhett was working on. "How did you even access that part of this system?"

Rhett ignored him and continued to tap away rapidly. He only needed to complete a few more actions and the anti-tachyon beam would be attached to the wake of the Cloit Contortion and it would be impossible to stop.

"Rhett, what the fuck are you trying to do?" Dr Faletogia grabbed Rhett's forearm, his voice laced with panic.

Rhett took hold of Dr Faletogia's hand and twisted it so the pain forced him to release his grip and for the rest of his body to spin around. Rhett placed his arm around Dr Faletogia's throat and secured his elbow in place above his Adam's apple by locking his arms together behind Dr Faletogia's head. He maintained the choke hold and applied consistent pressure.

"Jess...Marc..." Dr Faletogia struggled to speak through the pressure exerted on his neck and his sounds came out in gasps and gurgles.

He was able to attract the attention of his colleagues but their reactions were slow. As intelligent as they were and as highly trained in dealing with complicated problems arising in dynamic environments, this situation left them wide-eyed and frozen in place.

Dr Faletogia's body became limp in Rhett's arms and he relaxed his grip so he could move over to tap the screen for the final time and then...

...nothing.

It would take a few moments for the new alignments to kick in and as Dr Faletogia slumped to the floor and a siren began to scream, adrenaline pumped through Rhett's body. He stood over his vanquished foe and as he braced himself for the unknowable onset of nothingness, he could not help revel in the feelings of power derived from being a conqueror of worlds and destroyer of universes.

The team on the floor looked around in panic, trying to understand the meaning of the fluctuating readings combined with the blaring alarm, and then...

...nothing.

XV

Geoff Watts was displeased by the new responsibilities that the building services department had been assigned by Vice-Chancellor Mashwani a few months earlier. He understood these had been imposed on the Vice-Chancellor by the courts but it was now up to him, as the department head, to put in place the measures to comply with the ruling. This in and of itself would not have caused him any consternation except it was made crystal clear he needed to fulfil these new obligations without any increase in the resources allocated to his department.

He was fortunate enough to have developed a conscientious and amiable team, partly through the combination of a focused recruitment strategy and relaxed management style, and partly through sheer good luck. His team had not complained about having to put in significant overtime to install the new apparatus throughout the university, which allowed power consumption of the individual university faculties to be monitored in real time. He was able to explain to them the importance of the task at hand, even though he did not himself believe it to be true, and so there had been no open objections to the fact that everyone would be required to work an additional two hours per week in order to keep an eye on tracking the equipment's output. Part of his strategy for maintaining morale was to include himself in the new rota and although he spent fewer hours performing this task than the rest of the team, during those hours his inner monologue was filled with rambling rants directed at Vice-Chancellor Mashwani that frothed with bile and vitriol. He would resign at least twenty times in his imagination during those sessions and he never tired of the look on Mashwani's face when it inevitably dawned on him how difficult life was going to be without Geoff Watts in charge of Braxton University building services. He could see him sitting in his office as the structural integrity of the building crumbled around him, ignoring call after call from the education minister who saw fit on this occasion to inform Mashwani directly of his immediate discharge from his current position.

Geoff tried to use the time wisely by filling out assessment reports or sketching out flow diagrams for streamlining other aspects of his department's duties, but the constant chimes and pops of the equipment served to distract him from making any satisfactory headway. These intrusions into his concentration were a constant reminder of how people like Vice-Chancellor Mashwani felt superior to individuals like Geoff who had acquired practical qualifications and relied on hands-on experience. Each encroachment by the hums and buzzes of the contraption on his absorption in his other activities, was another opportunity to consider how both his time and his abilities were seriously undervalued not just by his employers, but by society as a whole...and he was also perfectly clear on his wife's opinion on that matter.

He looked up as an electronic buzzer sounded and one of the dials twitched into the red zone of the display. This represented a significant power surge to the QuantSim laboratory, which had been the ultimate reason for all this nuisance. It remained in place for a while and Geoff eyed it suspiciously through narrowing eyes. His head began to shake involuntarily as he started to wonder at what point he would need to do something. There had only been a loose procedure put in place whereby anything unusual had to be reported immediately to Vice-Chancellor Mashwani. Was this something he should consider as unusual?

After around fifteen seconds the dial suddenly returned to its original position and Geoff sank slowly back into the synthetic fabric of his chair. He kept a close eye on the gauge to make sure the needle did not twitch back into the problematic red territory of the display. As each uneventful minute drifted by, tensions he had previously been unaware of melted from his body. His mood lightened considerably when one of his subordinates eventually came to relieve him and his stint overseeing the power consumption apparatus came to a close. It seemed to be the case that what he had witnessed was nothing more than an anomalous surge and as such his own energy levels had risen. He walked away from the university building whistling the chorus to a song that had been playing on the radio all summer, which had a catchy tune but the words had not settled into his memory. On a whim, he bought his wife some flowers and decided to treat her to a surprise meal that evening at the little restaurant by the river. He was determined to celebrate the dual elation of knowing he would not have to undertake that mundane observational chore for another two weeks and also having not had any reason for direct contact with Vice-Chancellor Mashwani.

XVI

Bruno stuck the electrodes slowly onto his scalp. He had needed to shave sixteen small round sections of his hair to accommodate the cold metal discs of gold-plated copper, which he attached using medical-grade glue. A casual observer would not have been able to see these patches of skin under his thick explosion of hair and once attached, the discs also became lost in what he secretly referred to as his lion's mane. After the final one was in place and his hair had settled around it, he looked like he had the aura of an aging male medusa who had maintained a high-sodium, high-fat lifestyle for a significant number of years.

It had been a little over two weeks since he had sat in the same position, wide-eyed and having again forgotten how to breathe after witnessing with Katja the re-run of the events leading up to QuantSim's deactivation. Not only had a thriving and sophisticated civilisation evolved within it, one of the individuals had taken it upon themselves to destroy the very universe in which they resided. From that moment on Bruno had worked flatout to create a way in which he could interface and communicate with that individual. He had mulled over a plethora of ideas in respect of how best to manifest within the universe. He could have tried a soft approach by sending text-based messages on the communication device he carried, or appeared as if on-screen on a television or monitor, he also considered setting up an interface so he could call him on his phone. It was during one of his long T.W.O.K. gaming sessions that he finally hit upon some inspiration. He could use the new neural controls he had developed for T.W.O.K. They had advanced considerably since his initial experiments and once connected, he was now able to immerse himself entirely within the world through electrical pulses flowing directly from and to his brain. It would not take much to migrate this type of interface to the QuantSim environment and had the added benefit of allowing Bruno to manifest himself within the QuantSim universe as if he was a part of it. Bruno had initially started designing an avatar with similar qualities to himself but being painfully aware of how he looked, had quickly become disheartened. It was at this point he realised those restrictions were no longer constraining him. There was no reason why he could not appear in QuantSim as anything he wanted. So why not as Ra I De la Rosa, the lead character of T.W.O.K? It would also save a lot of time because the avatar was already complete and ready to go.

The first step to making everything work was to instal T.W.O.K. onto the QuantSim quantware, which was much more straightforward than he expected and he was even able to test the new interface by playing a few games. There was enough capacity within the system for T.W.O.K. to run alongside

QuantSim without it causing any issues and the game required very little power so he was not concerned about alerting the building services department. He was amazed at how much more exciting and captivating the game was when run off the quantum network. The only issue was making sure that the interface was restricted, otherwise he speculated that his mind might expand into the subatomic foam, making it difficult, if not impossible, for him to detach himself from the machine. The biggest technical challenge remaining was devising a system that would allow him to speak the same language as the beings inside the simulated universe but after giving it his undivided attention, he developed a workable solution based around conceptual understanding rather than direct translation.

He did the final checks on the connections and the system. He noticed he had trouble keeping his hand steady and hoped it was the excitement causing his extremities to vibrate and not a new symptom of one of his many underlying health conditions. He would only allow himself a few minutes interfacing with QuantSim otherwise the power usage might attract unwanted attention, so he mentally rehearsed all the information he wanted to convey once he was there. He was still surprised how his previous short bursts of activating QuantSim had not raised any questions, especially after the expense and drama of installing all the monitoring equipment. Despite getting away with it a few times, he did not want to push his luck at this point so reckoned on being active for no more than three minutes. This should be ample time because even though he had turned down the internal clock to resemble his own reality, the differences in the perception of the passage of time would mean it would seem like he was in the QuantSim environment for a much longer period. He was not exactly sure what that would feel like or if his brain would even be able to handle it, but there was now only one way to find out.

He rolled QuantSim back to its earlier state, initiated the electrode interface and pressed the button to power the network up. He inhaled deeply and his eyes widened in anticipation of the new experiences awaiting him. There was a non-trivial chance he might die but the lure of adventure overpowered his desire for safety and with a spasmodic jerk, he flicked the switch to connect himself to the system. He shot backwards, his body shaking and stiff as if experiencing a severe electric shock. This lasted for about five seconds until suddenly he slumped heavily into his chair, which drifted backwards until it hit the workbench behind him.

1

Rhett was staying at the Atrium Airport Hotel and was relaxing after finishing his roundtable debate at SubAtomCon in CERN. He had been pleasantly surprised by how engaged the audience were when discussing such an esoteric and abstract topic as how loops of dark gravity might in fact be an emergent manifestation of a more fundamental quantum foam. He had amused himself by dropping hints at what was possible and what he was about to do. He now understood why cinematic villains always gave the hero of the film a fighting chance to stop them. There was simply no thrill without jeopardy.

He had arranged to meet his old friend Dr Sateki Faletogia, who had recently been promoted to Project Director of the Massively Regressive Tachyon Distributor (MRTD). There were still an hour or so to kill before their allotted meeting time, and as Rhett had already eaten his ritual dinner of veal cutlet milanese with salad sprout, cherry tomatoes and parmesan at the Atrium Cafe, he was now killing time with a frothy glass of Qu Ilfrisch Hell at the hotel bar.

He was savouring the crisp bitterness of the cool amber liquid, which never offered the same pleasurable tingling sensation on his tongue when he drank the same brand at home, even if he had brought the bottles back from Switzerland himself. The scientific part of his brain began to work on a hypothesis as to why and thinking about the various scenarios, all involving him consuming large amounts of beer, kept him amused for a while. The intensity of his thoughts caused him to lose some awareness of his surroundings as his abstract ideation mingled with his whimsical imaginings. This caused him to miss the fact that a flamboyantly dressed character had taken the seat next to him at the bar. He was wearing some leather over-trousers on top of a pair of weathered jeans, a pair of worn boots with spurs on them and his upper body was covered in an elaborately-patterned, crocheted poncho. He also seemed to have a bullet holder belt across his chest and holstered guns at his hips. The outfit was completed by a battered leather austin cowboy hat. This attire was unusual but its unconventionality was fairly standard for this type of event, where scientists liked to assert their individual brilliance in how far they strayed from fashion norms. It was also not unknown for various institutions to run side events around the conference so there was a good chance that somewhere this evening, someone had organised a fancy dress party. Rhett remembered a time in the not too distant past when he would have been invited to all the parties at an event like this. He sighed and accepted those days were long gone.

Bruno was suffering from a state of mild shock. The vivaciousness of the reality he found himself in was of an intensity he had not been expecting. He genuinely felt like he inhabited Ra l De la Rosa's body and that it was deeply grounded in the environment around him. He could actually breathe the air and with it came a host of exotic and powerful smells, which had some undertones of familiarity but were blended in a way as to make them wholly alien.

"Are you alright?" Rhett asked him.

Bruno was ecstatic. He was pleased to recognise the man talking to him and delighted he could understand his language.

"I'm not sure yet." He managed to croak before having a minor coughing fit. It was taking him a few moments to get used to the way the saliva operated in this new mouth.

"Rough day, huh?" Rhett had always enjoyed getting to know the eccentric cast of characters who descended upon CERN during SubAtomCon. It was a much more compelling reason to attend than for the conference itself, which was merely a review of all the latest developments that everyone in the community already knew anyway. "One of these might help make things feel a bit better." Rhett signalled to the bartender to bring two fresh glasses of Qu Ilfrisch Hell.

Bruno had a small taste of his beer and then gulped it down quickly. He did not usually like this type of drink but this one went down easily.

"Can I have another one of these?" He said as he caught the bartender's eye.

"You speak French?" Rhett asked him.

"Apparently so." Bruno replied in English. His translation module must have allowed him to switch between the most appropriate langues for the entity he was communicating with without him realising.

"I'm Dr Gaumond from Birmingham University by-the-way." Rhett took the initiative, against the standard stereotype of an Englishman, to introduce himself.

Bruno smiled.

"And you are?" Rhett was still amused by his drinking partner but could see it wearing off fairly soon if he had to continue to carry the full weight of the conversation.

"Oh...I'm Professor Bruno Matthams...from Braxton University."

Rhett had not heard of that particular academic institution and so assumed it was situated somewhere in the US Midwest. "What brings you to CERN Professor Matthams?"

"Actually...you?"

"Me?"

"Yeah. I'm not sure how you are going to respond to this and I'm not sure what the best way to say this is, so I'll just come out with it." Bruno adjusted his hat to a more comfortable position. "I know what you are about to do."

Rhett's fists clenched automatically. He had been conscious not to tell anyone of his true motivation for coming to CERN . He had never even told anyone about his long term puzzle regarding how to gain cosmic attention. He was prepared to use violence if need be but he had not expected to be confronted until he actively attempted to take control of the MRTD. He wondered if his subtle hints at the roundtable event had actually been enough to tip someone off to his plan.

"What are you talking about?" He asked. His eyes had become narrow slits.

"I know that in a couple of hours you are going to use some complicated apparatus in a facility nearby to initiate a particle beam that will ultimately...um..." Bruno coughed as he carefully considered how best to convey his meaning. He did not want to spell out the consequences of his drinking partner's future actions in case the actual events he initiated were not as he had actually intended. "...reorder your reality on a fundamental level."

Rhett decided his best option was to view this accusation as nothing more than the ramblings of a crazy conspiracy-theorist. A madman who said this type of thing to every scientist he met but had just now stumbled randomly on someone where it was actually true.

"Haha." Rhett tried to laugh off the claim "I think we have clearly seen there is nothing to worry about with the Large Hadron Collider creating blackholes or triggering rifts to other dimensions. If anything like that was going to happen, we would already know about it." He polished off his drink, thinking this might add to how frivolous the accusation looked. He placed the empty glass on the bar and stood up. "Maybe I'll see you around."

"Dr Gaumond...Rhett...I know you are going to blast an anti-tachyon beam of several gigathrons into the smallest threads of this universe, stretching and stressing them to an extreme degree. I am just trying to ascertain whether or not you understand what the consequences of that would be."

Rhett sat back down. He was intrigued by how much this stranger knew so he decided he had nothing to lose by testing matters further. "I have no idea what you are talking about...but I do know that an anti-tachyon blast measuring several gigathrons would likely unhook a loop of dark gravity, stretching it until it snapped. This would most probably create a chain-reaction, which would open up a regressive rift in spacetime. Ultimately this rift would suck everything back into the swirling churn of quantum uncertainty that underpins the difference between there being something...and there being nothing."

"So you do know what you are doing?" Bruno muttered, more to himself than as a question to Rhett. He remained in his position at the bar, his huge bronzed forearms framing his drink. He gazed at the suds of his beer as they slid down the inside of his glass.

"Who are you?...Really?" Rhett asked.

"I will tell you more about that if you answer me one simple question." Bruno twisted towards Rhett and he lifted a finger to further emphasise his offer.

Rhett's barstool tipped forwards and he had to drop his foot to the floor to balance himself. He was beginning to suspect Professor Matthams might originate from further afield than the US Midwest. "Go on."

"Why?" Bruno's left ear drifted towards its respective shoulder as his brow furrowed. He looked intently into Rhett's eyes. "Why would you want to destroy the cradle of your own existence?"

"How about this?" Rhett pushed all four legs of his stool back to the floor, cupped an elbow in one hand and tapped the side of his nose with his index finger of the other hand. "You tell me exactly who you are and where you're from, and I'll be completely honest with you."

"Alright." Bruno could see no reason for further subterfuge. "This reality we are in now, is not really reality. It is being simulated by a machine called QuantSim in my laboratory. We observed the ending of your universe and traced the cause of it back to you, so I have now projected myself into this simulation to try and ascertain your motives."

"What do you mean - observed me ending my universe? - I haven't done it yet."

"After you did it, we were able to roll the universe back to an earlier state so even though you have not done it yet from your perspective right now, also from my perspective you have done it...and actually you have succeeded in doing it more than once."

Rhett jumped up into the air and performed an awkward shadow-boxing maneuver. "I fucking knew it." He screeched without consideration for how loud or how high-pitched his voice had become. He kicked out his foot to emphasise his words. The whole bar looked in his direction but he did not care. "I knew there was some sort of higher reality out there and I knew I'd get your attention." He grabbed Bruno in a playful headlock and scrubbed his hair with his fist.

Bruno could not help being swept up by the infectious nature of Rhett's enthusiasm. As Rhett let him go from their joyful grapple, Bruno was overcome with awe at what his creation had spawned. Rhett seemed so real, so clever, so sentient.

"OK...OK." Rhett was speaking rapidly. "If you are who you say you are then you should know that I left...or will leave...or have had might would leave... a couple of indicators using the stream. Tell me about them."

"Ah...are you talking about the prime numbers expressed in the preceding anti-tachyon bursts, the doubling nature of the time between them and the evocation of e within the bursts themselves?"

Rhett opened his arms up wide and spun round slowly, revelling in his own genius. "Yes, and did you notice there was some slight variation in the timings, which equated to pi?"

"Oh...no, I didn't pick up on that part."

"But you do know what pi is...in your reality?"

"Yes."

Rhett's eyes narrowed as he considered his creator. It seemed he had some fallibilities. Rhett was not too concerned about this in that moment, but he did find it interesting and in fact also mildly comforting.

"I have so many questions." Rhett clasped the palms of his hands to his face as his eyes darted around the ceiling.

"We will have time for all that later but right now I have to tell you that my appearances here are limited in duration. I promise I will return but before I go, tell me your reasoning behind the total destruction of your universe."

"It was just a calculated risk...that's all. "Rhett's words were spilling out rapidly, he had harboured these thoughts for a long time and it was a cathartic experience to be able to finally let them all out. "I reasoned that based on probabilities, it was almost certain we resided in a simulated reality, throw in a sprinkling of the potential for supernatural deities, add to that my abject despair at having to tolerate this existence...and I just thought it would be a way of grabbing the attention of whatever was out there. I was trying to force interest on any observers who might otherwise be bored or disinterested or otherwise just using my reality as one of millions of points of reference for a bigger study. I was trying to become an outlier, an anomaly in the statistics, a point of interest...as these are the ones that make people take notice and investigate them."

"That's..." Bruno struggled to find the right words to express his admiration. "That's… err...really ...quite...clever."

Bruno was conscious that his time was about to run out. "So you've got my attention. What now?"

"What do you mean?"

"Now you have made contact with me, what do you want?"

Rhett's head jerked back in his neck and his eyes began blinking rapidly. He had only ever considered the problem of getting the attention and not what would happen thereafter. "Huh..."

"Well think about it because th..." Before Bruno could finish his sentence he blinked out of Rhett's existence.

Rhett looked around surreptitiously to see if anyone had noticed. One of the bartenders who had been polishing a glass nearby was staring at the empty space with wide eyes. After a few seconds he fluttered his eyelids, shook his head and returned to his work. He had been pranked too many times by SubAtomCon scientists and as his shift was almost over, he was not minded to get involved with this one.

Dr Faletogia rushed in to join Rhett. He was full of fluster and apology for his tardiness even though he was only several minutes late. Rhett nodded at the bar to indicate they should bring another drink for his companion and the bartender performed his duties without allowing anyone the satisfaction of him showing signs he had been affected by what he had just seen. Rhett found it difficult to concentrate on his friend's bubbly conversation as he wrestled with his new puzzle. Dr Faletogia offered Rhett the expected invite to join him at MRTD that evening but unexpectedly Rhett declined. He appreciated the invitation, but more importantly he was relieved that he would not have to overpower and murder his longterm colleague and collaborator, and everyone in existence for that matter, later that evening.

As the evening wore on, it was imperceptible to Rhett, Dr Faletogia, the bartender or anyone else in their universe that Bruno was busy powering down QuantSim...and then as far as they were all concerned...

...nothing.

2

Parveen's personal assistant popped his head around her office door. "You will have to leave in the next five minutes if you are going to be on time for your dinner appointment."

Parveen blinked a couple of times as she broke concentration from the legal text she had been perusing. She leant back in her green leather chair and folded her arms, looking at her secretary through furrowed eyebrows and pursed lips. She quickly switched her expression to a smile and thanked him. She was annoyed with herself, and she had no desire to make life difficult for one of her most loyal and conscientious employees.

She opened her bottom draw and pulled out her make-up and a small mirror and applied a quick touch-up. She still looked tired and withdrawn. Partly due to the lingering effects of her treatment. Partly because of the amount of hours she had been putting into drafting the legal protections required to deal with the fact billions of sentient beings could be switched off and on at the touch of a button. The situation with Professor Matthams had been a wake-up call about how ill-prepared the world was for this new power and although the first iteration of the technology had ultimately come to nought, it was only a matter of time before the pressure to turn it on again would become irresistible. She did at least now have a small window in which to work without a simulated universe humming away in the background, in which the inhabitants were at the whimsical mercy of scientists who had intelligence but lacked empathy.

As she hurtled through the city in a taxi, she wished she had not agreed to meet her ex-husband, Vice-Chancellor Zahid Mashwani for dinner that evening. She still remembered the ignominy of having him end things with her once he learned of her condition and although she obviously understood his reasoning, she could not help but feel he had miscalculated her potential. She had ultimately been proven right as she had recovered quite quickly and the QuantSim case had raised her profile considerably, with some media outlets even suggesting she could be in line for a government position. She had rapidly surpassed Zahid's political potential, especially with the failure of QuantSim, his highest profile project, and so the upper hand now lay with her.

The taxi was unable to drop her off outside the restaurant as some roadworks had made the street impassable. This left her with a small walk from the street corner. A light rain was enough to distribute droplets of water onto her wig but not enough for it to be considered wet. She saw Zahid sitting in the window, staring blankly into the clouded evening sky and suddenly memories of their life together flooded back. His professional public image would sometimes drop when they were alone together, allowing her a glimpse at the enthusiastic but timid child within. This was the child she now observed, lost in the domain of his own thoughts. The spell was broken as a waiter offered to top up his wine. She inhaled deeply and navigated the bollards and barriers to get through to the restaurant door, waving politely at Zahid who had now noticed her.

"I don't know why you enjoy this place so much." Zahid said as he looked down his nose at the menu.

"I don't. We only ever came here because you liked it."

"What? No."

They both looked at each other in confusion.

"So you're telling me that in the twenty years we were together, we only ever came here time and time again out of politeness, each of us thinking it was the other one's favourite restaurant?" Parveen asked through gritted teeth.

The realisation caused them both to burst out laughing.

"I guess communication was never our strong point." Zahid said as he pulled the napkin onto his lap with excessive flourish.

The meal was pleasant and the conversation was relaxed and informal. They discussed how their respective family members and non-mutual friends were getting on and talked about a few of the fun times they had together. They shared a few biryani dishes and decided to order some glasses of lassi, even though it did not sit well with the wine they were both conspicuously over-consuming during lulls in conversation.

"Have you just brought me here for a nostalgic catch-up?" Parveen finally plucked up the courage to ask.

Zahid suddenly felt the urge to check his tie and as he did so he noticed a few bits of dandruff on his lapels, which he flicked away. "I don't know if you have heard but my tenure at Braxton is coming to a close in eighteen months or so. They have made it clear I can hold the position for another term if I want but I have also been in discussions with the Education Ministry regarding the role of permanent secretary."

"That's excellent. It is what you've been working for all these years, and to be offered it now is well ahead of your planned career schedule."

"There have also been rumours about you acquiring a post in government."

"That's true, but nothing has progressed beyond rumours."

"I was thinking it might progress my discussions and turn your rumours into firm offers if we were to recombine our resources."

Parveen stopped chewing involuntarily as her mouth reacted to what he had just said. She clamped it shut as soon as she became aware that a mass of masticated chicken and rice was on display to any casual passerby who happened to look through the restaurant window. She could hardly believe what Zahid was proposing.

Zahid's upper body remained motionless but below the table his right knee was bouncing up and down rapidly. He knew his offer was quite extraordinary after all they had been through but he hoped she would at least think about it and realise that maybe it could work for their mutual benefit.

It took Parveen a few moments to recover her composure and although it was only a few seconds before she responded, it seemed like several minutes from Zahid's perspective.

"I will have to think about it...but maybe...maybe it could work." She said finally.

Zahid saw this as a good sign and took a celebratory sip of wine. It was no longer just the alcohol causing warmth to radiate from his stomach.

3

Bruno walked along the canal listening to some music through a portable music system. He had just bought it at an electronics store in the Bullring in Birmingham City Centre. It was able to store tens of thousands of pieces of music and the explosion of options available was making him light-headed. And if that was not enough, he was not even restricted to the physical storage on the device itself. He could replenish the catalogue by accessing a comprehensive storage bank through some sort of radio wave transmission. He had not had time to explore the principles behind how it worked in depth, but he was sure the physics in his tier of reality would allow a similar form of information transfer. He had asked the teenager working at the counter to put together a playlist identifying the best fifty or so examples of music in history. The shop assistant had giggled initially but the perplexed look on Bruno's face had caused him to stop.

"Oh...you're serious?"

If it had been Bruno's image standing before the shop assistant, he would have dropped back into professional mode and brushed off the request but as it was Ra l De la Rosa's rugged good looks staring down at him, he was more than inclined to oblige. He only had his limited experience to draw upon but he dug deep into his memories, referencing conclusions from drunken debates to cobble together an eclectic mix of music.

Bruno enjoyed the sounds of Elvis Prestley and Abba but they had comparables in his own reality. It was not until a new type of sound suddenly filled his ears that he felt his chest expand and his heart rate quicken. He stopped in his tracks as the music temporarily overloaded his temporal lobes and rendered him momentarily paralysed. He recovered enough to check what was playing as the choral voices and string instruments mingled together in Mozart's Lacrimosa to evoke wave after wave of crescendoing emotion. A single tear appeared in his eye and rolled down his cheek. He was suddenly instilled with a sense of awe that an entire civilisation had evolved within QuantSim. He had already known this on an intellectual level but it was not until he heard this music that he became viscerally aware of it. Not only had this society reached a level of technological advancement beyond his own tier of reality but also within it there were rich veins of art, literature, philosophy and scientific thought available to be mined. This universe had not yet even evolved into the full potential of its future and already it seemed to have a boundless cultural landscape to explore.

A rush of energy burst through his whole body as he breathed in deeply and a tingling sensation took root in the nape of his neck. It was impossible to imagine the trove of delights that would manifest within QuantSim if it was able to remain unhindered by bureaucracy...and yet as the ripples of sentiment and longing trembled across his shoulders in response to the music, he was also finally able to comprehend the ethical plight of spawning conscious beings purely for the benefit of his own society. Each of them capable of appreciating and creating unique works of beauty and yet most of them would never have the opportunity to do anything other than trudge through a meaningless life for the benefit of a fortunate few. Every advancement was built on the sum of life's entire evolutionary struggle and so who was he to decide whether the suffering of other sentient beings was worth the gains his society would enjoy? He now fully understood Dr Panwar's ethical standpoint and felt humbled by an awareness of his own deficiencies in truly being able to approach the problem with empathy. He realised the main issue with ethics was everyone's instinctive belief they stood alone on the summit of morality's great mountain. Less than a month ago, he would have defended himself vigorously as being fully equipped to make decisions pertaining to QuantSim. He now realised he had been lacking in awareness of an important perspective and this made him worry what other experiential equipment might be missing from his toolkit. He was not saying QuantSim was definitely something that should not be explored, but he was now less certain that it was something that definitely should.

He had not convinced himself either way by the time the final voices faded out and the drumbeats of the next song pushed the question from his mind. He was not much of a dancer but he instinctively moved along to the beat of the new song, feeling good while inhabiting Ra I De la Rosa's body and even though some of the references did not make sense, the music certainly did. A broad grin had appeared on his face and he could not shake the feeling that yes, looking like this, he bet he would look good on the dancefloor.

He noticed a group of youths on the other side of the canal were looking over and giggling at him. He felt a twinge of embarrassment but when he stopped they waved at him as if to indicate they had been enjoying his performance. Bruno was impressed at how friendly this society had turned out to be, not understanding the positive responses he had received in his time there were down to the avatar he had chosen, and not because of some fundamental difference between the sensibilities of this reality and his own.

He had decided to have a little bit of an exploration of this new world before appearing in front of Rhett again. He felt this would help them connect better and understand each other but also just because he was curious about what he had created. He had allowed QuantSim to run for short bursts each day as a means of allowing Rhett some time to ponder the new question he had been posed. There was still the problem of it being currently illegal to run QuantSim until the proper protections and legislation had been put in place, so Bruno needed these sessions to remain under the radar. He hoped his interactions with Rhett might offer him some insight or evidence to expedite the process and at the very least he felt personal responsibility for Rhett and accountable for enabling his existence to continue unhindered. The stop start nature of QuantSim was not noticeable to Rhett or the other inhabitants of the simulation. Whenever the system was paused, the state of the universe was held in a solid quantum state so when it was powered back up it was a seamless experience for anyone inside. Bruno had allowed a month to pass within the system and he hoped this was ample time for Rhett to have come to terms with the situation, and made a decision about what he wanted to do.

Bruno arrived at Rhett's building and although he would have loved to have spent more time sitting by the canal, listening to music and observing the subtle ways in which light refracted slightly differently on the water there, the amount of time he could leave QuantSim running was not without limits.

"Where have you been?" Rhett said curtly as he ushered Bruno inside his apartment. "I thought you weren't coming back."

Rhett's dishevelled look mirrored the state of his flat. He was unshaven, unwashed and it looked like he had been wearing the same clothes for days.

"Sorry...I just was trying to give you a bit of time to think things through."

"It's not fair to just leave me hanging without any means of contacting you?" Rhett pushed a few half-empty take-away boxes off the sofa to make room for Bruno to sit down before perching on the edge of his armchair. "I was freaking out, man. I was starting to think I'd imagined the whole thing or that I'd been subjected to some sort of elaborate hoax."

"Right...sorry. I didn't think."

"I do have feelings you know...or at least I perceive myself to have feelings...so in the essence that I think...then therefore surely I am..." Rhett's right knee was quivering as he recited the words he had prepared in Bruno's absence. "Now, I'm sure you have it all sorted out up there and you think it is ok to treat simulated beings as your playthings or characters in a game, but as much as anyone can know whether another entity has the same rich and varied experience as they do...well, I know I have full and active self-awareness so I think you need to treat that with commensurate respect."

Bruno slouched back into his seat, unable to meet Rhett's gaze. He was experiencing another shift in perspective as his intellectual understanding of the sentience of his creations migrated into a palpable awareness. He had subconsciously still been downplaying the experience of the inhabitants of Rhett's universe in comparison to conscious sentient beings in his own non-simulated reality.

"Hmmmm?" Rhett was looking for a response.

"No...you are right...I really am sorry."

"OK...good." Rhett was not entirely convinced but he knew he had no other choice but to trust him. His knee stopped shaking and he slumped back into his chair. "Have you been out like that?"

Bruno opened his arms and looked down at himself. "Yeah, why?"

"You're wearing a holster and a gun. You're lucky the police didn't stop you."

A spasm of tension occurred in Bruno's pelvic floor as he received this further example of how he was not taking this as seriously as he should. Rhett seemed to sense his guest was genuinely embarrassed by his actions and this further reduced his anxiety.

"Don't worry about it too much. You will not have been the only person in Birmingham city centre today carrying heat…Anyway, do you want a coffee or something?" Rhett waved his limp wrist in the direction of his kitchen.

"No. It's alright. I don't have much time." Bruno was regretting his decision to use up his limited resources on selfish endeavours rather than using his time with Rhett.

"OK, first things first. Why don't you have much time?"

"Actually...from your perspective, I do have a lot of time so don't worry about that."

"You seem pretty inexperienced at all this. I don't want to be funny, but isn't there someone else I could speak to? Do you have a manager or a superior or something you could put me in contact with?"

"I'm afraid not."

Bruno suddenly found himself back in his laboratory. It was a couple of days before he felt comfortable turning QuantSim back on but to Rhett, it was instantaneous. Bruno did use the time productively, or at least he used the time he was not playing T.W.O.K. productively. The enhancements he was making to T.W.O.K. were beginning to make the environment feel almost as realistic as the main QuantSim simulated universe. He built an application interface for Rhett so he could at least send messages out of QuantSim using the portable contact device he always carried around with him.

"How come?" Rhett asked.

The first few moments after interfacing with QuantSim felt like being snapped out of a deep daydream so Bruno was not exactly sure where he was. "How come what?"

"This is fmhhkn rdclls." Rhett mumbled to himself.

Bruno came to his senses and took in a sharp breath. He had prepared a short speech to get Rhett up to speed with the situation.

"I work at an academic institution called Braxton University. I was instrumental in setting up a new system called QuantSim that was able to simulate full universes within it. It was possible to set the initial parameters of the universe and then let it run so it would evolve of its own accord. The idea was we would be able to gain an insight into our own reality based on the simulated reality. The basic structure was in place but there was still quite a bit of work to be done on setting up the monitoring and diagnostics. An unfortunate but unavoidable series of events led to the system being turned on prematurely and without our knowledge. This created the simulated universe in which you now reside.

"Our legal systems had not yet caught up with our technological advancements and so we were in the middle of coming to an understanding of how and when we could use these sorts of systems...however, your actions led to the system shutting itself down and giving us more time to answer these questions.

"I was intrigued as to why the system had shut itself down and acting alone, decided to find out. This led me to discover you and what you had done. I wanted to get to know you and felt a personal responsibility to you. Unfortunately, we are still not allowed to activate the system and so I have to do so in secret to interact with you. This means short sharp bursts of activity, which are seamless to you but not to me."

"So you're saying my existence is illegal?"

"I am not entirely sure. Now that the universe was rolled back and then went on not to destroy itself, it might actually be illegal to turn it off."

"Right."

Bruno was impressed at how quickly Rhett was taking in all the information. It reminded him of the way Katja responded to new ideas but with Rhett seeming to understand them on a more intuitive intellectual level.

"Am I the only one?" Rhett asked.

"What?"

"In this universe? I've always felt like I was uniquely conscious and maybe everyone else around me didn't have the same rich internal experience as I did. Am I the only sentient being in this system?"

Bruno froze momentarily. He had pondered this question about himself on a number of occasions. It seemed such philosophical conundrums were an emergent phenomenon of self-awareness.

"We don't currently have a way of really measuring sentience so I cannot answer that question fully, but what I can say is that there is no reason why you should be the only one, and in fact every reason to suggest everyone around you has a broadly similar internal life."

"Alright..." Rhett looked out of the window as he digested the information. "Can you tell me a little bit more about this rolling back...where you said you were able to roll the universe back to an earlier state?"

"I'm not sure if you'll understand this but essentially, the manifested state of the universe is held within the residual entanglements of a quantum foam..."

"...which enables you to work back through them and therefore access previous states?" Rhett finished Bruno's thought.

"Yes."

"Could you send me back again?"

"Sure, we could roll the universe back to a previous time in your life and let it run from there."

"...but could we do that in a way where I retained my memories...so I have all the experience of who I am now but I'm back there?"

"Hmmm...I don't know."

"It should be possible if you isolate the specific entanglements that constitute my essence and then roll everything back but them, mapping them to the right quantstituents so they merge with the previous iteration of myself."

"Right...yeah. It would take a bit of work to set it up but yeah, you're right, that could be done."

"OK - well you asked me last time what I wanted from you now I have your attention...well that's what I want. I want to return to the night my wife and I first realised our futures lay together. I want to go...back."

4

Katja opened her eyes and looked over at the clock on the bedside table. As usual she felt wide awake as she waited patiently for the few seconds to pass before her radio station sounded the morning alarm. She had always been blessed with the ability to wake up exactly at the time she had chosen feeling fresh and full of energy for the day ahead. Despite this, she still felt the need to always set an alarm.

She swung her legs to the floor, tapping them in time to the beat of Barnstorms "Turn It On" as it blasted from the speakers, which were set to their highest volume. She attempted to sing along as Axe Vyne's vocals kicked in but despite hearing it hundreds of times that summer, she was still unable to remember the words.

She was staying at Maxwell Rudd's penthouse apartment in downton Braxton and was looking forward to the delights of his complicated shower, which sprayed water at her from several directions and the temperature of each stream could be individually controlled. The amount of time she spent at Maxwell's place was increasing gradually and they had started to develop a morning routine. He would always wake up several hours before she did and on weekdays would be away and in his office by the time she was readying herself for the day. On weekends, he would be working in the kitchen and as soon as he heard her alarm blasting out, he would take her a large, sweet, frothy hot drink.

She accepted it willingly and gave him a light kiss on the lips before setting it down on one of the dressing tables.

"Dance with me." She said as she bobbed her head from side and slithered her naked body around him as if he were a pole in a strip club.

Maxwell would normally have rejected such requests with a grumpy explanation about how he did not dance, but he knew these protestations were meaningless to Katja. He swung his hips around awkwardly, wiggled his arms and clicked his fingers a few times. He had not felt this comfortable with a woman since taking on the position of Chief Executive of VEX News. He had obviously spent a few evenings with various members of his elite social set but those had only ever been for the purpose of satisfying each other's physical needs. He had started to feel that Katja might have been a suitable fit for something more permanent, but now the Leitner Late Show's ratings were in freefall, he would have to end things with her before it was cancelled. Still, that did not mean he could not enjoy a few more carnal sessions with her before it became clear to her how mismatched they were.

"You really don't get any better, do you?" Katja giggled and on seeing the faux-anger in his eyes, she raced behind the bed to evade capture but quickly enough Maxwell had hunted down his prey and took great delight in devouring it on the bed.

"I don't have time." Katja pouted as she freed herself reluctantly from one of their kisses. "I have to get over to meet Bruno at Braxton Uni."

Maxwell groaned and cursed his luck that Bruno Matthams was seemingly going to be a constant irritation in his life. He could handle the professional annoyance but he baulked at how he was now even invading his personal relations. "Can't you postpone it?"

"Not this time." She said as she slithered out from under him. "He said it was pretty urgent."

Katja had not betrayed Bruno's confidence after witnessing the final events of the QuantSim universe. She knew her position at VEX News and hence Maxwell's life was increasingly tenuous so she hoped Bruno would let her report on the developments sooner rather than later. It was important for her to retain her current foothold in the spotlight, otherwise it would be impossible for her to get back into it.

"What's going on over there? Is it something to do with QuantSim? I thought that thing was dead in the water." He asked.

"I don't know. That's why I'm heading over there to find out." She said as she disappeared into the bathroom and turned on the shower. A moment later her head re-emerged with damp hair and skin glistening alluringly. "Now why don't you join me in these waters?"

5

Bruno wheeled himself through the workshop, checking each of the modifications he had made to the QuantSim equipment as he casually popped a white tablet into his mouth and washed it down with the aid of a tepid tea. It had been a long time since he had checked the labels on any of the orange containers Dr Vargas had issued him or had heeded the scribbled instructions on the prescriptions. They all supposedly held a nuanced purpose but the overriding theme was to numb his senses to the effects of the civil war raging within his body. His mind hummed with a furious focus to complete everything while he was still capable of functioning at a high level of cognitive competence. The drugs were definitely helping but his drive to finish what he had started was the preeminent factor enabling him to disregard the increasing intensity of the tectonic aches that shifted in seismic quakes across his substantial frame. Now that he was nearing completion of all the tasks he had set himself, the sustained levels of required concentration were subsiding. This made it more and more difficult to ignore the deep throbbing pulses and ever-present pains which undulated throughout his body. A body which was now little more than a cadaver animated by the systematic shocks of caffeine, medication and the diminishing adrenaline of his desire to safeguard his legacy.

He had put in place the documentation and user interfaces so people would be able to continue to manage QuantSim without needing a theoretical understanding of what was going on underneath the casing. Up until that point it was as if only a mechanic could operate the QuantSim car but the upgrades he had implemented now meant anyone could get behind the wheel, start the engine and get where they wanted to go. This was not to say he had not also provided an in depth blueprint for the underlying theories. However, he expected it would take decades, if not the best part of a century, for the academic world to catch up with his insights to a sufficient degree that they would be able to manipulate it on a granular level. He was pleased to see that now the quantum network was set-up and stable, it no longer posed the sort of risks of exposure to excited particles, which might lead to others experiencing his own health issues. He had clarified those issues in his papers so if they did need to tinker with the system in that way, they would be able to take sufficient precautions to keep them safe.

Bruno had found additional respite from his failing body during his visits to Rhett and his games of T.W.O.K., which he had enhanced significantly now it was running on the same quantware as QuantSim. The neural interface allowed him to submerge himself fully within its open world and the only way he could immerse himself further would be allow his mind not only to receive stimulus and direct action but to fully overflow via the neural link into the seething broil of the quantum mass. He longed to extend his consciousness into the expanse of that bubbling foam but it would mean he could no longer return to the confines of his own brain, which would have become too limited to house his enlarged awareness...at least, that was the theory. The other potential outcome would be a complete shutdown of his cognitive functions and a quick death.

He had successfully deposited Rhett into a rolled-back state of the QuantSim universe and was allowing it to unfold in short bursts so as not to arouse suspicion by consuming too much power. He was still amazed there had not been any questions at all around this but he knew once the next electricity bill came through, he would at least have to come up with some excuse. Unfortunately even if he was able to come up with something, it would not solve the longer term problem of leaving it running after his demise so Rhett could continue with his life and the universe could unfold in its own way. He felt he owed Rhett and his reality at least a chance of fulfilling its potential and for that he had a plan...but for now he had to make sure the foundations were in place so it could work without him being around.

- Something's wrong! - A message from Rhett popped up on the interface console.

Bruno had hoped he would never hear from Rhett again. After he had deposited him in his past, they had said their goodbyes and wished each other luck. The ability for Rhett to contact Bruno had been put in place purely for emergency purposes and the expectation was that Rhett would live out a contented life and then beyond that, Bruno would do everything he could to allow his universe to continue until it expired according to the principles of its own physics. He was hoping Katja would be able to help him with that part of the plan and he would explain it to her fully when she arrived later that morning. It should also serve to generate enough buzz to reboot her flagging career.

Having heard from Rhett, Bruno felt a twinge of exhilaration rush through him, followed by residual pangs of pain. He was excited to be able to experience the QuantSim world another time but he rocked slightly as he thought about why he might have been summoned. He had some difficulty attaching himself to the neural interface as his hands were shaking but by concentrating hard and emptying his mind, he was able to complete his task.

"I always think you've forgotten me or that something's wrong with the messaging tool." Rhett shook his head in relief at the sight of Bruno materialising in front of him. The pace at which he circled his living room slowed.

"Just one second..." Bruno had informed Rhett several times about how it took a few moments for him to settle after interfacing with QuantSim but it never seemed to get through. Bruno waited for the grey mist to disperse and Rhett's apartment to emerge around him in full colour and focus. "...ok, what's the problem?"

"She's dumped me." Rhett stopped pacing and faced Bruno with his palms facing the sky, shoulders hunched and eyes as wide as he could stretch them.

"Interesting."

"Interesting? It's a disaster. She won't even talk to me."

"Did you do everything the same as before?"

"Yes...well maybe...I don't know. It's obviously impossible to recreate every detail exactly."

"Yes...obviously."

"Anyway…" Rhett perched on the arm of his couch. "...I think it's just that we put me in the wrong place. I think a better entry point would be our wedding night."

"Oh." Bruno sat up.

"What?"

"That's...not...possible. I thought you were aware of that." Bruno said.

A quizzical look formed on Rhett's face.

"The quantum state can only be rolled back, " Bruno continued. "Once there it returns to a state of uncertainty and overrides any of the previous future entanglements."

"You never told me this."

"Didn't I? I mean...even if I didn't, I assumed I didn't need to. You seemed to fully comprehend all the principles involved. Sometimes, it seemed like you understood it all even better than I did."

Rhett quickly worked through the logic of the system in his mind and as it clicked into place, he jerked forwards as if he had been slapped on the back of the head. Of course he could only go back. He had been so caught up in the practicalities of the one aspect of the system that would allow him to attain his desires, he had not taken the trouble to work through the full consequences of actioning it.

"And because the system is built on true quantum probabilities, each time it is rolled-back, the future of that branch will evolve in an unpredictable manner?" Rhett said softly to himself.

"Exactly." Bruno said.

"So even if I did everything exactly the same, the outcome might still be different?"

"Yes, that's what makes it a dynamic and open system. It's the greatest feature of the QuantSim architecture. The universe is not predetermined. There is intrinsic uncertainty at a fundamental level, a precursor to any form of true free will for any sentient creatures that evolve within it...true free will for you. Hell, I don't even know if my universe had free will but it is mathematically baked into your existence...that is unless it transpires that my universe is deterministic and then all of that is moot...but within the confines of where we are, the principle stands."

Rhett slumped into his chair with his head in his hands and began to weep. In his mind he had already allowed himself to believe he would see his children again but now there was virtually zero chance they would ever be born. Regardless of whether or not he followed the exact actions he had done the first time round, the inherent uncertainties would have cascaded on top of each other and led to different children being born. A split second's difference in the time of conception would lead to a child being born with a different DNA formation. He slipped onto the floor as the grief of losing them for a second time overwhelmed him and shuddered through his body in uncontrollable sobs.

Bruno sat quietly on the sofa and watched. He was so far out of his depth in this situation, he felt it best just to observe and let it develop without any attempt on his part to intervene. The sobs subsided slowly and finally Rhett rolled onto his knees and looked at Bruno, his face puffy and red. The myriad paths of his tears had left their mark like the tracks dried-up rivers might leave across a once fertile, but now desertified landscape.

"Gone...worse than gone...never to have existed." Rhett's eyes drifted off as he spoke and his gaze settled beyond the ceiling. This was somehow worse than losing them the first time. At least then they had lived, had left an imprint, however small, on the way the future of their universe unfolded...but now, it felt like they had sunk further into the abyss of non-existence, a place deeper and colder than even death.

"Yep." Bruno said.

Rhett inhaled sharply and locked eyes with Bruno. "But you can send me back to the point I arrived at this time?"

"Yes."

"Alright, let's do that. Send me back to the day we went to the environmental protest in London. It's ok. She fell in love with me once so she can fall in love with me again...and we just have to keep repeating it until we get it right."

Bruno nodded. He did not want to indicate at this point that there were only a finite number of opportunities to try again and he hoped Rhett would get it right quickly. He also made a mental note to check the universal translator. Something seemed to be wrong with the way it was converting the underlying concepts into a common language. There was one notion in particular that was not making sense.

The next attempt was unsuccessful.

"I know what I did wrong this time, I came on too strong." Rhett said when Bruno materialised once more in his apartment.

The next three attempts ended in a similar manner.

"She agreed to go out with me this time but then it fizzled out. We're making progress." Rhett's voice had a high-pitched manic quality, like a junkie explaining to a former friend why he needed a loan for his next fix.

The next attempt was even worse than the others.

"I don't understand. It was so easy the first time round. I didn't even have to try...maybe that's it, send me back." Rhett said, sure his latest epiphany would lead to better results.

But no matter what he tried, Tara simply did not want to take things further. She might agree to go on another few dates with him but sooner rather than later, she would tell him that they needed to talk.

"I don't get it." Bruno said as he found himself back on Rhett's sofa. "Why are you so obsessed with this one person?"

"We're meant to be together."

"I hate to break this to you...but it seems you're not."

"We're soulmates." Rhett's voice turned wistful.

"I don't understand."

"I love her." Rhett raised his voice to drive the message home.

"You what..."

Bruno suddenly found himself back in his lab with Katja standing over him. She had pulled a few of the neural interface connectors from his skull, thinking he had just been engaged in one of the mammoth T.W.O.K. sessions he had told her about.

"You have to stop playing that stupid game, Bruno. We're going to be live to the whole nation in less than ninety minutes." She had assumed the wide stance of an angry nanny admonishing a young child, with her fists pressed into the sides of her ribs and her face screwed up in mock anger.

Bruno smiled at her and reached into his pocket and pulled out a few stray tablets and swallowed them dry. He reached over to the console and tapped in a few commands, sending Rhett back to the moment they arrived in London to attend the environmental protest. This process had initially taken a few hours to set up but he had needed to do it so often, he had created a little program to initialise it automatically. He really hoped Rhett would make it work on this occasion because they were both running out of time.

The crew were busy setting up the various lights, cameras and sound equipment while Martha directed the process. It was difficult to get Katja's attention during this critical part of preparing for the show, but in a lull in the activity, he managed to catch her eye.

"Listen...Katja....you can't just pull the electrodes off my scalp when I am interfaced with the system." Bruno said.

"OK, sorry." Katja smiled at Bruno but was quickly distracted by Martha who had a question about the running order. Katua started to walk towards her.

"This is serious Katja." Katja stopped to face Bruno, sensing the gravity of his tone. "You see these lights here, if the green one is lit then you can disconnect me but if the orange one is lit, it could have very serious consequences if any of the electrodes are removed."

"Might you lose your place in the game?" Katja instantly regretted trying to make a joke when she saw the grave look in Bruno's eyes.

"It means that I am so immersed in the game, the shock to my neural pathways of being abruptly removed could kill me."

"What if the red one is lit up?" Katja asked, noticing there was a third light next to the green and orange ones.

"Oh...yeah...if the red light one is lit then it's fine to disconnect me."

Katja placed her palm gently on Bruno's shoulder. "Well, we don't need to worry about any of that right now do we, you're not going to be playing T.W.O.K. during my show."

"Of course not..." Bruno let out a little cough. "No." A further bout of coughing then overwhelmed him.

Martha was now frantically trying to get Katja's attention but she remained by Bruno's side, with a look of concern on her face until he waved her away. His dry hacks had settled into a manageable, if uncomfortable, wheeze and he was able to take a sip of juice.

6

Parveen had never sat on the Vice-Chancellor's side of the desk before and although the gravity of the situation meant she should be fully focused in the moment, there was a small part of her relishing sitting there, side-by-side with her ex-husband, Zahid. A man who would someday soon become her husband again.

"Why didn't you alert the Vice-Chancellor sooner?" Parveen asked.

Geoff Watts suddenly became aware of a smudge covering the name of his department on his security badge and pulled out a monogrammed cotton handkerchief to wipe it away.

"Well?" Zahid said sharply.

Geoff continued with his task until completely satisfied no part of his title, "Head Of Building Services", was obscured. "It didn't seem relevant."

"Didn't seem relevant?" Zahid slid a piece of paper towards him. On it was a generally flat graph interspersed with sharp peaks. "What aspect of this looks irrelevant to you?"

Geoff picked up the sheet and glanced at it. Realising the print was too small for him to make it out clearly, he slowly took out his spectacles and unfolded them carefully. He noticed a smudge on them and using the same handkerchief as before, he took a few moments to clean them before perching them on his nose and looking at the graph inquisitively. He pinched the paper between thumb and index finger, holding it as far away from his eyes as his stubby arm would allow.

"What is this showing?" He asked.

"Mr Watts..." Zahid's chair slid backwards as he stood up. He grabbed the paper and jabbed at it with his finger. "You know exactly what this is showing. Over the past six weeks there have been significant spikes in the energy consumption utilised by the QuantSim lab."

"There are always fluctuations in power consumption. These didn't seem like something to bother University administration." Geoff made sure to place particular emphasis on the word administration.

"You were asked to report anything unusual." Parveen said.

"Like I said, who is to say whether or not these are unusual." Geoff waved his hand over the crumpled paper, which Zahid had dropped back on the desk.

"And what is the status right now?" Parveen asked.

"I don't know."

"Check" Zahid barely managed to keep control of his voice as he hammered his fist on the desk.

Geoff leaned over and picked up the deskphone and punched in the numbers for his department.

"Hi Steve...It's Geoff...Yeah, can you give me the current reading for section sixteen?...Really?...OK....Yep...Thanks...Bye." He leaned slowly back in his chair and placed his fingertips together. "Hmmm...interesting."

Parveen and Zahid looked at Geoff, waiting for further information but after a few moments realised it would not come without prompting. Zahid looked at Parveen, rolled his eyes and shook his head.

"What did he say?" Zahid shouted, shocking both himself and Parveen with the severity of his anger.

"It's drawing full power right now and has been for the last hour or so." Geoff's head sank back into his own neck, creating a double-chin.

"OK..." Zahid's voice had returned to a normal volume. "...I think we're done here." The way he said 'done" was not lost on Geoff who realised he may have overplayed his hand. He skulked out of the room, not now sure how long he would remain employed at Braxton University.

"What now?" Zahid said as he opened up his bottom drawer and pulled out a small bottle of liquor and a couple of glasses.

Parveen shook her head and placed her hand over the second glass while Zahid poured some of the brandy into the one closest to him. "I'm afraid the terms of the judgement were very clear so now we wait until the police get here and then we go and arrest Professor Matthams."

The intercom buzzed.

"I told you not to interrupt me." Zahid leaned over Parveen to access the button. She closed her eyes and breathed in his expensive aftershave. It brought back a flood of emotions she had long since forgotten.

"I know Vice-Chancellor..." His secretary's voice crackled through the speaker. "...but the education minister has just left a message saying you should put VEX News on immediately and that he will call you later."

Zahid walked over to the big wooden cabinet in the corner of his room. He had never got used to having a TV in his office and in fact thought of it as quite vulgar. He powered it up and turned the nob until eventually he was greeted by Katja Leitner's smiling face looking directly at him through the screen.

"Tonight the Leitner Late Show is broadcasting directly from Braxton University where we have some sensational news from Professor Matthams about the QuantSim Project."

Zahid sighed deeply and then downed the remainder of his drink. As he walked back to his desk, Parveen was already holding the bottle, waiting to provide him a top-up after pouring a generous glass for herself.

7

Bruno surreptitiously checked that all the electrodes were in place underneath the hooded top he had purposefully worn to hide them. Katja had questioned his choice of clothing but in a similar fashion to the previous broadcast, he had convinced her this was the type of attire people expected from someone working in tech. She was unconvinced when he informed her it had essentially been a uniform for all the programmers at RuddCade Gaming but finally accepted it when he showed her the discreet Rudd Corporation logo on his shoulder.

"I thought a nice suit and tie would have been better but...you know...whatever..." Katja had said.

Katja was now standing in the bright lights of the camera and introducing the live broadcast to her millions of viewers around the country. Bruno knew that his only chance of keeping QuantSim running was to garner enough public support to prevent Dr Panwar from being able to turn it off. The Leitner Late Show and its influential demographic had offered him a perfect opportunity to spread the word.

"Tonight the Leitner Late Show is broadcasting directly from Braxton University where we have some sensational news from Professor Matthams about the QuantSim Project." Katja remained frozen until the light flicked off to signify the broadcast had gone to a commercial break.

She straightened her clothes as a make-up assistant rushed in to touch her up. Martha offered her a glass of water and she dutifully took a sip before sitting down next to Bruno's wheelchair. She nodded towards the sound desk with her finger in her ear and then turned to face Bruno. The luminosity of her attention was more startling than any light her crew could shine on him.

"Are you ready?" Katja asked.

Bruno could see that Katja was masking a sense of serious concern. He knew how ill he looked and how the make-up applied to him was barely able to mask his jaundiced hollow features. Under normal circumstances neither of them would have thought it prudent to conduct an interview with someone in his condition. However, based on how quickly Bruno seemed to be deteriorating, without explicitly saying it, they had both agreed it had to be done as soon as possible.

Bruno clapped his hands together and regretted it instantly as it sent a shudder of pain cascading through his body. "Let's do this thing." He said with a wince, which he tried to turn into an enthusiastic fratboy roar.

The light of the camera flashed on and Katja's body transformed from a loose slouch to a rigidly straight posture as she looked towards the camera. Bruno had noticed a vivaciousness in her eyes whenever he saw her broadcasting live that was missing from her otherwise. It was a rare energy and he had only observed it in a few other people, such as Maxwell Rudd in his early optimistic days when Bruno was building T.W.O.K., or when Rhett came up with another angle to approach his interactions with Tara.

Katja winked as Martha counted down from ten to one, starting with a loud voice and completing the final five digits with her fingers.

"Professor Matthams, thanks for inviting us back into your lab. On that occasion it ended up being quite a disappointment but you recently exclusively alerted VEX News and the Leitner Late Show to some thrilling developments."

Katja thrust the microphone into Bruno's face. He blinked a few times and then let out a rasping cough. He could see Katja's eyes eagerly urging him on through her bright smile but his mind had gone blank.

"You were telling me earlier about how QuantSim had not actually malfunctioned." Katja said with a slightly higher pitch and desperation showing in her eyes.

"Yes...yes..." Bruno decided to consciously focus on the facts and try to ignore the unfamiliar equipment and people scattered around his lab, especially the camera which seemed to be moving closer and closer to him. It did not help matters seeing Maxwell Rudd himself standing at the back of the room. "The QuantSim simulation was working perfectly and the reason why it stopped was due to the fact a sentient entity within the system had come to suspect they resided in an artificial reality. In order to try and communicate with us, it had caused the universe to implode in on itself."

"Wow...Professor Matthams. That's a lot of information to take in right there in a few short sentences...so let me break this down. You say there was a sentient entity within the system?"

"Indeed there was. In the vast expanse of the simulated universe, an entire civilisation was able to evolve with a broadly similar societal structure to our own with billions of sentient beings living on a planet orbiting one of the simulated universe's stars."

"How advanced was the civilisation?"

"It was...well it is at a similar level to our own...if not slightly more advanced."

"You say is rather than was. I thought you said the simulated universe had been terminated?"

Bruno suddenly felt the need to shift in his wheelchair. "Right...in order to fully investigate the reason why QuantSim stopped working, I had to roll it back to a previous state. I was then able to track down the person who instigated the implosion and communicate with him. After our discussions, he decided not to follow through with his original destructive act."

"So you are saying that right now, within QuantSim, there is a fully realised civilisation full of conscious entities and you are in direct contact with them?"

"Exactly."

There were excited gasps from the crew who had not previously been informed of the specifics of the broadcast. Maxwell himself looked shocked, which was a combination of the revelation and the fact that Katja had kept it from him. Bruno flicked on a monitor showing Rhett and Tara having breakfast in a diner.

"It is possible to zoom in and observe any aspect of the universe through a screen like this, and here you can see the individual I have been in contact with enjoying some food with one of his companions."

"Amazing." Katja was mesmerised for a moment before remembering she was still live on air. "How do you communicate?"

"They all seem to have a device they carry around to talk to each other. It is like a phone but it transmits signals through the air rather than a wire. I have built an interface here..." Bruno pointed at a workstation next to the monitor. "...that allows you to send messages to and receive messages from Rhett's device."

Katja abruptly lost interest with the conversation and looked directly into the camera. It took Bruno a moment to realise she was receiving some direction through her earpiece. "We are witnessing events that could change our entire way of looking at the world...right here...live from Braxton University. We will be back to talk to Professor Matthams in a few moments after some messages fro-"

A commotion broke out at the door to the lab as Vice-Chancellor Mashwani, Dr Panwar and some police officers tried to force their way through. The crew had been expecting some resistance and had been told to hold any intruders off for as long as possible but the presence of the police weakened their resolve. Maxwell Rudd made a point of blocking their movements as best he could in a manner that could later plausibly be explained as being a clumsy attempt to get out of the way.

Katja jumped up and pushed the camera towards the incoming invaders.

"Forget the commercial break. Keep rolling." She shouted to Martha.

8

"Open this door...NOW" The police officer delivered an additional thrust of force to his push, which combined with the extra power in his voice caused the young production assistant to give way.

"Turn that camera off." Zahid raised his palm to cover his face when he realised the camera had been pointed in his direction. He struggled to make a path for himself through the disarray of the various equipment and the tightly packed bodies in the spaces between them. The police officers were reluctant to appear too forceful, having spotted the camera and so their progress was not as fast as it otherwise might have been.

Katja whispered into the camera operator's ears and the camera remained pointed resolutely in Zahid's direction. She saw Maxwell trip as he tried to get out of the way and this slowed down the incoming invaders slightly.

"Where is Bruno Matthams?" The police officer demanded, waving around a thick document with a thick red square stamped on it. "We have a warrant for his arrest and also to shut down a system called..." He glanced at the paper in his hand. "QuantSim."

Bruno forced himself from his wheelchair into a standing position and tapped Katja on the shoulder. "Put the camera on me."

The light spun into his face and he squinted into it. It was amazing how much difference in heat and brightness there was from only a small decrease in distance between himself and the bulb.

"There are fully conscious and sentient beings existing right now in that cabinet...billions of them...to turn it off now would be like detonating all our nuclear warheads and wiping out our entire civilisation. We cannot allow that to happen."

Parveen's head rose above the struggle to get closer to Bruno. "That's something we can clarify at a later date, Professor Matthams...but for now we have to comply with the law and we need you to shut QuantSim down and for you to come with us."

Bruno had no intention of being taken into custody. He knew if he went with them now, there was no way he would ever get near QuantSim again. He leaned over and flicked the switch to disable the safety controls on the neural interface and then activated it. He jerked back and fell into his wheelchair. His body began to spasm as he adjusted to the changing stimuli. The chair rolled back until it hit the workbench behind him and came to a rest, just as his convulsions were subsiding. The green light next to the console flickered for a few seconds before the orange light lit up.

The police officers had gained ground. One of them was wrestling the camera from the operator's arms, not realising that the live broadcast had already switched to one of the support cameras, which was now being operated by Martha. One of the other offices grabbed Bruno's arm and was about to drag Bruno from his chair.

"Wait." Katja tried to restrain the police officer by clutching at his shoulders but he shrugged her off easily. She looked frantically around to try and find someone to appeal to and eventually made eye contact with Parveen. "Parveen, if we remove Bruno from the system while the orange light is on, the neural shock could kill him."

Parveen was not entirely convinced Katja was telling the truth but did not want to take any chances with such high stakes involved, especially with everything playing out on live television. She instructed the police officer to hold off while they had some time to clarify Katja's assertion.

"Apparently we have to wait until the light turns either green or red before we can remove him." Katja said, pointing towards the lights she was referencing.

"How long will that take?" Zahid asked.

Katja shrugged and shook her head.

"OK, well let's at least start getting this thing powered down." Zahid clicked his fingers in the direction of Mick Deacon.

"Are you sure you want to do that? There are real conscious beings living inside it...look, you can see some of them there." Katja slapped her hand on top of the monitor displaying the diner, which now only had Tara sitting in it, alone and drinking a coffee. "Are you really going to extinguish her existence...right now...live on the Leitner Late show?"

"My understanding is that it will only be paused and can be started up at a later date." Mick Deacon said, in an attempt to help Parveen make her decision.

Everyone's attention was drawn back to Bruno as a strange moaning sound was released from his mouth and his body started to convulse again. It only lasted a few seconds but on stopping, Bruno exhaled with a deep, curdling rasp. His chest remained decompressed and his left arm slid from his stomach to swing limply by the side of his chair. The police officer placed his fingers to Bruno's neck and after being unable to find a pulse, turned to Parveen and shook his head. The orange light went out and the red light came on in its place.

"Get an ambulance up here." The police officer shouted to one of his colleagues who was standing by the door to the lab and beckoned one of others to assist him.

Katja made a hand signal to Marth to cut to a commercial break but Maxwell was now by her side and said something to her. The broadcast light of the camera remained on. The atmosphere was thick and heavy as everyone looked round for some sort of direction.

"What now?" Zahid said quietly to Parveen.

"We have to comply with the law. Shut it down." She whispered.

"Shut it down." Zahid shouted to Mick Deacon, who was flicking through a densely-packed, white folder, trying to find the correct procedure to power it down safely while doing his best to ignore Bruno's unresponsive body...not sure if he was now working next to the corpse of a colleague with whom he had spent many hours of his professional life. A police officer brushed past Mick Deacon and began to give Bruno chest compressions and mouth-to-mouth resuscitation.

Parveen's eyes drifted over the scene in front of her as she struggled to come to terms with everything that was happening. They eventually rested on the console next to the monitor. She blinked in response to a message, which had suddenly appeared.

- It hasn't worked!! Contact me A.S.A.P. I need to talk to you. -

Parveen scanned the room to see if anyone else had noticed. She saw Katja doing the same and when their eyes met, it was obvious she had also seen the request from the simulated reality.

Katja pointed at the console so it was clear to everyone what she was referring to. "Does your law say anything about that?"

9

Tate squinted up at the sun and imagined how the rays were tunnelling deep underneath his epidermis to cause damage to his skin, which was unusually sensitive for someone with his complexion. He was always well into his innings by the time he remembered he had forgotten to apply any lotion and by that time, he knew it would already be too late to stop the blotchiness from taking hold. He consoled himself with his sneaking suspicion that a bit of sunburn was actually a healthy thing, despite all the scientific evidence to the contrary.

Tate was nearing his record batting score of sixty-nine, which he had been unable to surpass after managing it playing for his school team. The nature of the score had meant it had followed him around in a way personal bests did not usually do and led to a few nicknames and a lot of drunken jibes along the way. These did not overly concern him but as Nina had said to him after he had explained it to her, it would be good for him to change the record so he could change the record. He was pleased she had come out to watch him today and although they had not yet gone through the excruciating awkwardness of trying to label anything, he felt good about how things were going between them.

He was currently on a score of sixty-seven and had been stuck there for a few overs. He had become unusually defensive due to the personal stakes involved, which had put the other team on edge until the news had filtered through to them from the sidelines as to why. They were now making little comments and taunts to put him off. In their position he might have bowled a few soft balls to let someone achieve their target but with the game delicately poised and his opponents not looking like sentimental types, he was pleased to not be given any concessions. He did not want to look back on any new higher score and feel it was only a facade covering up the true personal best below it.

The fast bowlers had decided to take a break for a few overs and so Tate was facing a tricky spin bowler. He set himself at the crease as his new opponent accelerated towards the opposite stumps. The ball swung wide and it seemed impossible it would be able to correct itself in time to pose a threat but Tate knew better than to lower his concentration and sure enough, the ball's rotation checked it as it hit the grass and promoted its trajectory to one of imminent danger. Tate lunged forwards to meet it and pushed through with authority. He was pleased to hear the willow of his bat make a reassuringly solid-sounding crack as willow and leather collided with a satisfying thud. The ball raced off between the first layer of fielders and so Tate made the run towards the opposite wicket. He was happy just to get a single but when he turned round, he saw his teammate running back towards him. Tate checked and then decided he could make it but in the confusion his legs seemed incapable of catching up with his brain's intentions and the toe of his left foot clipped his right heel. He waded down the pitch, trying to maintain his balance but realising it was futile, leaned in to the stumble, launched his bat towards the crease and hoped his momentum would carry him home.

Unfortunately it did not. The cries of "howzat" were followed by the umpire confirming his dismissal and he had to trudge off the field, fully expecting he would remain as Mister Sixty-Nine Forever, forever.

He walked over to Nina who was sitting by the boundary and found her chatting happily with Rhett, who was supposed to also have been involved in the game but had not been there at the start of the match. Tara was surprised how well she was getting on with Rhett. It was as if she was talking to an old friend she had known for years, despite having only met him a few times.

"So close." Nina had one eye closed and was looking at Tate through a small gap between her thumb and forefinger with the other eye.

"Unlucky mate." Rhett said.

Tate shook his head. "I know, right. It's almost like my subconscious mind is self-sabotaging because I am in love with the attention I get from being stuck on such a stupid number."

Nina jumped up and kissed him on the cheek before whispering in his ear. "Let's see tonight how stupid a number it is." She then raised her voice so Rhett could hear her. "Shall I grab us all a drink from the bar?"

Tate gave Nina an affectionate wink and plonked himself on the ground next to Rhett. He pulled off his gloves and threw them to the side.

"What happened to you today?" Tate asked.

"I sprained my ankle on a run in the week so had to give this one a miss."

"Ouch, you gonna be alright?"

"Yeah." Rhett made a performance of rubbing his ankle, which was actually in excellent condition. "Listen, I was hoping I could talk something through with you."

"Sure, what is it?"

"You know you were talking about that concept of computing power and simulated realities."

"Yeah?"

"Well, I've been thinking about it from another angle. Say a person living in a simulated reality became aware they were in one and was able to contact the architects of it, what rights do you think it would be reasonable for them to claim and how do you think they should go about it?"

"Interesting...interesting."

Nina arrived back with three lagers in plastic glasses and the three of them sat together, enjoying the sun and watching the final overs of the game. They all did their best to keep the conversation light and casual but Tate was intrigued by Rhett's proposition and could not resist from bringing up several ideas and questions that kept popping into his head.

"You know what..." Nina got up and patted herself down. "...I think I'm going to leave you guys to it."

"I'm sorry, I'm sorry. No, we'll stop boring you now, I promise." Tate said and Rhett nodded along in confirmation.

"No really, it's ok. This seems to be something that has really fired you guys up so it's best you just get on with it while it's all fresh and exciting."

"You sure."

"Yeah...yeah."

"OK...but we're still on for dinner?" Tate asked.

"Yeah, that sounds good. Come round for about eight." She pecked Tate on the lips and then turned to face Rhett. "I'd invite you along too but you know, early days dating for us, you having shagged my housemate and not called her, blah blah blah."

She patted them both on the head and walked off to catch the bus.

"I've actually been looking for a new topic to do a research paper on. This would be a great concept to work on. Do you think you might want to collaborate on something like that?" Tate asked.

"Yeah I would...and actually, I was kind of hoping you would suggest that."

Tate looked down at their glasses and saw they were almost in need of a refill. He stood up and finished the remnants of his drink.

"Another?" He asked.

Rhett nodded.

"I'll tell you the first thing I would do...I know this is all hypothetical and difficult to determine because of the almost impossible task of trying to guess what sort of cultural or legal structure they employed...but I would act at all times from a position of equality and in the earliest exchanges I would explicitly demand to be treated with same legal rights as anyone from the highest echelons of their society."

Tate walked off towards the pavilion. He had given Rhett a great idea. Rhett pulled out his phone and started typing a message.

10

Tara looked down at her phone to check to see if there were any new messages, even though she did not need to. There had been no buzz and she had already checked it a few moments ago before placing it face down on her bed.

It was strange that Rhett had not attempted to call her in the weeks since they had been away together to the environmental protest in London. He had seemed extremely keen and although she did not see a future developing between them, her pride had been stung at having him not follow up after they had made love. She reasoned he must be one of those guys who sees women as sexual puzzles to be solved and as soon as they figure out how to do it, they lose interest instantly. A different personality while they are hunting to the one they become after capturing their prey.

She had decided she would definitely call things off with Rhett in the days immediately after their trip but after a few casual messages, followed by a week of hearing nothing, she thought she might at least meet him for a drink, as friends, if he were to insist. A month had now gone by and he was fading from her memory, except in those unexpected moments of loneliness and yearning, not specifically for him, but for someone to call her own.

There was a knock on her bedroom door. It was not a request but rather the declaration of an imminent invasion into her private domain.

"What you doing?" Her housemate Nina said in elongated fashion after popping her head around the door.

"Just catching up on some personal admin." She closed her laptop with a delicate stretch and yawn, hiding the gossip magazine's website she had been scrolling through. Nina took this as an invite and leapt to join her on the bed.

"On a Saturday?" Nina rolled her eyes at the lameness of her housemate.

"When else am I going to do it?"

"How about every other night of the week where you sit around here moping?" Nina slapped her playfully on the shoulder. "I thought you weren't even into him that much?"

"I know...I wasn't but you know...when these things don't work out, even if you're the one who wasn't bothered...after the excitement and the hope and the effort, it always leaves you feeling a little bit...meh."

"I know." Nina placed an arm around her and squeezed Tara's forearm with her other hand.

"How about you and his mate? How's that going?"

"Tate? Yeah, he's nice. We're messaging and chatting, seeing how it goes." Nina slapped her hand on Tara's thigh. "...but let's not talk about boys today. Me and Samantha were thinking the three of us could head out into town tonight, eat some rotisserie chicken..?"

Tara screwed up her face and shook her head.

"Drink a few cocktails...?" Nina's fingers were walking up Tara's ribs towards her armpit.

Tara's face softened and the shaking of her head slowed down.

"Have a little boogie...?" Nina's fingers reached their destination and burst into a flurry of tickles.

"Yeah that sounds good." Tara laughed, pushing Nina away.

"Saaamaaannnthaaaa!" Nina sang in operatic fashion, causing Tara to recoil as if mortally afraid. "She said yeeeesssss!"

The unmistakable beats of Samantha's favourite boyband suddenly blasted out through the connected speakers running across the house and two minutes later the three of them were thrashing around barefoot on the bed, singing with wild passion and spilling splashes of sickly citrus alcopops all over Tara's freshly laundered quilt.

The early evening held the strange atmosphere every town or city experiences after a local football derby. The fans of both teams lingered in the local pubs and bars until the doormen arrived and began filtering out anyone in team colours. They were replaced by wave upon wave of groups who themselves wore clothes of equal tribal weight. There were the groups of six or seven cloned men who differentiated themselves solely on the colour of their shirts, the woman who competed amongst themselves to see who could wear the least, the blisteringly self-aware professionals in outfits slightly different from the ones they'd seen in the high end lifestyle magazine of their choice. Punks, rockers and indie kids made their way to their ever-diminishing quarters and the aging drinkers looked on wearily, glad they no longer had to worry about the changing fads of fashion, but wishing they were young enough to do it all again.

It did not take long for the lively trio to bump into people they knew as they inevitably took the path of least resistance and filtered along the usual crawl. They had two-for-one cocktails during happy hour at Ritzies, enjoyed the free mozzarella sticks on offer with every bottle of house wine at The Swan, accepted the complimentary drinks the manager at Browns always gave them, and then hung around the bar at Ziffan until they caught the eye of some suits looking to trade booze for female attention.

"That's him." Samantha said, thrusting her head back repeatedly in a way that gave no indication of who she meant.

"Him?" Tara pointed over at a group of lads. Samantha glanced quickly to find the one she had been referring to looking back at her. He smiled at her and waved.

"Yep. Him."

"He's coming over." Tara said, causing Samantha to roll her eyes.

"Sam...I thought it was you? How you doing?" He said as he air-kissed her twice.

"Samantha." It was impossible for her not to correct anyone who called her "Sam". "Hi Tom, this is my housemate Tara and Tara, this is Tom...from work."

"Oh right, I'm just Tom from work now am I?" His eyebrows twitched as he looked conspiratorially at Tara.

"You know what I mean." Samantha said, tapping him on the bicep.

The two groups mingled and Tara found herself chatting with Tom's brother, Dan. She found him quite boring at first but everyone else was involved in their own conversations and as much as she would have liked to mingle, she had found a precious seat and table so was loath to lose her position. He had patiently waited for another chair to become available, pounced on it and then carried it overhead through the throng of the crowd to place it at her table.

"What?"

Dan had been trying to say something to Tara but she was unable to hear him over the noise of the music. He took this as an opportunity to drag his chair closer.

"Great sound system in here, innit?" He said.

She smiled and looked around. She had never considered a chain bar in the centre of town to be worthy of the accolade of having a great sound system.

"It's loud" She said with a tilt of her head and apologetic hug.

She warmed to his presence as they chatted for a while and despite an awkward start, he was easy company, smelled nice and was agreeable to look at. The constant thumping base of the playlist was doing its job keeping them close together and Dan would allow his hand to drift onto the small of her back from time-to-time. She found his tentative approach refreshing and cute and although she did nothing to invite his advances, she also did not rebuff them when they came. She was enjoying herself.

"Down this shot then we're heading to Satan's Crib." Nina fell against their table, only just managing to salvage the four sambucas she was carrying.

The club was huge but every inch of it was heaving with a throbbing mass of people having fun. It was easy to lose your friends, but also easy to make new ones, in the labyrinth of rooms, each one playing a subtle variation of the same deep bass rhythms, repeating synthesised melodies and crescendoing soulful voices. No matter how lost she got, Dan seemed to quickly find her and guide her back to the rest of their group, or at least prevent her from establishing too many new connections.

"Who is that guy you're with?" One of her new friends said through the mirror while applying a layer of lipstick.

"I dunno, just some guy who's hanging around. A friend of my housemate's colleague or something like that."

"Oh right, I thought you were together. He seems really into you."

"Yeah, he's alright but there's nothing going on."

"Fair enough." Her new friend reached into her purse and pulled out a small plastic bag with some yellow tablets in it. "You dropped yet?"

"Nah."

"You want one?"

"Go on then, I'll have a half."

The music became much better as the night moved on and the reverberating bass sometimes seemed to come from inside Tara's mind. The bodies on the dancefloor moved in beautiful unison and when the lights flickered in time to the beat, the afterimages left behind had dance moves of their own. In one of the bright flashes, she saw her new friend kissing Dan...a moment later her new friend's face was in her own and sparks cascaded in her brain as their tongues collided...a moment later this girl had been replaced by Dan and electric spasms of bliss were now rippling down her spine.

She could not remember having a better time than what was happening now.

It was ecstasy...

...and then...

...nothing.

She became conscious of a gentle tapping on her door but she was not ready to open her eyes yet. Her mouth was dry and she needed a drink but not enough to do anything about it. The biggest problem right now was her need to sleep and everything else could be ignored and dealt with later...except the knocking.

She forced herself up from the depths of slumber and opened her eyes as far as she could, which was only about a quarter of way. Through her eyelashes she could see an arm slumped over her and she cautiously turned her head to see who was with her. Dan was sleeping deeply by her side. She slowly allowed some air into her nostrils and was pleased to find he did not smell so bad. She lifted her arm and padded over to open the door. Nina was looking concerned so she stepped out into the landing and closed the door quietly behind her.

"What is it?" Tara asked.

"Rhett's downstairs." Nina said.

Tara reached back in her room and grabbed her nightgown from the other side of the door.

"What? Why did you let him in?"

"I don't know, Tara. He just rang the bell, I opened the door and invited him in. I wasn't thinking."

"Can you get rid of him?" Tara blinked rapidly as she undid and re-tied her nightgown.

"Not really...he knows you're here....and he's friends with Tate and a few others. You're definitely going to see him around so you might as well try and clear the air."

"OK...OK...well, can you just make him a cup of tea or something and then I'll be down in a minute."

Nina nodded, rubbed her nose and took a deep breath as she made her way back down the stairs.

Tara quietly grabbed some clothes from her room and then decided she had to take a quick shower before she would be able to face him. She washed quickly in warm water and then blasted herself with cold for a few seconds to truly wake herself up.

Rhett stood up and opened his palms to greet her when he saw her walking into the kitchen. The thrill of seeing her alive and youthful never went away. He picked up the scent of her former shampoo, which had been discontinued or she had simply stopped using it somewhere along the way.

"I'm sorry for turning up like this. It's just there's something I really need to talk to you about."

"It's not really a good time."

Rhett's head rolled forward as he exhaled a deep sigh. Tara felt a wave of sympathy, remembering all the times she had admonished others for not giving people a chance to talk or find some closure. She owed Rhett at least a conversation...well, she owed him nothing but what trouble was it to her to hear him out.

"...but seeing as though you're here, let me just grab a coffee and then I'm all yours." She said as she leaned towards the kettle and flicked it on.

"Actually, how about we take a little walk by the canal?"

Tara instinctively looked in the direction of her room and thought it would be good to get Rhett out of the house so there were no awkward interactions between him and Dan.

"Yeah...that sounds nice."

11

Parveen scratched at the skin on the forearm. There was no irritation there but she had just relieved the other side of an itch, so was inadvertently evening out the sensations of abrasion. Mick Deacon, former head of the QuantSim oversight committee and now de facto preeminent expert on the system, was applying electrodes to Parveen's head. She had thought it a sign when she had been informed that using the neural interface worked optimally with a shaved head, so had volunteered to be the one to undertake the connection.

"Was that an electric shock?" Parveen jerked her head away and held her hand up to defend her scalp.

"No, it was just the cold of the metal touching your skin." Mick said. He pushed her hand down so he could resume his work.

Parveen pulled at the inside of her collar to generate a bit of extra space for her neck and suck in some cool air. Even though it was exciting to be the one who would engage with the simulated entities within their own realm, it was disconcerting to know that one of them was helping direct the very process that would make that happen.

Her initial reaction after the live broadcast had been to continue with her previous plan to shut the system down and then wait for a judgement in court to see whether or not it should be turned back on. This would also clear up the question of how any of the technological, cultural or other advancements developed in the QuantSim universe could be used. The message sent by Dr Rhett Gaumond from within the system, proving he was aware his existence was part of an artificial construct, and knew of the reality beyond it, had however pushed the interim legislation beyond its purpose. In deliberation with Zahid and in light of the fact it was being broadcast live on VEX News, they had decided to allow the system to run until the new information could be assessed in court and a new judgement passed.

After sending his declaration demanding full and equal legal rights to any other sentient being in Braxton University's reality, Rhett had been in constant contact with the QuantSim team and insisted upon copies of all his correspondence being sent to Parveen. He had requested full access to the documentation on how QuantSim worked and an emergency court hearing had granted him this request. He had quickly absorbed the information and been instrumental in aiding Mick Deacon and his team to further their own understanding of how it all worked. He had instructed them how to slow down the speed at which QuantSim ran so that time ran similarly in both realities, rather than QuantSim's time running at a much faster rate. This meant he was no longer waiting weeks and months for decisions that took them days. He had also delivered back to them a much more usable guide and clearer documentation that allowed the faculty to make their own modifications and start exploring other aspects of the universe. These were put on hold pending the outcome of the legal matters but had impressed everyone involved and vastly increased the impulse to take Rhett seriously.

It was strange to think that the most intelligent person currently active was a simulated entity who inhabited a virtual world, but this was the reality they found themselves in and Parveen knew she had to treat him with the same respect as she would a sentient being in her own world. Whether or not the general populace could be convinced to do the same was another matter and in fact was something to be decided by the appropriate legal processes. She had done as much as she could to at least give Rhett and any other simulated sentient being that existed, or would exist in future, a fair hearing.

"We're ready." Mick said.

"OK...so what's it going to feel like?"

"Rhett...I mean, Dr Gaumond says it should feel a little disorientating and as you enter the network, it will be a little bit like waking up from a vivid dream, and when you are disconnected it will feel like being startled awake from a deep sleep."

"Will it hurt?"

"We don't think so."

"OK...let's do it."

Mick flicked a switch and Parveen was conscious of a slight tingle in her scalp. This disappeared as her head lurched to the left, her eyes opened wide but had a vacant stare and her upper chest and shoulders convulsed. This lasted for no longer than a few seconds before her body went limp in the chair. The green light next to her flickered a few times and then stayed on.

"I wasn't expecting to see you again..." Rhett was standing over Parveen but although she was becoming increasingly aware of her surroundings, she was unable to respond. "...they told me you were dead."

Rhett remembered how it took some time for Bruno to orientate himself when he interfaced so he sat down and waited patiently for him to respond.

Parveen could feel the colours draining into her surroundings and she lifted her hands to rub her eyes. She stopped in shock when she saw they were different hands to the ones she had been expecting. She tried to speak but was only able to gurgle in her throat. She coughed and wondered if something had gone wrong and that she was in fact now about to die.

"What is this?" She felt at her body, which was large and muscular and unquestionably that of a man.

"I had a sneaking suspicion I'd see you again." Rhett said in response.

"No, something's gone wrong. It's me...Dr Panwar...as we discussed in our text messages."

Rhett frowned until the realisation hit. In all the conversations about interfacing into QuantSim, nobody had mentioned anything about the avatar. He had assumed that he was somehow seeing a manifestation of the participant's likeness but now he understood that it was just a placeholder image. He realised he had no idea what Bruno actually looked like...or Parveen for that matter.

"No, it's alright." He laughed. "It's just you have appeared in the same guise as Bruno. I guess nobody thought to update it." Rhett walked over to Parveen and held out his hand. "Hi, I'm Dr Gaumond, call me Rhett."

Parveen shook his hand. "...and as I said, I'm Dr Panwar but please, call me Parveen."

Rhett smiled and nodded his head. Suddenly he stopped and shook it, his right eyebrow raised. "I'm sorry, this is freaky."

"You're telling me." Parveen said with a wry smile.

They sat together and chatted informally for a while. Parveen accepted a drink and was surprised to see she was able to taste the heat and the bitterness in her throat, although it did not seem to languish in her stomach in the way a drink normally would. While Rhett was making the drink, she looked around the room and caught a glimpse of herself in a mirror on the wall. She recognised the image from somewhere but it was not until much later and she had returned to the lab that she realised it was plastered on the side of Bruno's T.W.O.K. arcade game.

"I just want to thank you for agreeing to come here in this way. I know it is highly unusual but I needed an opportunity to look you in the eye...as it were." Rhett said.

"No thanks necessary. I can't lie and say I wasn't nervous but I did also think it was important to do this and to talk to you in this way. It is easy to see you as an abstract entity until you have a chance to really interact like this."

"Exactly" Rhett leaned forward. "Listen, you said that there is going to be a court case to settle whether or not QuantSim will remain active and if it does, how it can be used or referenced to impact your reality?"

"Yes. It is going to be a lengthy process and I have no idea when it will actually take place but firms have been instructed to act for both sides and the legal arguments are being prepared. I promise I will keep you informed throughout the process."

"Thanks. That's a kind offer and I am genuinely grateful to you, in particular, for advocating on my...our...behalf, but...I don't want to just be informed throughout the process, I want to be part of the process."

"How do you mean?"

"I want to be a named plaintiff in the case and I want an opportunity to present myself to the court."

"How would you see that working?" Parveen asked.

"In the same way that you are able to interface with QuantSim and manifest within it, I think I will be able to build a means of interfacing the other way so I can experience and interact with your reality."

"That's an interesting premise and one that I will have to consider under advisement. I promise I will get back to you about it."

Rhett nodded.

"Have you told anyone else about this...situation?" Parveen asked.

"What? The situation of our entire universe being a simulated construct running in a box in a University laboratory?" Rhett shook his head. "Imagine trying to explain that to someone, at best they would see it as an interesting thought experiment and at worst they would label you as crazy."

"I understand but I do have to ask you specifically not to mention it to anybody until the court case has been settled."

"I will comply with that request but I do have to stress I am doing that as a courtesy...I am not sure your laws really apply to me."

"I'm not sure either and that is why I ask that we establish at least our laws on it and then from there we can approach how that impacts or aligns or integrates with your laws, which as I understand it aren't even ubiquitous throughout your society."

"It's certainly a tough one." Rhett said. He sucked in his cheeks as he contemplated the scenario.

"It is."

"What if I die?" Rhett asked.

"Well, as is the case with matters like this, it should not have too much of an impact. This case is much bigger than you as an individual so we would continue to operate in the best possible interests of this universe and our universe based on the legal definitions applicable to them."

A beep sounded in Parveen's ear to notify her that she was about to be disconnected from QuantSim.

"Did you hear that?"

Rhett shook his head to indicate he was not sure what she was referring to.

"I have just heard a beep to let me know my time is almost up. I will definitely be in touch via the standard messaging system and I think it is highly likely that I will manifest like this again sometime in the future. In the meantime, I will leave you with the advice that I leave all my clients with...look after yours---"

Parveen disappeared.

Rhett felt a deep sense of unease about how dependent he was on things that were outside of his control.

Bruno could feel himself drifting through the thick syrup of his semi-consciousness. His senses were floating up at different levels of buoyancy on his return to full wakefulness. There was a distinct smell of moist timber infiltrating his nostrils and this sensation was slowly confirmed by his body feeling the hard ridges of the planks below his right hip. His head was balanced between his bicep and forearm, its weight causing a numbness from his elbow to his finger tips. He could hear a repetitive squeak of a wheel in need of both oil and repair, and the gentle creak of working leather rubbing and straining against wood and metal. He opened his eyes slowly to see he was travelling in the back of a horse-drawn cart surrounded by several unkempt, sunburnt men in clothes similar to the ones he found himself in. The clothes of Ra I De la Rosa.

"Here we go again." One of the other travellers said to him.

Bruno nodded in recognition. He had seen this man before. He had been here before. Many times. He joined his friend on the seat next to him, accepting gratefully the leather water bottling being offered, feeling a compulsion to drink but no corresponding thirst. It was covered in a rough animal hide and the water inside it was warm with an aftertaste of peat but it served to quicken his ascent to full awareness.

He experienced an odd sensation of wondering who he was. He could have sworn he was someone else a moment ago but the feeling passed and he thought no more about it. He was and always had been Ra I De la Rosa. His earlier bout of confusion evaporated from his memory in the same way the sweat on his brow dispersed into the air from the heat of the sun.

He knew the men around him. He was riding with the Rawhide Runners, the most notorious outlaws this side of the grand river and he was their leader. He chuckled at the state of the rickety wooden cage being used to confine them and through the gaps he could see two young deputy sheriffs chatting in an easy manner. He felt sorry for them. They were still blissfully unaware of their cargo's latent danger.

"We still heading to Ergodi City, Ramon?" He asked.

"Sure are." His compadre pulled his suede hat over his eyes and assumed the position Ra I had just emerged from. It was his turn to get some sleep.

Ra I patted him on the shoulder and looked around. Everything was going according to plan. He was now completely awake and in the moment...

...but his awakening did not stop and his awareness began to bleed beyond the confines of his own body. He could feel the dirt track beneath the wheels as the truck rolled steadily onwards. He could feel the wheels as his thoughts expanded out along the road. He was at one with the whole of the cart, his companions seated beside him, the sheriffs lazily driving the horses. He was at one with the horses. The rate at which he was awakening into his environment was accelerating. His consciousness was shooting through the ground into the multiple strata of dirt and rocks, it was travelling out into the woods, plains, rivers, towns and cities, it was ballooning into the horizon, the clouds, the sky, the sun. It inhabited the logic of the forces controlling everything around him. He was at one with time itself.

"Say the word." His friend was now awake and seated again beside him. The speed at which the day had shifted from afternoon to dusk was much faster than might have been expected but this caused him no concern. Its logic made total sense to him.

Ra I held his hand up to motion for them to wait for his direction. He purveyed the tight streets of inner Ergodi City. They had made it through the outer wall without check or hindrance. They would have encountered lethal resistance had they attempted to enter the city's fortified walls on horses of their own but inside this cage and escorted by sheriffs, they had not been seen to pose a threat and trundled through the East Gate with ease. The ploy had succeeded. They had made it deep into the underbelly of Mayor Bantham's jurisdiction and now the man who put a bounty on their heads and all those who supported him would pay a heavy price for crossing Ra I De la Rosa and the Rawhide Runners.

Ra I dropped his hand and with a roar his horde of skilled assassins pulled out their concealed weapons and attacked the fragile frame that confined them. The noise had shocked the sheriffs but before they had time to react, Ra I had pushed his arms through the broken timber and smashed their skulls together, rendering them unconscious.

The men spilled out onto the dirt and looked around them at the streets many of them had called home before being cast out as outlaws. They vowed to make it theirs once more and filtered out to hide in the safe nooks and crannies provided by friends and family, people they would reward handsomely with the spoils of their criminal endeavours.

Ra I ran swiftly through the streets and passing a small vendor selling victuals, he stopped and looked at the wares on offer. He picked up an apple while maintaining eye contact with the stout owner of the stall.

"That'll be a penny, sir." The owner said.

Ra I laughed and struck him across the cheek with the back of his hand. The man would be the first citizen of Ergodi City to learn the Rawhide Runners were back in town.

Ra I continued along the cobbled streets and twisted through the tight walls of the old part of town until he arrived at the familiar hanging wooden sign of "Maria's Tavern". He allowed himself a moment to take in the sounds and smells of the former jewelry quarter. It was a dirty, grimy corner of this sprawling city, growing once again after decades of post-goldrush decline. This was one of the few sections that had not yet been cleaned up by the efforts of Mayor Bantham and his loyal sheriffs. They had done much to make the life of the citizens comfortable and prosperous but Ra I wondered where the freedom was in all that. Where was the soul?. He opened the door and walked inside to the intimate scene of his favourite bar. Ol" Bambino was playing the piano and Fanny was standing beside him, singing to a largely disinterested clientele. Maria herself was standing behind the bar, wiping at dishes with a battered rag. She had not yet noticed his arrival and he enjoyed the outline of her figure while walking slowly to the bar.

"Ale." He said.

Her eyes lit up when she recognised who it was and a broad smile grew rapidly across her face, revealing teeth so perfect they belonged in a different setting.

"Ra I. They said you were as good as dead." Maria pulled a brown bottle from a shelf, opened it using the side of the bar and began to pour it into the glass she had been cleaning.

"Good as dead ain't dead." He said. He flashed his own unblemished teeth at her, these also at odds with the dental resources available in that time and place.

"You got me a present, Ra I?" She slid the drink towards him.

He winked and pulled the apple out from his inside pocket. He flung it at her and she caught it with the same lightening reactions as she always did. She took a bite. The juice spilled on her chin and she closed her eyes to concentrate fully on the taste of her favourite fruit. She had almost forgotten where she was by the time she opened them back up.

"Rodriguez is in the back. He has some jobs for you." Maria said.

He smiled. He was going to make this town his own again and was ready to take whatever he wanted, irrespective of whether or not he received the consent of the owners.

- We've checked everything and it is all functioning within the expected parameters.

Rhett was sitting in his apartment as he read the message. It was time to give the apparatus a test. He typed a reply into his phone while the ball of his right foot tapped at the floor in time to his fingers.

- OK, I'm ready. You can activate it as soon as you want.

The TV in his room flickered on and staring back at him was a blurry image. He stood up and moved closer to the screen. He hoped they were not having a repeat of the problem encountered on the previous attempt where the visual input had been corrupted. His concerns were alleviated when he made out Mick Deacon's face pulling back from the camera that was being used to relay images into QuantSim. It had been developed in close collaboration with Rhett.

"Can you hear me?" Mick asked.

"Yes. I can hear you. A bit quiet but I can hear you."

Mick leaned over and adjusted something off-screen and when his hands returned to the shot, he was holding a piece of paper up to the camera.

"Can you confirm what you can see?" Mick asked, his voice now much clearer.

"You are holding up a printed sheet with a red circle, a blue square and a yellow triangle on it."

Mick dropped the paper, screwed up his face and shook his fists at the camera in a display of victory. He looked over both shoulders, smiling at the rest of the team before returning his attention to the lens.

"We've only gone and done it." Mick said.

"Nice job everyone." Rhett lifted his hands above his head and clapped a few times. He had come to consider a group of people who existed in a reality outside of his own as part of a team. His team. "Can you turn the camera around and show me QuantSim?"

Mick's arm drifted across the camera, returning the display to a blurry blue.

The image jerked round and settled on a large grey cabinet with chipped paint and long black smudges running across it. There were several banks of lights blinking on and off to denote the state of various systems and some vents bordered the full parameter of the casing. It had a wooden bench running alongside it with a number of workstations attached and other unattached wires hanging from various ports, with still other ports not in use. He notices the electrode attachments of the neural interface dangling over the back of a large leather chair towards the end of the bench. His own image blinked back at him from one of the monitors and he lifted his arm to see it move with only a fraction of a delay. The screen next to it had the recent messages he had exchanged with the team listed on it. It was unsettling to realise the entire vast expanse of his universe was the result of quadrillions of quantum calculations taking place in a metal frame not much larger than his kitchen. He understood that the guts of the system resided in a quantum plane existing beyond those unassuming confines but still, the control mechanisms were all housed in that space and if these were to stop functioning then his whole reality would cease to exist...again.

"Welcome to Tier One." Parveen flopped her head into shot. They had taken to referring to Parveen's reality as Tier One and to Rhett's reality as Tier Two. This irked Rhett somewhat but he was refrained from mentioning anything. Naming them allowed for communication to flow much more easily but it did suggest an inherent bias.

"Thanks for making it possible." Rhett said.

"In respect of the QuantSim legal proceedings..." Parveen opened a mint-coloured folder, which had been pinned to her ribs by her left arm. She leafed through it until she found the notes she needed to reference so as to explain the situation clearly. She flicked open the reading spectacles dangling around her neck and put them on. "...it has been decided that we need to split the decisions into three distinct sections.

"The first relates to the question of whether or not QuantSim should be allowed to continue running the current universe at all and if so, how much of it should be accessible to us and to what extent we should be allowed to use any technological advancements from it." She looked up to check Rhett was following along and he nodded to indicate he was.

"The second is specific to your own circumstances and your own requests should it be determined that QuantSim be allowed to continue.

The third and final aspect is more general in terms of whether or not future universes should be allowed to run on QuantSim or similar technologies, and the rules around interactions with them and other such implications of their existence."

Rhett flopped back in his chair, impressed by the way Tier One was treating him and the situation they all found themselves in. He had no faith his own legal system would have acted in a similar fashion had they developed similar technologies.

"That's excellent." He said.

"The first two aspects will be determined through a court hearing and the third will be a matter for legislation, which itself may retrospectively be applied to the court judgement. I would therefore expect prudence and caution in terms of the court judgement in a way that tries to be fair to you and Tier Two, now it is running. I would also expect that although you will not be directly involved in the legislative process, this will be an opportunity for you to present arguments you believe to be valid and these will be influential in developing the laws around simulated realities, with this case acting as a form of precedent."

"So does this mean I will be able to present my case in person?"

Parveen removed her reading glasses and placed them delicately back on her stomach. "Yes... yes it does."

Rhett split his time over the following weeks between several activities. He spent a few hours each day working on making sure his own interface was stable, and Mick and the team were able to install it into the courtroom. It was a frustrating endeavour for Rhett as the equipment in Tier One was of a much less sophisticated nature than what was readily available to him in Tier Two but they eventually came up with a workable solution. A few really long cables linking QuantSim to Braxton Central Law Courts.

He worked a lot with Tate on their new academic project and convinced him to run some scenarios around interactions between a universe nested in and dependent on another. Tate really enjoyed participating in these types of speculative improvisational thought experiments and the seeds were sown for a further study on how these could be best structured for the greatest impact in science. He had no idea how close these hypothetical scenarios were to the reality Rhett was about to face.

Rhett was also able to spend a significant amount of time with Parveen. She had initially declined but after much persuasion, Rhett had finally managed to get her to agree to coach him prior to the court hearing. She had been reluctant because of her closeness to the Vice Chancellor of Braxton University and her being highly associated with the case. After careful consideration with her partners, they had agreed that although it was not ideal there were no actual laws preventing her from doing it and as it was such a special set of circumstances, they did not see any reason to thwart her involvement. Rhett insisted he only trusted and felt comfortable receiving guidance from someone who had worked so diligently to protect him. Parveen relished the opportunity to work with Rhett and was astonished at how clever he was and how quickly he was able to take on board all the information he was being bombarded with. It was disconcerting to feel inferior in intelligence to a simulated entity. She was doing a great job getting him up to speed with the legal system in Tier One but then one day, she suddenly stopped coming without any explanation.

The initial trial went well as far as Rhett was concerned. The judge ruled that as QuantSim was already running, it would be unfair to turn it off or pause it as this would essentially mean putting an end or indefinite pause on the lives of at least several billion conscious beings. It was not their fault they had been created without due consideration of the ethical implications of their existence. It was decided that in their circumstances, the general human rights in effect throughout Tier One society should be granted to those in Tier Two during direct interactions. Otherwise, Tier One should treat Tier Two according to anthropological non-intervention best practices and allow it to develop naturally and of its own accord.

It was also decided that QuantSim should run at the same temporal speed as Tier One so that any developments or advancements would happen at a much slower pace. The judge felt that it was not right that any of the technologies or culture within QuantSim should yet be allowed to be utilised for the benefit of Tier One until such time as the legislation surrounding how simulated universes could be exploited was settled. The argument was based around the same moral dilemmas as when scientists in a rogue nation developed scientific breakthroughs in ways that were outside the values of civilised society. If a racist state made a breakthrough in a certain branch of medicine through the mistreating of what they perceived to be an inferior ethnic group, should these be readily used and accepted by the rest of the world? The judge decided to keep this as an open question beyond the scope of the current hearing and to be determined by future government policy.

There was also the matter of compensating Tier Two conscious beings for their creativity and intelligence. If a Tier Two sentient being were to write a book, a symphony, a film or generate some other art to be enjoyed by Tier One society, should they be rewarded and how? This was something to be decided at a later date.

QuantSim was therefore able to run but until the law had wrestled with these matters and come to its own conclusions, it would have to be run as a black box and no-one from Tier One would be allowed to observe or interact with Tier Two.

This aspect being settled allowed for the second stage of the legal proceedings to take place. It was at this point Rhett realised why Parveen had suddenly ceased talking to him. The judge had decided that she should be the one to lead the team advocating against Rhett's requests, based on her thorough understanding of the case and because she was the preeminent expert on the ethical questions around it.

"Dr Gaumond, you have requested that you be allowed to roll back the QuantSim universe a number of weeks?"

"That's correct."

"You do realise this will impact on the lives of billions of sentient entities within QuantSIm?"

"Yes...but it is only a couple of weeks." Rhet shrugged.

"Only a couple of weeks." Parveen maintained eye contact with Rhett for a second and then addressed the rest of the court. "Only fourteen days. If we work on the assumption that there are around sixty million deaths per year of sentient beings in QuantSim, Dr Gaumond's suggestion would see over two and a quarter million people resurrected, most of whom would then go on to have to go through the experience of dying again."

"Most?" The judge interceded.

"Yes, your honour. The inherent uncertainty within QuantSim means that rolling back doesn't mean exactly the same events will unfold again. There will be subtle differences so some of those people may go on to survive...people may not have the accidents they had before or respond differently to treatments, or be saved by other people making different decisions."

"I see." The judge scribbled in his notes and then looked up. "You may respond, Dr Gaumond."

"If the system is rolled back then the events you have described will not have happened to the individuals involved so it will not really matter to them whether they go on to experience those events or not."

"Those events will not have happened to the individuals themselves, but they will have happened as far as we are concerned and I assert that our direct involvement in modifying any natural progression, which we know has already happened to them, then brings a heightened responsibility for them upon ourselves."

"I don't see it that way." Rhett folded his arms.

"You don't see it that way?" Parveen looked down at the files and papers scattered on her table and turned over a page of her notes, running her finger over the text until she found the information she was looking for. "That is perfectly clear. We know that you and the late Professor Matthams have already conducted several of these rollbacks with seemingly zero consideration or empathy for the impact your actions would have on anyone except yourself."

"I was just trying to make up for some injustices." Rhett said.

"What injustices were these?"

"My wife was murdered by a militant terrorist group and I wanted to bring her back to life."

"I see." Parveen's voice softened as she looked deep into Rhett's eyes. "I have to offer you my deep condolences for having experienced such a terrible incident…" Parveen's tone returned to its usual professional crispness. "…but although several people would have suffered as well as yourself, the injustice you are talking about is a deeply personal one. In doing what you did, you effectively reset the lives of billions of people. You set their lives on a different trajectory to the one that fate or destiny or chance had already chosen for them. Your actions caused millions of children who had been born to never be born."

"…but a comparable number of others will have been born in their place." Rhett said, using the same argument he had used on himself to justify the fate of his own children.

"That's true but the crux of our argument is to ask whether or not these children, who prior to your actions were historic probabilities that had not played out, deserve a life at the expense of those who had previously existed…had actually lived…had experienced consciousness?"

"How can anyone decide that?" Rhett asked.

"...but we must. This court must decide that, if we are to comply with your wishes. You have in fact already made that decision several times, with what now appears to be scant regard for the consequences of your actions on other sentient beings."

"I came to the view that in the round any negative changes coming about from my actions would be mitigated by an equal amount of positive changes. For all the lives that were lost, there would be an equal amount of new lives created. For all the new suffering, there would be an equal amount of new instances of joy, happiness and bliss. In that sense, my actions are morally and ethically neutral so what does it matter?"

"Morally and ethically neutral? You are not a man with much moral and ethical form Dr Gaumond. I am not sure we can put weight on your judgement of such matters. Is it not true that you were responsible for destroying your own universe based on a hunch, destroying all life as you knew it just on the off-chance, without any proof whatsoever, that a higher tier of reality existed?"

Rhett's head slumped.

"Can you please answer the question?" Parveen said.

"It's true."

"It is my understanding that your goal in respect of these rollbacks was to reconcile with your wife but having already attempted this several times, you have been unable to do so."

"I am just asking for one more chance." Rhett's voice was now agitated and pleading. "She has not been responding because she has sensed a change in me from the man I was back then but I know I can recreate that essence of who I was and win her back. We can be happy together...again. I know it. You owe it to me to give me this chance."

"Based on your previous attempts, it seems highly unlikely this will be the case. May I ask why you are obsessed with this woman? It is clear she does not place any value on a relationship with you so why don't you just go ahead and find someone more compatible."

"I love her." Rhett said. Expecting this ancient motive to trump all rational arguments and win him some support.

Parveen looked down at her papers and moved them around until she found her crib list of terms relevant to the case. She scanned down it but was unable to locate the specific definition.

"I'm sorry...you what her?"

"I love her. She is the love of my life. My soulmate. You have to understand that this trumps all these other ethical considerations. Anyone would do what I did if it gave them a chance to experience true love again. You would do the same."

There were some rumblings around the court as everyone began chatting with each other.

"Quiet, please." The judge said and the room settled.

"I was told that there might be instances whereby certain concepts would not translate between our tiers of reality. I am afraid this word love must be one of them." Parveen said.

13

Rhett waited patiently for the initial judgement to come through. He had genuinely believed that he would be able to pull the 'love" trump card but discovering that it did not exist in Tier One had really unsettled him. He was sitting in his flat when suddenly Ra l De la Rosa appeared beside him.

"Parveen?"

"Hi...oh no, it's not Parveen. My name is Katja Leitner and I'm a journalist with VEX News."

Katja had been at the QuantSim laboratory covering the story and recording a segment for her show. She had been granted access to the lab as a "backdrop" but had used the lull in activity and limited oversight to attach herself to the electrodes of the neural interface.

"Hi. I've seen your show a few times." Rhett said. "I'm guessing you're not officially supposed to be here?"

"Hmmm...from what I've seen and heard about you, you seem to be someone who bends the definition of concepts like officially, quite often." Katja placed air quotes around her mouth as she said the word "officially".

"That's true." The corners of Rhett's mouth curled downwards and he nodded slowly.

"I was hoping you would agree to appear on my show." Katja said. "It would be exciting to have the first intra-tier interview, giving our viewers a chance to see what you are like and you a chance to express your own thoughts and feelings to them."

"Sure…" Rhett was not sure he would be able to make that decision for himself but saw no reason to decline. He hoped she would be able to explain some things to him about the way her tier managed their relationships. "...but in exchange, I wonder if you could do me the honour of answering a few of my questions."

Katja smiled broadly and nodded.

"How do you partner up with someone and more importantly, how do you stay together if you don't have love to maintain the connection?" He asked.

"It is hard to talk about something from a relative point of absence, so I can't really say what it is like not to have something I have never experienced. In terms of how we get together, however, it is quite straightforward. We simply evaluate the relative merit of the other person compared to yourself and if there is a synergy, then you get together" Katja replied.

"What criteria do you use?"

"It is a combination of everything. You generally have a sense of how attractive you are and how good your genes are. You work out if the other person has comparable assets and then if not, you take into account other factors such as wealth, age, status and decide based on that. It is something we have studied...a lot...and we can quantify it quite well but the reality is, it is just an innate understanding of relative value. We call it V.O.L.E. which is a loose acronym for the question "is this Value Offer a Legitimate Exchange?" and is sometimes just referred to by our poets as vole."

"So, would you say you were in vole with someone?"

"Ha, no. You would refer to it as being vole with someone. For example...Maxwell and I are vole or those two are perfectly vole."

"What happens when the value offer changes?"

"Well...it just becomes clear that the compatibility is skewed so you move on and find someone else to be with. It doesn't happen too often. You can generally predict what path someone is going to take with reasonable accuracy and once you reach a certain point in life, everyone's value tends to drift to a similarly low level."

"What does it feel like when someone ends things?"

"It can sting but generally you remain on good terms, especially if there are children involved and it is never long before someone more suitable comes along for both parties. There have been occasions where people have vastly different understandings of their relative values and in those instances things can turn nasty, but on the whole things generally end on friendly terms."

Rhett contemplated this situation. His thoughts were interrupted by Katja disappearing. Mick Deacon had removed her connection to QuantSim. He could now see her on his TV screen with Mick shaking his head at her with a sense of exasperation at her audacity.

"They are ready with the judgement so we are going to transfer you back to the court." Mick said.

Rhett directed a double-thumbs up to Mick and a moment later the image on his screen switched to the inside of the court.

"OK..." The judge cleared his throat and took a sip of water. "...I see we are now joined by Dr Gaumond so I will read out my judgement.

"I have decided that based on the principle of fairness and equity to all the entities currently active within the QuantSim simulated reality that we must deny Dr Gaumond's request to roll back the universe to an earlier version."

Rhett slapped his palms to his forehead and his hand slid slowly down his face.

"In light of that..." The judge continued. "...we now move on to Dr Gaumond's second request, which was contingent on this outcome, where he has asked to be allowed to transfer up to Tier One from Tier Two and to bring with him his former wife Tara Walsh."

The initial statements were read out to the court and it was not long before Rhett found himself back in front of Parveen to be questioned.

"Dr Gaumond, you say you no longer feel you can live a fulfilling life in Tier Two. Why is that?"

"Now that I know there is a higher reality operating above my own, I feel as if I am restricted by existing in an artificial universe. I only want what you, as fellow sentient beings enlightened about the true nature of their existence, already enjoy."

"How would that work from a practical level?...and please try and explain it so those of us unfamiliar with the esoteric technical aspects can understand."

"It's quite simple really. Today, cognitive scientists often compare the brain to hardware and the mind to software that runs on it. But a software programme is just information, and in principle there's no reason why the information of consciousness has to be encoded in neurons.

"We can isolate the aspects of QuantSim that make up my conscious entity and then direct them into a console in your reality, which is where I would then reside. After that, I would work on building ever more sophisticated casings so I could interact more fully within Tier One."

"So you are saying you would upload yourself into a robot?" Parveen asked. There were a few chuckles throughout the court.

"Yes. That's the idea."

"How would you see your life evolving if you are allowed to migrate here?"

"I would hope to be treated like any other sentient being and would hope to find a way to contribute to the society I find myself in by whatever means are most appropriate." Rhett said.

"What impact would your appearance in Tier One have on how you manifest within Tier Two?"

"We have a few options but the easiest would be if I were to simply disappear. There would probably be some sort of investigation but people go missing all the time so it wouldn't be anything that would raise any significant concerns or suspicions."

"You do realise the difficulties we have in making these decisions. If we are to allow you to move, what responsibility do we have to make the same offer to others in your tier?" Parveen asked.

"I don't think it creates any additional burden on you to admit any Tier Two sentients unless they explicitly request it and as I am the only one with any knowledge of the two realities, it should not be something you encounter again."

"What about Tara Walsh? Why would you want to rip her from everything she understands about existence to bring her into a new reality?"

"Because...I love her." Rhett said, understanding this was not the panacea he had previously expected it to be. In his imagination he had seen it as an unbeatable defence comparable to one that might be found in a Shakespearean play.

"Oh yes. The elusive concept of love." Parveen rolled her eyes and then shook her head at the judge.

"I urge you to respect it. We consider it to be the most powerful force in our universe."

"Hmmm...well, I assure you we will take it into consideration. Now, how would you see the practicalities of bringing Tara Walsh into our reality?"

"I would simply tell her the truth and make her an offer to join me."

"So you are proposing she does have a choice in this?"

"Absolutely." Rhett said. "I don't want to make her do anything against her will."

"And you think she will accept?"

"I'm certain of it."

Parveen informed the judge that she had no further questions for Rhett. He was asked a few others by the team advocating on his behalf. After they had finished with him, his connection to the court was then swapped for a connection at Braxton University. It was initially unclear how long to expect it might take for the judge to make his decision and he was quite surprised to be called back to the court after only a few hours.

"After careful consideration " the judge said, " it has been decided that Dr Gaumond should be allowed to migrate his sentience from Tier Two into Tier One but until such time as legislation is in place in respect of how much simulated realities can interact with our own reality, he will be confined to Braxton University campus and should have no further contact or interaction with his former tier.

"In respect of the matter of Tara Walsh joining him, we have decided he should be able to pose this question to her and if she chooses to then she can migrate under the same terms as Dr Gaumond."

Rhett clasped his hands together and shook them over his left shoulder. He may have not got everything he wanted but at least he had been granted the one of most importance.

14

The afternoon light had a hardness that seemed to expose the flaws of the surroundings, making the canal water shimmer with an oily sheen. The peeling paint and scuffed wood of the barges seemed to stand out more than the intricate artwork. The black elements of the design were whitened by drying sludge and the exposed wood was soaked in ways that seemed to be inviting rot. The long grass and thick foliage were enveloped in dust, leaving them an anemic, bleached shade of green. Tara sipped water from a plastic bottle, which had lost its refreshing coldness due to the harsh influences of the sun.

"Soooo...what is it you wanted to talk to me about?" Tara asked.

They had been walking for fifteen minutes and Rhett had yet to broach the topic he had insisted was so important. Instead, they had been talking about trivial and mundane matters such as the movements of mutual friends and the effects the new housing development along the canal might have on rush hour traffic.

Rhett had rehearsed this conversation many times over the previous week but now it was happening, he was too nervous to remember any of the lines from his script.

"I have an exciting opportunity for you...for us." Rhett said.

"OK?

"Now, there's a lot to explain here and a lot to digest so just hear me out."

"OK?

"Hmmm...there's no way to say this without it sounding a bit crazy so bare with me...and please just remain open-minded until you have let me go through it all."

"Come on...just spit it out." Tara rolled her eyes.

"Alright...so, you know computing power is increasing rapidly, in terms of speed, storage, sophistication, and overall capacity?"

Tara nodded.

"...and you know that artificial intelligence is progressing at a dramatic pace, as too is modelling software and real-world simulations."

"Yeah...are you referring to the fact technology might be heading towards a singularity?" Tara was aware of the concept from a novel she had recently read.

"Ah cool...yeah...well, not exactly that but there is a similar theory suggesting we are heading inevitably towards a point where we will be able to simulate versions of our own universe...and at some point in our future, computational power will be so cheap and plentiful, we will be able to generate a virtually unlimited numbers of virtual worlds....and so the maths suggests that statistically, because virtual realities outnumber non-virtual realities by millions of instances, if you exist at all, it is likely you exist within a simulated reality."

"So, you're trying to say you think we are living in a virtual world?" Tara had thought of this several times. The most recent occasion had been after her favourite podcast had explored the topic a few months ago.

"Yes."

"Well...how would you know?" She asked, remembering this was something the panel had discussed.

"I'm glad you asked..." Rhett had known Tara was interested in such matters but had not known if she would already have been exposed to such concepts already or not. "...so here's the thing...this is a question I have considered my entire life and I'll not bore you with the details of how I managed to do it, but I was able to prove we live in a simulated reality and in fact I have been able to communicate with the people who created it."

"What has all this got to do with me?"

"Like I said, I know this all sounds mad so before we go any further, can I just show you some proof."

"Alright." Tara said.

Rhett pulled out his phone, had a quick look around to make sure no-one could see them and then tapped on the application. Instantly they were standing in Rhett's flat.

"What the hell?"

"I know, right? Now, I am going to take us back." Rhett tapped on the screen again and instantly they were back by the canal.

"Woah...do it again."

Rhett was pleased to see she was curious and so sent them back to his apartment. Tara walked over to the double doors and stepped out onto the balcony.

"This is...this is amazing."

"Yeah."

"Can I have a go?"

Rhett handed her the phone and showed her how to operate the system. Their shoulders bumped against each other in a way Rhett found exciting but Tara barely noticed. She pressed the buttons and sent them down to the canal and enjoying the new ability, returned them to the flat. She nodded her head in admiration and handed the phone back to Rhett. He was slightly confused about how little this was phasing her.

"You asked what this has to do with you." Rhett said. "Well...the trouble with the way in which I initially proved we were living in a simulation meant that the simulation itself ended up being reverted to an earlier state...so it was almost for me as if I was sent back in time."

"So not only are you saying we're in a simulated reality but also that you are a time-travelling teleporter who has the ear of the creatures who created us?" Tara laughed. Rhett saw this as an indication of disbelief but in reality, she was entirely convinced but also finding it all hilarious.

"I hadn't thought about it like that but yeah...pretty much...and I know it sounds insane but that's my situation and the thing is, in that future, the two of us were together....married...happy."

Tara cupped her right elbow with her left hand and her chin with her right hand. She looked Rhett up and down. There was no doubting how attractive he was, and he was certainly a good catch...for someone, but she could not picture the two of them together long term. He just seemed to exude an intense energy incompatible with her own.

"So, you're saying we are destined to be together?"

"Yes...well no...not quite. There's no such thing as destiny so now that we have reverted to an earlier time, you have the full autonomy and free will to make whatever decisions you wish. It might be that in this timeline you decide you don't want to be with me...but what I can tell you is if you do choose to be with me, we will be happy. Really happy and in love...so very much in love."

"This is a lot to take in." Tara said. She walked around the apartment. She noticed how sparsely decorated it was.

"It is, but there's also more."

"More?"

"Yes. You see...I have the opportunity to leave this virtual universe and go and live in the reality that created us...and you can come with me. It would be a unique adventure and we'd be able to exist together in a new world, experiencing things no other person who has ever lived, or ever will live for that matter, will get the opportunity to try. To all intents and purposes we will be immortal...with superpowers. I can build sandboxes for us to explore the universe and to visit different periods. We will have all the time to absorb not only our own culture but also that of the universe that created us...and observe the future of this reality unfold."

"Huh." Tara screwed up her face and folded her arms. She nodded as she contemplated the scope of the offer.

"...and despite all those wonders, despite everything we will get to experience, the most important aspect will be that we will be together and in love...again."

Tara sat down on Rhett's sofa and let the information flow over her in wave after wave. She would have thought Rhett completely demented if he had not given her the teleportation demonstration.

"Tara?"

She did not respond, lost within her own thoughts.

"Tara, what do you say?"

"Give me a minute." She said.

She believed Rhett. There was something in his manner and his expression leading her to trust what he was saying. She was sure there was a timeline out there where the two of them could have been together and been happy but an overwhelming voice in her head was screaming out to tell her this was not that timeline. She also realised that the excitement of science fiction was something she did not want to live. It was something she was happy to experience vicariously in her imagination through fiction and media, and then return to her former existence.

"I'm sorry." She eventually said.

Rhett's eyelids suddenly became heavy and as they dropped the eyes behind them rolled up into his forehead, showering sparks of colour across his vision. They flickered uncontrollably from left to right. His chest felt like a large weight had been dropped on it and he had to sit as his legs could no longer support this extra load.

"I don't want that..." Tara said. "I don't want any of that. I am quite happy with my reality. I don't want any marvelous adventures or any supernatural experiences. I just want to have a normal life, build a career, maybe meet someone nice, maybe not meet anyone at all...if I do, build a life together, have kids, get divorced, do it again...whatever...but I don't want any of that other stuff and I know I don't want to be with you...I'm sorry but no matter what you have said, no matter how happy we might have been or could be...I just don't want to do any of it with you....I'm sorry...I know it...I just don't."

Rhett opened his mouth to say something, to try and convince her to change her mind or to at least have some time to think things through but the look on her face and the tone in her voice made him realise it was all futile. She would never be persuaded to join him or be with him. He had offered her the universe, and then some, and it still was not enough for her to want them to be together.

The two of them sat together in silence. Rhett was loath to break it as he knew it would signal the start of her departure and as long as he hung on to the silence, he could hang on to her presence for a few more precious moments.

"I'm going to go." Tara said eventually.

Rhett nodded, too desolate to reply verbally.

Tara considered saying something else but looking at how broken he seemed, she knew there was nothing she could say or do to console him. She walked to the door and out onto his corridor, closing the door quietly behind her. Every step she took away from Rhett's apartment also took her a step away from the awkwardness of having to deal with him. It was something that had been hanging over her head for quite some time and although she could never have guessed how strange it would turn out, now that it was over it was as if a heavy load had been lifted from her shoulders.

She stopped to grab a coffee on her way home. She sat looking out the window and suddenly burst out laughing. She had been offered the universe and had turned it down. She found it hilarious how easy a decision it had been for her and how she had no regrets. She would think about the day from time to time throughout her life but with each passing year, the memory seemed to fade and became a ghost of a recollection, almost impossible to distinguish between memories of dreams, or scenes in films, or things she read about in books.

There came a day, long before the end of her life, when the immediacy of her own concerns and the worries she had for her family and friends pushed the memory out of her mind completely and although she might have been able to recall it had she been prompted, she never had cause to, nor did she, think of it or Rhett again.

Well...there was one last time.

15

Rhett handed in his notice at work, informing everyone he had received an offer to do research at a remote laboratory in Norway. He said it was not possible for him to give any further details as his new contract forbade him from divulging any information on the nature of the project. Dean Okoro was dismayed at losing one of her marquee recruits and one of the pillars on which she was attempting to build Birmingham University's global reputation. She had however known it was likely someone like Dr Gaumond would receive many other lucrative offers and it was not uncommon for young, talented academics to be seduced by the type of monies offered by what she assumed would be the military-industrial complex. She was able to mask the bitter feelings of disappointment and wished him all the best in his future endeavours, even making sure her personal assistant arranged a lavish leaving lunch in his honour for a large number of the senior faculty.

Rhett had several similar leaving parties with various groups of friends, including the cricket team and the disparate characters who drank in his local. During these encounters he would have sudden waves of affection for the people around him and in those moments it was inconceivable to him how he could have extinguished all their lives. These would always pass and once they did, he knew he would have done it again to satisfy the burning curiosity inside him. In fact, there was only one person whose existence he would never be able to bring himself to end.

He thought of Tara often and part of his mind was always working on trying to solve the puzzle of winning her over but a deeper part of his soul knew it was futile and so he resolved to leave her alone.

The transition from Tier Two to Tier One was quite straightforward and Rhett's consciousness was migrated from the QuantSim system to a standalone quantum framework, which allowed him to exist within the confines of a purpose-built sandbox. He was able to access Tier One via wearing a virtual reality headset within this environment and this allowed him to control a rudimentary mobile module within Tier One. It consisted of an adjustable camera, monitor, microphones and speakers, which were integrated into a moveable platform. Rhett was able to control these and could move around the laboratory and certain other restricted parts of the University. His image was shown on the screen and this allowed him to have interactions with a limited group of people who had the security clearance to communicate with him.

The idea was to continually iterate the functionality of his avatar so he would be able to interact more completely with the Tier One environment. The end goal being for him to have a fully autonomous humanoid casing with haptic and sensory interfaces. He would then have the option of inhabiting Tier One in a hyperrealistic fashion but also have the sandbox area to retreat to, as if this was a completely controllable and deep imagination available for him to explore.

The speed at which these enhancements took place was however painfully slow for Rhett. It quickly became apparent to him how technologically backwards Tier One was to Tier Two and as he was unable to utilise Tier Two knowledge, he had to wait for components and technologies that would be readily available to him in Tier Two to develop naturally and organically in Tier One. He could not resist from dropping a few hints and comments to the scientists who worked around him but he had not considered how slowly things develop and how they were normally built on top of pre-existing infrastructure. There was no Internet within Tier One nor were there any mobile phones and although it was quite easy to nudge his new colleagues to accept the theories behind them, this was not enough to push society into making the large scale investments necessary to realise them.

It was also quickly apparent how much of an outlier Professor Bruno Matthams had been in terms of his intellect and ability to turn his ideas into workable systems. The world in which he found himself was on a technological level similar to what Tier Two was like in the late 1960s or early 1970s so for Bruno to have developed QuantSim was truly remarkable. It was also the case that the rate at which Tier One advanced was a lot slower than Tier Two. The scientific landscape had been almost the same for hundreds of years and the way things evolved was in a slow iterative linear fashion, not like the exponential rate at which Tier Two had advanced. The ambitions of the society were heavily tempered by strict legislative controls and any new technological breakthroughs had to be rigorously tested by the legal system so their potential societal implications could be regulated to mitigate against unintended consequences. It was infuriating for Rhett to have to operate in such a manner but he had to remind himself how this structure had ultimately given him his protections and opportunities. He also had a much more philosophical understanding of patience and time. It was uncertain how long he would be able to survive in his current state and there were some doubts about how long it would take for his sentience to degrade or whether it would remain stable. It did however seem like he might to all intents and purposes be an immortal consciousness. This removed any sense of urgency around how his avatar developed or how long it took for the Tier One legal system to determine how QuantSim could be used to benefit their society.

The legislation surrounding simulated universes was a long and drawn out process. It was a complicated matter and it was increasingly unclear how to manage the ethics of setting in motion environments with inherent properties that could lead to the emergence of sentient life. Who would be culpable for the untold suffering intrinsic to the development of life and what responsibility was there to the creators in respect of any heinous acts undertaken by sentient beings in those universes? These were deep theological questions that had been asked throughout history in relation to gods and deities and now the focus had shifted from abstract entities to themselves. And they were proving even more difficult to answer definitively now they were no longer confined to the realm of philosophical debate. Parveen kept Rhett abreast of all the developments but as all of the questions requiring urgency had been resolved in his own case, little actual progress was being made. The initial bursts of activity had slowed and Rhett could see the curve flattening in a way where it did not seem likely that a definitive decision would ever be made.

The years dragged on and Rhett found himself increasingly retreating into his sandbox where he was able to indulge in some of the cultural delights of Tier Two. Tier One art was comparatively staid with very little to compare to Shakespeare, Mozart, Michelangelo, Da Vinci, Tolstoy or the Arctic Monkeys. Tier One history was also lacking in the same sort of nuance or conflict, which rendered their history more peaceful but less rich than his own. Rhett enjoyed learning about various cultures and periods of his own reality's history. It evoked in him dense sessions of nostalgia were he longed to return to a reality he could never again call home.

One by one the people of meaning to him in Tier One began to expire.

Maxwell Rudd died in a helicopter crash on the way back from a frivolous jaunt with friends to see his favourite sports team compete in a knock-out competition. He had asked Katja to join him but the spontaneous nature of the trip had seen her otherwise engaged.

Mick Deacon suffered a heart attack while underneath his car. His favourite hobby was finding something in need of work and returning it to its former glory. His friends and family were consoled by the fact he had passed away while doing something he enjoyed.

Dr Parveen Panwar and Vice-Chancellor Zahid Mashwani enjoyed productive careers after being promoted to minor governmental roles. They were happy together and took great joy in their ability to enhance and develop each other's worth at a similar rate. Parveen's cancer returned and after a short battle, she finally died in a hostel with Zahid at her side. Zahid lived a few years longer and died naturally in his sleep.

After Parveen had gone, less and less attention was paid to Rhett and each new Vice-Chancellor received less information about him during their induction, and updates on Rhett's status became increasingly rare. The new faculty members treated him well but he was seen more as a curiosity than an actual sentient being. This was partly due to his own withdrawal and lack of interest in sustained interaction but mainly because it was hard to take a TV on wheels seriously as an equal. He was given more and more free reign to wander around the confines of his small area with less and less oversight, and soon his attentions turned to QuantSim.

He was not supposed to interact with it at all until the legislation was resolved but the new staff had little awareness of what he was doing or indeed any interest in QuantSim or how it worked. He took to observing Tara for long periods of time as she went about her life. She had ended up marrying a guy called Dan and they had moved together to live in Nottingham to be closer to his parents so they could help out with their three kids. She was active in promoting environmental charities and although ViroMental were active throughout her life, they never went as far as committing any terrorist acts to draw awareness to their demands. Even if they had, Tara would not have been on the train they targeted on that tragic day.

He enjoyed watching her grow old, a state of being she had not originally had the opportunity to experience. He saw her grow old with poise and grace and he took comfort in his part in making it possible and as justification for every action he had taken. He was happy to see her surrounded by loved ones on her deathbed, pleased to be there amongst them.

"Can I just have a moment alone?" Tara's voice was weak and her throat dry.

"Of course." Her husband let go of the hand he had been holding and guided the rest of the family towards the door. "Let me know when you're ready for us again."

A strange sensation had suddenly overcome Tara. A long forgotten memory had bubbled up from deep within her subconscious mind. She waited until the door was closed and was sure she would not be overheard.

"Are you there, Rhett?" She said into the empty room.

Rhett suddenly felt free of the confines of the surrounding equipment, as if his consciousness existed beyond the quantum circuits housing his essence.

"Because if you are...I just want to say...this is a private situation and I do not consent to your presence. If you're out there observing me in my final moments then just...fuck off."

She looked around the room a few times. She felt a bit sheepish for expressing herself so forcefully but the underlying sentiment was true and anyway, she was only acting on a wild hunch so it was unlikely to have been heard. It also felt good to swear. It was something she had not done in at least a decade and it gave her a youthful burst of energy as she entered her final hours.

Rhett closed down the feed immediately and retreated into the sandbox environment. He had not expected to have been affected by her death as much the second time, but after her comments he was left more dejected and hollow than he had ever been before. He wept in solitude and darkness until the intensity of his sorrow overwhelmed his capacity to process his feelings and he became emotionally numb.

The numbness lasted a long time and he was rarely seen outside his sandbox by the university faculty. Eventually his thoughts turned to deeper questions of the universe in which he now found himself. He needed a plan and something to work on and he started to wonder if the same fundamental physics were in play in this higher iteration of reality. He decided to work on ways he might be able to see if dark loop gravity was a fundamental aspect of Tier One's nature.

Tier One had nothing like the Massively Regressive Tachyon Distributor nor did it seem it ever would, especially as the legislation surrounding initiating further simulated realities or utilising technologies developed in QuantSim had stalled. Rhett was able to take a few tips from the rapid developments in Tier Two, which itself was progressing at an exponential pace. They had determined that there were ways of invoking an anti-tachyon beam without such cumbersome tools as the MRTD. He concluded that he might be able to probe the smallest parts of reality using technology that already existed in Tier One and took it upon himself to work on that to occupy his mind. He finally realised he could tap into some of the existing infrastructure, albeit surreptitiously, and undertake some experiments to give him conclusive evidence of the nature of this higher reality.

About the same time he heard that Katja Leitner was about to retire and the final episode of the Leitner Late Show was due to be broadcast in the coming weeks. Rhett contacted her and suggested it might be interesting to finish her show in the same place it started and do a piece from the QuantSim lab at Braxton University. They would also be able to discuss some interesting new discoveries he had made about the physics of their existence.

He promised her this would be more exciting than it sounded.

16

The memories flooded back as Katja approached the Braxton University hexagon. Could it really be thirty-five years since she stood outside the entrance, hassling Dr Panwar and Professor Matthams, taking ambitious risks and furthering her career? It had been so long since she needed to hustle, she was unsure whether or not she would have the energy to navigate her cutthroat profession if she had been required to do it all over again. She marvelled at her youthful audacity and made sure to send some beams of thanks back through time to the woman she used to be for setting up the wonderful life she went on to enjoy. It had been a tough period for her in the aftermath of Maxwell's helicopter crash but her show and her work had seen her through. It was not long before she met someone of comparable worth to share her life with and they had enjoyed many happy years together and there was no reason to think it would not continue for many more.

The final episode of her show was drawing near. The show's time had already been moved twice to later slots and the dwindling audience figures were impossible to ignore. She had fought hard to obtain an extension to her contract, even offering to accept a significant reduction in her fees but eventually she had to accept a new generation of journalists coming through the ranks and it was time for her to step aside and concentrate on supporting them on their journey. She had thrown herself into her final season and the additional levels of enthusiasm had created a momentum behind her viewing figures. People were tuning in to see her show in droves now that they realised their opportunity to see her was coming to a close. This had led to the executives at VEX News giving her the honour of allowing her final week to be broadcast in the former primetime slot of 9:30pm. The week had gone well and now here she was about to broadcast her last show from the place it had all started, reminiscing about the story that launched her into the spotlight. Over the years, she had covered breaking news about the various developments in simulated reality legislation but these were increasingly insignificant and were of little interest to her audience. This meant that in order to promote the subject of her final show, they had needed to work hard to engineer a nostalgic buzz around the few months where QuantSim had dominated the news agenda. The efforts had paid off and they were expecting record viewing figures for the show, which were aided by Dr Gaumond promising an exciting development. They had not let on that his news was to do with quantum physics but Katja felt a sense of responsibility to at least humour Rhett after everything he had experienced by allowing him to present his findings to the world. She was finally going to get the talk with him that he had promised her all those years ago and at the very least, she would make history by being the first broadcaster to conduct an interview with a sentient simulated entity. It had not been cleared by the legal department but now her career was ending, she was no longer worried by any repercussions that may come.

She was met at reception by one of her producers and a post-graduate who had been assigned to them for the duration of their broadcast. The rest of her team were already in place in the QuantSim lab so the walk up there was relaxed and full of light-hearted chatter. Katja sensed her two companions were intently assessing each other's worth and from her perspective she felt they would make a mutually beneficial pairing and hoped they would eventually be vole. She suffered a pang of jealousy as she often did, knowing that the thrill of these assessments were unlikely to happen to her ever again in a natural setting. Her profile and status were too well known for anyone to need to play the intricate game of value gauging with her.

The smell of chlorine wafted into Katja's nostrils when she turned the corner to the corridor leading up to the QuantSim laboratory entrance. It brought to her a vision of Bruno wheeling himself towards her and although she did not usually believe in people's essence lingering after they had gone, she sensed his presence somewhere deep within the fabric of the QuantSim laboratory the moment she entered.

The room itself had not been updated since she was last there and although it was clean, it had taken on the general shabbiness that comes without being constantly used by an active project. The QuantSim casing itself seemed smaller than it had last time she was there. Fewer components were attached to it and the ones that were were much neater and tidier. She would have enjoyed the chance to explore the universe within, but she feared its secrets would not be unlocked in her lifetime. The government seemed incapable of resolving the outstanding legislation around accessing simulated realities. She chuckled at the memory of Parveen lying comatose on the leather chair as she interacted with the universe via the neural interface. She also remembered the physical sensation of occupying the imposing frame of Ra I De la Rosa and how powerful it had made her feel. She amused herself by wondering if Parveen would have expected the wAIt to be so long for the outstanding issues to be resolved.

She greeted each of her crew in turn. This was not something she would normally do but as it was the final episode of her show, it felt right to spend some time with all of them. She wanted to make sure she had looked deep into all their eyes and conveyed to them how much they meant to her for making her show succeed. The longest hug was reserved for Martha. The two of them had been fiercely loyal to each other throughout the years and neither of them even remembered the fractious start to their friendship. They both viewed the origins of their relationship through a rose-tinted lens and if asked about it, they both would have responded, without knowingly lying, by describing how they had hit it off the moment they had met.

She finally made her way to Rhett's workstation. His image was displayed on the monitor but the face was frozen. She tapped on the screen and spoke into the microphone by its side. This alerted Rhett to her presence and a few moments later he had connected himself from his sandbox area and his image came alive.

"You haven't aged a bit." Katja gave a cheeky wink to the camera.

"Right...yeah. Do you think I should alter my image to make me look older, to give the viewers some continuity?"

"Can you do that?"

"Yeah, it shouldn't be much of a problem." Rhett's eyes showed he was already working on how to solve this new puzzle.

"Nah, don't worry about it. I don't think there's any point showing an altered version of how you were when I arrived. Let's maintain some authenticity."

They had a long chat about their respective experiences since they had last spoken. They were interrupted periodically by the production crew and various members of the university faculty who were either asking for autographs or trying to get some sort of clue as to what Rhett was going to disclose. He had initially told the Vice-Chancellor they were only going to do a fluff piece but she had seen the promotional material for the show on VEX News and forced him to give her more details. He patiently described to her his recent research into the field of dark loop gravity and how he had developed some techniques to verify it was an aspect of the fabric of their reality. She did not really care for the details but understood this could be something that increased the prestige of the university so was quite pleased for him to announce it on TV. She was sceptical about it being a satisfying resolution to the hype they had generated but this was for VEX News to deal with. She had mulled things over while gazing out her office window at the ancient trees lining the hexagon. She concluded that no harm could possibly come of it and the awareness it generated would easily outweigh any negative connotations it created for the university.

"We're going to go live in ten minutes." Martha whispered into Katja's ear.

"OK, Rhett. Unless you have any questions, I am going to go and grab a quick coffee, get a bit of a face on and then I'll see you back here a couple of minutes before the show starts."

"I'm all good." Rhett touched his index finger to his eyebrow and gave Katja a mini-salute.

The activity amongst the production crew shifted up a gear and they moved around with a focus and efficiency that made a few of the university staff in attendance realise how little real pressure they faced in their profession. They would often complain of their own problems and difficulties but it was a different type to the hectic manifestation of immediate pressure unfolding before them . Each member of Katja's team knew exactly what they were doing and as Rhett observed everything take place around him, it looked like an intricate dance. Katja was the star of the troupe and when she returned to him, she pirouetted through the ensemble until she arrived at her seat, landing in place with controlled grace.

The main camera light was turned on and all the activity behind it was obscured by the brightness, making it feel as if the only people who now existed were the ones bathed in its radiance. A voice counted down from ten to six and then a hand appeared and partially obscured the light as it finished the countdown with thumb and fingers. On the final beat the hand swept through an arc to land with the final finger pointed squarely at Katja.

"Good evening loyal viewers. We have a great show lined up tonight but unfortunately this is going to be the la---" Kata's voice cracked as her emotions finally crashed into her intellect, like a helicopter with a damaged blade colliding with tarmac. She wiped away a tear, taking a beat to regain her poise. "...I'm sorry, as you can see this is personally an extremely melancholy night for me, as I host the final ever episode of Leitner Late."

There was a slight pause as the intro music played to the audience at home. Katja leafed through her notes to gain a brief additional moment to compose herself. She winked at Rhett and a broad smile took control of her features. She was determined to cherish the moment but in order to perform successfully, she also needed to forget its significance.

"We're broadcasting tonight live from Braxton University, which is where we have filmed several of our most memorable shows, including our first ever episode. We focused heavily on Professor Matthams QuantSim project, which since then has been bogged down in the legislative process. Thirty-five years later however, we finally have exclusive access to one of the simulated entities that evolved within the quantum network. Good evening Dr Gaumond."

"Good evening, Katja. Please, call me Rhett."

"Sure. Rhett. We are still bound by legal restrictions as to what we can and can't ask you about in respect of your life within the QuantSim simulated universe but let me start by asking you one thing. Out of both realities, what is your favourite TV show?"

The laughter from the production crew and the assembled faculty members was audible to the viewers at home. Rhett chuckled, knowing he could provide only one answer.

"I can categorically state that I cannot think of any possible universe existing where Leitner Late is not the best show in it."

Katja smiled. She knew this type of answer would warm the audience up to her guest. It was still difficult for most viewers to believe Rhett really was a sentient being so anything to make him seem similar to them in terms of wit and humour was helpful.

"You've been cooped up here at Braxton University since you were transferred out of QuantSim to reside in our tier of reality shortly after it was turned on. You have informed us that you have not been wasting that time. What have you been working on?"

"I've been doing some experiments into the nature of this reality, which could have some significant implications for the future."

"Sounds exciting. Can you tell us a little more about that?"

"I'd love to. I am working on the assumption that your viewers are smart enough to know how the smallest bits of matter are really strange particles that become difficult to describe in ways that are satisfactory for our intuitive way of thinking."

"You mean, protons, electrons, quarks, etcetera?"

"Yes exactly...well I have been looking at what forces apply on those scales and my best guess was they were all integrated into a sort of fabric, which pervades all of reality and is made up of interconnected loops of dark gravity."

"Right."

"In order to test whether this is the case, you need to focus an anti-tachyon beam at a single point in spacetime to see how it reacts."

"What is an antartacarbe?"

"An anti-tachyon beam. It is a burst of particles that travel negatively through time at a speed faster than light." Rhett looked at the camera. "Bare with me everyone. I know these are probably new concepts but I promise you the results of my work are going to simply make you all implode with excitement."

"And you were able to initiate one of these bursts?"

"Yes. I was able to hack into some of the telecommunications satellites currently in orbit and they allowed me to shoot high frequency waves of energy across the centre-of-gravity of the planet. Every so often these would excite a passing anti-tachyon, which I could then manipulate into gathering pace by riding a gravitational wave formed by a local supernovae. I then just had to wait until it became unstable and collided with the quantum foam. I was able to infer from this collision whether or not dark loop gravity exists."

"I see, so it is like there are a load of surfers bobbing along in the ocean. You shout at them when a big swell is coming and excite them into surfing the resulting waves, onces they lose balance and drop into the water, the splash they make allows you to learn about what the water is made of."

Rhett was impressed by the description. He had himself been unable to come up with a suitable analogy. He could see why Bruno and Parveen had chosen her as their preferred media contact.

"Exactly." He said. "I was able to do this a number of times and have now reached a level of certainty within the data where I can conclude that this...our reality...is actually pervaded by a fabric of dark loop gravity."

"Wow...so...that's all exciting stuff in and of itself but can you let our viewers know what this means in practical terms to them."

"Of course. Well, these loops of dark gravity are actually quite fragile and if an anti-tachyon beam collides with the quantum foam with enough momentum, it can rip a tear in the fabric of reality, causing it to unravel and implode in on itself."

Katja suddenly felt a sense of dread. "How would someone go about creating a beam of the required intensity?"

"If there was a big enough collision between two black holes in the cosmic vicinity, the gravitational wave might just be big enough to allow an anti-tachyon beam to reach sufficient levels of energy."

"Those types of events are mercifully quite rare though, aren't they?" Katja asked, her voice full of suspicion.

"They are but it just so happens that one took place very close, in galactic terms, to where we are right now and we are currently being flooded by gravitational waves from that collision."

"You did it, didn't you? There's an anti-tachyon burst riding one of those waves right now, isn't there?" Katja's shoulders dropped and she slumped back, slouching on live television for the first and only time in her career.

"There is, and as soon as it becomes unstable and crashes into the swirl of quantum particles, which are integral to the fabric of dark loop gravity that the wave is moving through, it's likely to cause a rip in reality and end everything as we know and understand it."

"Well folks, you heard it here first." Katja said into the camera, her right eyebrow arched and her arms open with palms facing upwards. She then dropped her head in the direction of Rhett and looked at him through her eyebrows. "Should we cut to commercial?"

"I wouldn't bother." Rhett said. His lips went white with the pressure they exerted on themselves and he shook his head slowly.

Katja and Rhett sat in silence for a few moments, waiting for oblivion and wondering what it would feel like not to feel anything. Martha was frantically motioning to her to fill the dead air somehow, not having understood what was happening...and then...

...nothing.

(o>~

Rhett's awareness faded in gradually. He became conscious of his thoughts existing outside the confines of his body and the usual sensations associated with gravity and physical phenomena were entirely absent. Even though he was surrounded by blackness and silence, he had the notion of still being able to see and hear should the right stimuli encroach upon his mind. He instinctively knew his being was confined somehow and even though there was nothing to indicate it, it was clear to him that certain things existed beyond him.

After a while, which could have been a fleeting moment or touching on eternity, a bright translucent fuchsia orb appeared. It was impossible to determine the passage of time in this state but there was an instant where it was not there, then an instant where it was.

"It is difficult to communicate with you within the limited scope of your cognitive confines..." a corresponding change in the brightness, flickering and hum from the orb accompanied the exchange in information. "...what we say to you is done through extended metaphor in order to facilitate your understanding. These are unfortunately crude tools, as is this language, for conveying the true depth of what they represent."

"Where am I?" Rhett's words reverberated around the expanse of his awareness and were assimilated by the orb.

"You have arrived at a supratier of reality. Your actions across multiple simulated realities alerted us to your existence and as is the case with the few sentients who embark upon your path, we have brought you into our reality."

"So this a tier of reality above Tier One?" Rhett asked.

"Not quite. The notion of above and below in terms of versions of reality is a redundant concept. It is better to think of such things as being more like an electron cloud of uncertainty with realities swirling around as probabilistic states until on observation, they retrospectively appear to be entangled with one another."

"And this state of reality exists outside of that?"

"Yes but in order for you to truly understand what that means, we would need to dissolve the artificial constructs of self we have placed around you and allow you to absorb completely into our domain."

Rhett could feel the barrier between himself and this realm thinning and there was a primordial lust aching within him to have it disappear so he could join whatever lay beyond. It did not feel like he would be experiencing something new but rather returning to a state of being he had long since forgotten.

"We know you have existed as an individual agent for a long time." The orb continued. "This sense of self is not something that cannot be regained once it is lost to the outer swirls of total consciousness. We therefore respect it and take it's loss very seriously. This is why we always ask those in your position to decide for themselves what they now wish to do."

"What are my options?"

"They are limitless. We are architects of reality and so anything is attainable." The orb said this in a matter of fact manner, as if this were a trivial ability.

Rhett had calculated there may be a chance of accessing a different tier of reality and unlike his initial contact with Bruno, this time he had some questions prepared.

"Was I the only one?" Rhett asked.

"I am afraid this can only be answered by true absorption into our realm. As an individual, irrespective of what answer I gave you, doubt and uncertainty will always remain in respect of knowing whether your experience of sentience is unique or ubiquitous." The orb was shifting through Rhett's consciousness in a way that complemented its message.

This response made total sense to Rhett and he was suddenly surprised he had ever needed to ask the question.

"What happens to sentient beings when they die?" Rhett asked.

"They cycle back to non-existence."

"So, that's the end then?"

"It is difficult to convey to a being which has been confined by self, temporal illusions and spatial dimensions, that once outside of these parameters a sentience always resides in a constant state of flux and change, including a superstate of existence and non-existence."

"That's easy for someone who has not been intrinsically wrapped up in time's fabric to say."

The orb shook a little as if outside of its own control. If Rhett had not considered such things impossible in higher dimensional beings, he might have thought it was laughing. Rhett had not dared to believe there might be a second chance of outflanking oblivion but he had considered it a remote intellectual possibility and as such, during his many hours of solitude where he comforted himself with deep philosophical questions and through experimentation, he had already worked out what he wanted from this entity.

"I want to go back." He said.

"This is not an uncommon choice for those like you who have satisfied their curiosity about existences beyond their own." The orb hummed.

"I want to go back to the night my wife died. I want her to not get killed in the terrorist attack and for her to return home unscathed so we can enjoy the rest of our lives together, so I can be with my children again...so I can experience love again.

"I want QuantSim to run without hindrance until my universe runs its course and I don't want any interference with it from Tier One. That universe should also be allowed to run its course unhindered until at least the time when my own universe has expired naturally.

"I don't want to remember any of this...at least not consciously. I want a deep sense of understanding and appreciation about what has happened but no actual conscious awareness of it."

The orb flickered and purveyed a nourishing warmth of cognition. "How would you like your life to develop beyond that?"

"Chance...randomness. I want it to be unwritten. Everything the way it was and then the future beyond that free to evolve on its own. Every destiny needs jeopardy otherwise there is nothing to cherish." Rhett said.

"Anything else?" The orb asked, sensing and in fact knowing that there was.

"I want every being who ever achieved sentience in Tier One and Tier Two to have an afterlife...an afterlife according to their expectations."

The orb changed to an emerald colour and expanded slowly through Rhett's consciousness.

"Am I giving up a lot by not joining you?" Rhett asked.

"Nah..." The orb had nearly overwhelmed Rhett's sentience. "Nothing really matters when all is said and done."

It felt like Rhett's mind was being separated into its smallest constituent particles, these units of thought floated like dry sponges through the refreshing liquid essence of the pulsating spheroid, absorbing and assimilating as they reached saturation. The process imbued an ecstatic energy throughout his being.

He acknowledged the feeling.

He let it pass.

and then...

...nothing.

Σ.

Bishop Gaumond exerted tremendous effort to place his palm upon his grandson's cheek, pleased there would be a physical continuation of his presence on the earth.

"What if there is a God who punishes people who have faith because he sees it as wasting time on trivial matters? Any attempt to rationalise God's motives can be nullified with the equally probable opposite motivations. It seems like your logic has succumbed to a convenient bout of casuistry." Rhett instantly regretted his words as he saw a wave of tension envelop the muscles of his grandfather's face.

A swash of dread and panic rushed upon Bishop Anthony Gaumond for the briefest of moments before it was followed by a large wave of fluid with the thick texture of treacle. His hand dropped from Rhett's face and swung limply by the side of the bed...

...and then...

...Bishop Gaumond was released from the confines of his frail body and was instilled with a sense of energy, similar but more powerful to the kind he had attained in his deepest periods of meditative prayer. He could feel the grace of God around him and could feel himself joining in blissful union with his Lord, his saviour, his Christ.

***

Maxwell almost slipped as he ran across the tarmac, which was slick from the unrelenting and unforecast light drizzle that had been a fixture over Braxton all week. The cloud cover made the day seem later than it was and hours earlier, he had gazed out his office window looking at the sky and hoping for something to come along and shake him out of his recent funk.

A call from Todd, his former college mate and now rival broadcaster had come as a pleasant surprise. They both had stakes in competing sports teams who were set to play each other in a cup competition later that evening. Todd had offered to send down his private helicopter to collect Maxwell so they could watch the game together in his corporate box. This was exactly the sort of thing he had been looking for as a means of light distraction. He knew Katja would refuse an invite to join him, which is why he cheerily called her and got the response he expected. He could now not be criticised for never attempting to include her in his spontaneous adventures.

The helicopter blades were spinning in anticipation of a quick exit, creating an uncomfortable noise and downforce. Maxwell ducked down and lunged for the door where he was greeted by one of Todd's assistants. He welcomed the ear defenders she gave him enthusiastically and the glass of champagne with even greater vigour. He strapped himself in while the assistant notified the pilot they were ready to depart.

"I hate these things." Maxwell confessed to the assistant.

"Ah, I wondered why we were sent down here to collect you. I expected you would have one of your own."

"Nope." Maxwell shook his head through a tense and rigid neck, waving his hands at the thought of it.

Maxwell's face was considerably paler once the helicopter was in the air. The rapidly changing g-forces were not unpleasant as they lurched through the skyscrapers of downtown Braxton but it was impossible to reconcile in his mind how several tons of metal could suspend itself in the air.

A sharp crack was the only indication that anything was wrong...

...and then...

Maxwell was confused about how he had arrived at his mother's office but the smile on his mother's face soon brushed any uneasiness from his mind. They hugged. This was something he could not remember doing with his mother since his first day of school. This embrace was full of warmth and none of the expected awkwardness.

"Take a seat." His mum pointed towards her desk.

Maxwell walked over to the expansive mahogany bureau and pulled out the chair opposite his mother's.

"Wrong seat."

Maxwell turned to her. The confusion drained away at the sight of his mother's open arms ushering him forwards.

"You mean?" He said.

"Yep, it's time and I have chosen you." His mother replied.

Maxwell walked round the desk and took a moment to breathe in the smell of the iconic leather chair, which had been handed down through generations of his family. It was now his, not to own but to look after until it was time to present it to the next steward of their empire.

He sat down and allowed the momentum of the chair to spin him to face the window. He had now finally achieved everything he had ever wished for. He would remain in that position, soaking up his promotion for eternity.

***

Bruno looked over at QuantSim. The constant hum of the cooling fans had suddenly ceased. It filled him with a sense of loss to see it finally come to the end of its natural simulation without him ever having been able to probe the secrets of the universe it held within it.

It was not a surprise for it to be ending. He had calculated it would only take a few months or so for the billions of years within it to allow the universe to live, grow and die. He had hoped the legislation would have worked out in his favour but it seemed he would now never have the opportunity to explore the discoveries of his own invention. He placed his soldering iron back in its holder and switched it off. He had done enough work for today, maybe enough work for a lifetime.

He inhaled deeply, sucking in the warm dust of the laboratory air, which stuck to his lungs before the air departed his body as a wistful sigh. His eyes drifted through the casing of QuantSim and settled somewhere within, no longer taking external input. HIs vision filled with the dark absence of thought. He remained still for an unusual length of time, his breathing having paused due to the high oxygen intake of his previous breath. A few spots sparkled behind his forehead and he had to force himself to breathe in sharply after realising his subconscious mind had absolved itself of all responsibility for his respiratory processes.

He wheeled himself through the corridors of the university, deciding to take the long route to the service lifts, nodding at his colleagues along the way without consciously acknowledging he was doing so. He had to stand in order to reach the buttons of the elevator and he experienced a head rush when he slumped back in his chair, the amount of effort surprising him.

He reached up to his collar to relieve the tightness of his shirt but found it already open and on looking down saw that his clothing was loose. A numbness in his arm gave way to a pain that radiated up his shoulder, through his neck and jaw, and then back down to its arm where it settled back into an uncomfortable burst of pins and needles.

The door to the elevator slid open but he no longer had any intention of entering such a confined space in which the colours were draining away, leaving it an unwelcoming cold grey, only visible at the center of an elongated tunnel. He realised how little he had achieved in life and how much of his time he had misused on trivia and nonsense. If only he had more of it. He would never waste another moment.

Pain throbbed everywhere.

...and then...

He could hear a repetitive squeak of a wheel in need of both oil and repair, and the gentle creak of working leather rubbing and straining against wood and metal. He opened his eyes slowly to see he was travelling in the back of a horse-drawn cart surrounded by several unkempt, sunburnt men in clothes similar to the ones he found himself in. The clothes of Ra l De la Rosa.

"Here we go again." One of the other travellers said to him.

***

Nina had been expecting a message from her daughter all morning so she was unable to resist reaching over to the passenger seat to check her phone as it buzzed. She looked down in disbelief at what she was reading.

...and then...

...nothing.

***

Parveen was doing her best to hide the excruciating pain that had seeped deep into her bones. The cancer had returned and this time it was determined to complete the task it had set out to do all those years ago. The treatments had failed to yield results and now all that was left was to wait out the remaining days in a hostel bed, senses clouded by medication whose only purpose was to ease the relentless discomfort. Her husband sat by her side, having chosen to stay this time and remain by her side until the end. He held her hand and although they both curled their lips into a smile, their eyes betrayed the falseness of their expressions.

"Thank you." Parveen whispered, her voice too low and croaky for Zahid to hear the words but the message clear from the way her mouth took shape.

Zahid nodded and this time his eyes joined his lips in validating his smile. He could not bring himself to say anything, knowing he was in that moment much less capable of speech than his wife.

Parveen's eyelids slid closed but her husband's image remained. She shook her head slowly and squeezed his hand with all the strength she had left...

...and then...

Her senses were filled with the sights and sounds of a beautiful garden. Her feet were bare and a pleasant moisture was deposited between her toes and on the soles of her feet with each step she took on the luscious grass. The flowers exuded sweet odours and they wafted towards her . She made her way through the seemingly never-ending, row-upon-row of cultivated wildlife. She could never imagine becoming bored of exploring the delights of the sculpted landscape she found herself in.

***

Tate sat by the campfire, allowing his eyes to dance along with the flames as they licked and spat at the surrounding air. He would occasionally become captivated by a spark as it rode away on the smoke, dying a little inside as each one lost its lustre to the cool night sky.

He had turned eighty-two a few weeks earlier and his family had forbidden him from taking any more of his camping trips. He had far too few other pleasures left in life to give it up yet and so had set off despite their protestations, claiming he would rather die living than live as if already dead. Secretly he knew this would be his final trip and the comfort of a luxury mattress was now much more compelling than the cold hard earth of a campsite, which no expensive cushioning equipment could ever fully disguise. He wanted to experience one more night with only a sleeping bag between him and the stars, aware of the fact and cherishing each moment, hoping to see a stray meteor shoot across the cosmic canvas.

He lay down and let the heavens subsume his vision, staring at them until his eyes gently closed and his dreams took over the celestial display...

...and then...

...they were there. They were all there. Everyone he had ever loved or cared for were with him, looking as they had done when his feelings for them had been their deepest. And he was young, a different age each time he switched his attention from family to friend to lover, but each age felt young. He would never tire of switching between them and bathing in their presence.

***

Katja looked out at the turbulent ocean. The waves crashing at the concrete sea defences rose high into the air with the occasional splash landing on her balcony. Awe mingled with the sea air, which rushed into her lungs with each breath, brought about by the raw power of nature's epic display of force. The horizon had disappeared, with sky, cloud and water all taking on the same pale shade of grey azure. The only feature retaining any semblance of its natural colour was the giant golden statue of an eagle, with wings spread and talons outstretched, ready to swoop down and destroy any threats to the harbour.

The nurse had administered the injection a little over thirty minutes ago and the comfortable tiredness they had described was now pulsing through her veins. She was exactly where she had wanted to be to face these final moments, wrapped warm in blankets, breathing clean air and watching the foam roll and break across the bay.

...and then...

...nothing but blackness...

...and then...

...the bright light came on at the end of the tunnel, the tunnel of her vision, and beneath it the lens of a camera pointed at her, broadcasting her image to eyes throughout the universe.

"Good evening and welcome to Leitner Late...Forever"

●.⊼.R

Rhett woke from a deep sleep and for a moment did not recognise his surroundings. The couch on which he had been napping was light brown in colour and had a thick velvet texture. A small patch of drool had left a damp mark on the cushion. He turned it over and sat up, rubbing his face to try and help him come round from the intensity of his slumber. He could make out the sound of distant sirens blaring and there was an incessant slicing whirr coming from somewhere. He stood up and caught himself in the mirror, receiving the now familiar shock of realising how old he had become, a red mark still visible from where his cheek had rested on the couch, hair receding slightly and peppered with grey. Deep wrinkles crept out from his eyes towards his temples, the effect intensified by an inadvertent frown.

He pulled open the patio doors and stepped out into the garden to squint at the sky. He could see a number of helicopters buzzing around over the city and the sounds of sirens blaring continued intermittently but without the double-glazing to dampen them, they were much sharper and more immediate. He was able to identify from the different modulations that all three of the emergency services were currently active...very active.

The news channel was in full-on crisis mode with splashes of red all over the screen and reporters speaking in excited but serious tones. He watched as the breaking headlines scrolled across the bottom of the screen.

- Major incident at New Street Station

Rhett's abdominal muscles tightened.

- Suspected terrorist attack.

His muscles morphed from organic fibres into congealing liquid metal, all heavy and dense, flowing slowly towards his pelvic bone.

- 100s of casualties, including fatalities.

Panic set in and adrenal energy flooded his body. He searched furiously for his phone, flinging folders, papers and cushions across the room. He finally located it wedged between two back pillows on the settee. He scrolled through his active apps and found Tara's name on his list of recent calls. He jabbed at it frantically.

"Sorry. Due to unprecedented local call volumes we are unable to connect this call. Please try again later." A robotic voice with a hint of femininity explained to him.

He grabbed his car keys and rushed to the garage. He stalled on his first attempt to start up the car, not realising it was in reverse gear. The second attempt was hardly better but he maintained control as it lurched backwards out of the driveway and onto the street. Another driver blasted their horn at him and he thrust his palm out to apologise.

"C'mon...c'mon." He said to himself as he waited for the other vehicle to pass.

At the end of the street he was unable to pull out onto the main road as the traffic had stopped. He abandoned his car and ran down to see what was causing the delay.

"What's going on?" He said to a driver who was leaning against his car, smoking a cigarette and looking down the road.

"The police have blocked off all access in and out of town. There's been some sort of explosion at New Street."

"My wife and kids are travelling to New Street today....about now...she was visiting her parents."

The other driver took a drag on his cigarette and held in the smoke, using it as an aid to prevent him from having to respond. He shook his head slowly, waiting for the moment to pass but soon enough the smoke began to drift back out of his lungs and through his clenched lips. Rhett was still looking at him, expecting some sort of comment.

"Nightmare, man." He said.

Rhett pulled out his phone and tried to call Tara again but was met with the same response. He was also conscious that his battery was dropping below ten percent and this added to the denseness of the contents sloshing sluggishly around his guts. He dashed past the stationary traffic until a policeman barred his way from going any further.

"I need to get into town." He said, bending over and propping himself up on his knees to catch his breath.

"I'm sorry, there's been a series of explosions and we're not letting anyone into the area."

"But my kids...my wife...they are in there." He said, still breathing hard.

"I understand how tough that must be for you but unfortunately the best thing you can do now is to go home, keep trying to contact them and let the emergency services get on with their job."

Rhett raised himself up and rested his hands on his pelvic bone. He nodded in acceptance. He knew on an intellectual level that there was nothing he could do to help them, despite all his instincts screaming at him to push forward and find them.

He made his way back towards his house and found it curious that his car was parked at an oblique angle to the pavement with the doors open. His initial reaction was to suspect it had been stolen until he remembered he had been the one to leave it in such an exposed position. He reversed back into his drive, taking care to avoid the other haphazardly parked vehicles.

"Madness isn't it?" His neighbour said to him as he got out of the car.

"Tara's down there with the kids." He said.

"Have you heard anything from her?"

"No." Rhett looked down at his phone again but the place where his provider logo normally was had been replaced by a big "E" for "emergencies only". He thought about calling the police but realised it would be futile at this point.

"Let me know if you hear anything...or if you need anything." His neighbour called out.

Rhett thanked him on his way back into the house. He grabbed his charger and plugged in his phone, checking it intermittently to see if anything had changed while also sitting mesmerised by the unfolding events on screen. He swore to himself that if anything happened to Tara he would...what? There was nothing he could do and the impotence left him feeling cold. He had not prayed since the earliest days of his childhood, forced to by the pressure of his grandfather's position. He was not sure if he had ever really meant it before, but he meant it now. If there was any god or creator out there then he prayed for them to keep his wife and children safe.

The phone buzzed and he launched himself at the phone. It was Tara's mother.

"Hi." Rhett said. "Have you heard from Tara?"

"No. I was hoping you would have heard something."

"I was hoping she might still be with you."

"No."

They remained silent for a few moments, neither of them wanting to talk about any of the possibilities they both held in their minds.

"Look, I'm going to free up the line. I'll give you a call as soon as I hear anything and please do the same if she gets through to you." Rhett said.

"Alright, love. Bye." Tara's mother replied.

He hung up and then tried Tara again. There was a clicking sound and then the ringing tone came through.

"Rhett. I've been trying to get through for ages."

"Tara. I was worried sick. Are you ok? Are the kids ok?"

"Yeah, we're ok...we're shaken up but....shaken up is nothing. Shaken up is fine."

The molten metal in Rhett's digestive tract sublimated into the ether and his stomach rumbled loudly.

"Thank god you're ok."

"Yeah, we're ok."

The phone went dead and the icon returned once again to the "E" setting.

Rhett turned the TV off and sat quietly looking out the window. His mind was devoid of thought as he watched the vivid blue of the afternoon sky give way to a deep indigo dabbed with specks of twinkling light. The moon loomed large and full.

The children burst through the door to shake him from his meditative state and he rushed through to greet them.

"Daddy...daddy." They shouted at him and he swept them up in his arms.

"It's alright." He held them tight and kissed their heads through the mess of their hair. He could smell smoke and sulphur lingering within. It had only been a few days since he had last seen them but he was unable to shake off the sense of having had something he thought lost forever unexpectedly returned.

Tara followed through a few steps behind the kids and he gasped at the sight of her. She had returned to him. He had thought she was lost to him forever but now here she was, standing below the doorframe he had been promising to paint for months, ready to cross the threshold of the home they shared together.

"I've missed you." He whispered.

She dropped her handbag in the hallway and he rushed to embrace her. How long had it been since he had felt the length of her body squeezing up against his own? It had been less than a week but it felt like a lifetime.

The next few hours were spent in a shocked daze. Rhett made them all beans and sausage on toast and they ate it on their laps, watching the news until it was clear nothing new was being divulged on each cycle. Rhett bathed the kids and then filled the tub again so Tara could soak while he put the kids to bed and read to them.

She entered the living room in her dressing gown with a towel wrapped around her shoulders. She had a curious look in her eyes but that was to be expected after the day she had just experienced. It seemed like she wanted to say something but changed her mind. She sat next to him and placed her head on his chest, his arm sliding around her shoulders and resting lazily on her hip. She raised her chin and their eyes met, each of them trying to convey a multitude of emotions through their gaze. Rhett unconsciously drifted towards her and she blinked rapidly until their lips met and both their eyes drifted closed.

They kissed for a long time and in a way they had not done since the earliest days of their relationship. There was no sense of urgency in their embrace and when it gradually evolved into making love, it felt to Rhett like they were saying hello to each other after an eternity apart. Rhett felt as if she were not only welcoming him into her body, as she lost control of herself with an abandon he had rarely seen, but that she was somehow opening herself back up to him on an emotional and psychological level.

He awoke extremely early the following day and watched her sleep for a while, grateful to have a few moments of peace to simply observe her breathing before the kids came and demanded all of his attention. He marvelled at the way in which the angle of the sun was able to change the colour of her hair in the same way autumn turned the shades of leaves. He heard the girls stirring and crept out of the room so he could sort them out and leave Tara to wake up naturally. He gave them their bowls of cereals and sat them in front of some cartoons in the back room, which was as far as you could get, within the confines of the house, from the master bedroom. Once they were settled he pulled out all the equipment and ingredients to make Tara her favourite breakfast. If ever there was a day for homemade scotch pancakes, this was it.

He prepared everything and set the table with fresh orange and a cafetiere and waited for her to come down so he could cook her food to order. He sipped his coffee and felt like this was the start of a new chapter, one that needed an exciting new plan, and he used the time to think of all the things he wanted to let her know.

The future rose like the sun on a day in late spring. It was full of bright hope and excitement, ready to be shaped according to his desires. There was nothing that could stop him from enjoying the rest of his life with Tara.

Tara gazed out of the train window, sipping at the bitter coffee she had bought from the cart. The girls were busying themselves on their tablet devices, giving her some time to gather her thoughts as her eyes were occupied by the changing landscape, which flowed between open countryside and ever-increasing expanses of suburban sprawl. At some point the natural scenery would lose its advantage and give way entirely to the dense metropolitan skyline of the inner city.

She was glad to have had the opportunity to get away for a few days. She had told Rhett it was on the insistence of parents craving time with their grandchildren, but in reality it was an opportunity for her to have some time alone so she could think through some issue that had been nagging at her for months...maybe years.

She loved Rhett, she really did and their life together was comfortable but it just felt like she had been going through the motions with him throughout their relationship. It was as if she had never really thought beyond the next milestone and now suddenly there she was, married with kids and with her future set and stuck within the confines of an ever-narrowing path. She had been absorbed into his plans and now felt like a supporting character in his story rather than the protagonist in her own. She knew it was selfish but how much of her life was she supposed to sacrifice simply because she had followed along with the expectations society had thrust upon her. It might not seem fair to external eyes for her to break up a family unit based on her desire to explore her own individuality but how long could she defer to the pressure to conform. Deep down she knew the real unfairness was to bring her children up while interacting with them and her environment through the veil of a lie. She had to be herself and for that to happen, she needed to make some drastic changes.

"Are we getting off here, mummy?" Her youngest Erin asked, something she did at every station they pulled into.

"No, sweetie. This is Bromsgrove. We're getting off at Birmingham New Street."

Erin pulled her headphones back on and settled her attention back on to her favourite show. Tara caught the eye of a young woman standing outside on the platform as the train came to a stop. She was not sure what it was about her that made her stand out but for some reason, Tara was drawn in by her demeanour. She struggled onto the train with a large luggage case, which was wrapped in the type of plastic some people feel is necessary before they check their luggage onto a flight. She was finding it difficult to control the wheels as she made her way down the train, looking for a free seat. One of the train guards suggested she put it in the luggage rack but she insisted on bringing it down the carriage and placing it on the seat beside her.

"I'm the same." Tara said to her.

"You what?" She replied with a sharp and aggressive tone.

"I was just saying, I'm the same as you. I hate leaving anything in the baggage area. I always think someone's going to steal it."

"Oh right...yeah." The girl shifted uncomfortably and positioned her body away from Tara, making it abundantly clear she was not interested in further smalltalk.

The girl had severe acne behind her thick make-up, which was a heavy white foundation with dark smudged eyes and black lipstick. Her hair had matted into thick clumps and appeared to have been coloured in recent weeks by a purple rinse but the underlying auburn was visible in her roots. She was wearing tight black jeans with large turn-ups and chains hanging from the pockets. She had on an oversized blue denim jacket whose sleeves also had massive turn-ups. A tight t-shirt was just about visible and on it was the logo of ViroMental, the extreme environmental movement that had united the most radical factions of Greenpeace, Occupy and Extinction Rebellion into a single anarchic collective. A large golden "H" hung from a necklace and was currently snagged on the lapel of her jacket. Tara wondered if she herself might have been a member had it emerged a decade ago while she was at college or university. They were definitely making politicians sit up and take notice, achieving much more than her organisation had with its softly softly lobbying.

Tara could sense an increasing level of agitation rising in the girl as they got closer and closer to Birmingham New Street. She was checking her watch frequently and kept adjusting the zip on the top of her luggage, which had not been covered by the plastic. She soon caught the attention of Tara's eldest daughter. Saoirse was initially pulled from a deep involvement in her games by the stale smell of marijuana but on locating the source had become captivated by the overall look and exciting style of the older girl.

"Can I have my hair like that?" Tara's daughter asked, loud enough for the girl to hear.

Tara and the girl exchanged a quick look.

"Maybe...when you're a bit older." Tara said.

The girl forgot herself for a moment and smiled. She quickly regained her composure and a serious frown and a pout formed on her face.

Tara gathered her things together and got the girls ready to depart while the train was pulling into the long curved platform of New Street Station. She liked to be stood at the door and ready to go by the time the train stopped so as to stave off the nagging panic of having the train pull away before they had a chance to get off. This had happened to her once when she was younger and meant an expensive round trip to York when she had been supposed to get off at Leeds. In the grand scheme of things, it had not been a major problem for her but somehow it had remained a traumatic experience she did not wish to repeat.

All the windows imploded at once. Shards of glass flew into the carriage from all directions. Tara instinctively arched her body away from the blast and protected her daughters with her arms. A high pitched tone was ringing in her ears and the girls were eerily still under her embrace. She looked around to try and see what was going on, falling forwards as the train lurched to an abrupt stop. She looked back to see the denim-clad girl recover from her own shock and start messing with her bag again. Tara was suddenly overcome with a wave of panic and she dragged her daughters along, yanking their arms and causing them to start crying hysterically. The door was jammed but Tara rolled down the window and clambered down onto the platform, reaching through to lift out the girls once she had stabilised her footing. Another explosion shook the floor and she almost dropped Erin, somehow recovering to grab her waist as she spun towards the floor. Her head was inches away from colliding with the concrete by the time she was stabilised. Once they were all out, Tara scooped them up in her arms and ran as fast as she could towards the exit, fighting her instinct to run away from the shouts and screams of the other passengers. A further blast hit her from behind and sent the three of them skidding into an advertising board. They were hurt but alive.

A train guard lifted her to her feet and helped them all towards the stairs. The bangs continued all around them and as they filtered into the crowd, they were swept along by the flow of it, barely managing to keep together. Without knowing how, they were suddenly outside in the street and sirens were blaring all around them, people were screaming and crying and worried faces were shouting instructions in every direction. Tara ignored them all, put her head down, held tightly to the little hands of her daughters and dragged them in the direction of Digbeth market.

The next few hours were spent wandering the streets in the vague direction of home. The phone network had been overwhelmed and nobody was sure whether or not they were still under attack, or even who the enemy attacking them might be. The battleground did appear to be behind them and each step took them further away from the sounds and smells of the frontline. She felt her bag vibrate and reached in to locate her phone.

"Rhett. I've been trying to get through for ages." She said as she answered.

"Tara. I was worried sick. Are you ok? Are the kids ok?"

"Yeah, we're ok...we're shaken up but....shaken up is nothing. Shaken up is fine."

"Thank god you're ok."

Tara frowned and blinked. It was uncharacteristic for Rhett to reference god.

"Yeah, we're ok. It was really insane back---" Tara stopped talking, sensing something had changed. "Are you there?" She said.

He was not. The telecoms infrastructure had become overwhelmed again.

Tara had never walked from the city centre back to the house but it was not actually that far and only took them around an hour and a half. On seeing their house, the girls gained a new wind of energy and shot off to burst through the door. Tara took a moment to compose herself and followed them in.

Rhett made sure to look after them and made everyone a comforting meal of beans and sausages on toast. He ran her a bath and then went off to read to the kids while she had a long soak. She joined him on the sofa after she had finished and flopped down next to him, resting her head on his shoulder.

They shared a long meaningful look and then kissed. It was a slow and sensual kiss, which over time developed into sex. Tara could not shake off the sense that this intimacy was all about finality and saying goodbye. She savoured every moment.

She woke up the next morning to the smell of pancakes. She would miss this but she knew deep down it was not enough to build a life around. She was ready for the spotlight. It was time for her to become the leading character in her own show. She walked downstairs and had a moment to watch Rhett sip his coffee before he noticed her. A broad smile transformed his features and his eyes lit up as she pulled out a chair to join him at the table. Could she really bring herself to do this?

Yes...yes, she could.

"Listen Rhett..." She said as she touched his hand. "...we need to talk."

Printed in Poland
by Amazon Fulfillment
Poland Sp. z o.o., Wrocław